THESE

JAMES TARR

TROUBLED

DAYS

Cover and interior design by Nuno Moreira, NM DESIGN

ISBN Paperback: 978-1-7369761-0-4

ISBN Ebook: 978-1-7369761-1-1

THESE

JAMES TARR

TROUBLED

DAYS

WINTER

CHAPTER I

Harold Maguire watched from the corner of the sidewalk as two policemen beat a man across the street. The man was cowering on his side in front of a flower shop, screaming at each blow. One baton fell on his neck and the other was raised and ready to strike. As the other baton hit the man in the gut the first one was raised and ready to hit him again. The man lay crumpled in a thin layer of snow as the blows came down on him. Harold waited as the police finished their arrest, dragging the man off. Harold crossed the street and entered the flower shop. The door jingled as Harold opened it. He was greeted by a woman at the counter in a worn green apron, her coarse hands sorting an arrangement.

"Hi there, I'm picking up some flowers. I called about an hour ago. The name is Harold. Are they ready?"

"Yes; I can make up a message for you. Any special occasion?"

"My daughter is coming home for winter break." A timid grin grew on Harold's face.

"Lovely."

The woman disappeared. Harold stared out the window and lost some of the joy that had struck him so suddenly. As he leaned further toward the window, he noticed the sidewalk stained red leading up to the patrol car just a few parking spaces up the street. The florist came back and held up a brilliant looking bouquet, a swirl of reds, oranges, and pinks. The woman put them on the counter and offered up a card with a personal message.

"Did you see the police outside?" said Harold.

"I did. What can be done of it? He was lucky it wasn't Protection Services; they'd have done more than roughed him up."

"Nasty business."

"Someone has to do it." The florist was curt.

Harold put some cash on the table and waited for change. The florist called out to Harold as he opened the door with a jingle.

"Happy Christmas – keep safe."

"You too." Harold went back into the cold. Happy Christmas? Harold thought. He still wasn't used to hearing it. Something they say in England? Or used to say, he thought. She was one of the lucky ones. She made it out.

Harold walked down the sidewalk, avoiding the pink stains in the fresh snow. The stuff had started falling fast, winds picking up around him and offering only howls and a biting chill. Sirens wailed past him, and Harold glanced at the patrol car. The beaten man was slumped in the back with his head against the window. The car was gone in a flurry of white. Harold kept on down the street and noticed one of the digital billboards on a crumbling brick building, taking up a large portion of the side. The face of a dejected soldier in camouflage, grains of sand embedded in the lines on his face. Text started scrawling across the bottom. DISSENT HURTS THE TROOPS…YOU KNOW IT WHEN YOU SEE IT… REPORT DISSENT WHEREVER YOU FIND IT.

Just as he finished reading it, the image shifted. A Protection Serviceman, standing tall and strapping, proud and painfully white. Clad in the gray uniform, stupid grin on his face as he motioned to point at whoever might be walking by. DO YOUR PART…DO WHAT IT TAKES…JOIN PROTECTION SERVICES TODAY…GENEROUS PAY…HONORABLE WORK. Jesus Christ, Harold thought. I'll never get away from this. At least I'll have Aiden back soon. He shielded the flowers from the wind and the snow and trudged on.

Harold was finally out of the range of the surveillance cameras and close to home. The unmanned aerial cameras never wandered onto his street – at least not usually – even though Harold's place was one of the last single-family houses left on the block. Many of them had been converted to triple-deckers over time. He glanced at one of the three-story buildings and saw the national flag hanging from the porch of the third floor. Looking further down he saw the same flag hanging from the second-floor porch, and another at mast jutting out from the first floor of the house. He noticed for the first time that more than half of the houses on the street had similar flags hanging from them. Most of them looked ragged. Harold couldn't help mumbling under his breath.

"What the hell are we so proud of?"

* * *

Lieutenant Frederick Eckart and Officer David Blair were driving, tooling around winding streets as the snow accumulated. Eckart put the windshield wipers on. It didn't do much. The gusts had become unpredictable, nearly blizzard conditions.

"Maybe you should pull over?" said Blair.

"No. Why people in Massachusetts can't drive in snow is mystifying to me. You grew up here, you should be able to handle it. You should especially be able to handle it if you want to keep doing this."

"It's been six months; I think I've got an understanding of what Protection Services expects of me."

Eckart sneered. "Right. You're lucky I let you ride with me today."

"I feel lucky."

The vehicle console buzzed. *"2E54, this is Dispatch. Reports of a dissent criminal in police custody. You're closest to Malden PD. Can you take it?"*

Eckart picked up his radio. "Dispatch, this is 2E54. You have a description?"

"Darker complexion, black hair, brown eyes. Approximately five foot seven and 160 pounds. ID suggests he's a British refugee. Emigrated after the outbreaks. That's all we have so far."

"Copy that. We're on it."

* * *

Harold was at his doorstep. He clutched at his knitted hat to keep it from flying off his head. Juggling the flowers, he searched in his coat pocket for his house keys. He jammed his house key in the lock, stepped into the warmth of his home, and locked the door. Harold had set aside a vase filled halfway with tap water before leaving. As he unwrapped the flowers and placed them in the vase one by one, Harold noticed a small and weak looking little one. The flower was a sickly-looking light powder blue and had yet to bloom.. Harold thought about plucking it out so it didn't distract from the others. He wondered if it would bloom by the time Aiden got home. I'll give it a chance, Harold thought, as he placed it in the vase along with all the rest.

He moved from the living room into the kitchen and took off his heavy winter coat, spotted with melting flakes of snow, and placed it on the kitchen heater as it hissed and pinged. The silver monstrosity was an old heap, and large sections of paint had been scorched off. A filthy orange rust that was rough to the touch was steadily advancing. Harold removed his hat and set it on the heater's last bit of free space. He ran the hot water at the kitchen sink, splashed some on his face, grabbed a towel, and dried himself before he made his way to the living room.

Harold went over to his record collection at the far side of the room and began rummaging—an exercise from his youth. He remembered looking through his parents' collection as a child and becoming a connoisseur of everything from the '70s to the '90s before his tenth birthday. The best rock bands, the alternative stuff, punk and postpunk. Every time he listened to vinyl, Harold relived that first time he had ever heard the low scratching of an album as he placed the needle in the grooves, just before the music started. It was why he kept the records and bought a new player, discarding the new technologies constantly released one on top of the other. An analog music set was harder to keep tabs on to boot.

Harold settled on The Chameleon's *Strange Times*. He removed it from his bookcase along the wall, took the record out of its sleeve and made his way to the player, lifting the needle and placing it with care on the side that read A+. He put the needle down, and the first track began to fill up his living room. Harold made his way to the chair at the center of the room and fell into the cushions. What artists, he thought. They're not even capable of producing B-sides. Only A-level work. Harold reached for his remote control and clicked his television on. Robert Wright filled up the screen in his three-piece suit and mainstay flag pin on his lapel. That man the country was supposed to admire and obey above all others. The one people were now calling the Leader.

He was mid-speech, droning on about the trials of top Party members for treachery, cowardice, and other deep intractable moral failings. The necessity of suspending elections, new deployments in Tanzania, bombing campaign in Pakistan, the expansion of internment to include dissent crimes, blah blah blah. Somehow different but always the same. The drumbeats and meandering guitar riffs tumbled out of the record player and filled Harold's head like a sinister soundtrack for the words of Robert Wilson Wright, founder of the Party, architect of the Restoration at home and the Great Liberation in countless foreign lands. The man who had mobilized the whole of the country against all those who would do us harm, without pause or shame. The man who did all that was necessary and required. The President of the United States.

*   *   *

11

"We're with ProServ. We're here for the one you just picked up." Lieutenant Eckart spat out the words, showing his SubCrimes Division ID to the policeman at the entrance desk, who stopped his paperwork and rose to his feet. Officer Blair looked on, raising a clenched fist to his yawning mouth.

"You got it," said the policeman. "He's in one of our interview rooms. I'll let you in at the end over there."

Blair and Eckart walked towards the door leading to the rest of the station as it buzzed open. "Just follow me," the policeman said, as Eckart held the door open for Blair. The partitions in the station made the hallways feel too tight and Blair felt he was barely squeezing through. They walked single file past a large bullpen with desks, ringing phones and busy police officers on one side and marked office rooms on the other. Old, warped, faded oak doors of the offices reeked of wood treatment. Blair grabbed his dark overcoat by the collar and shook off flakes of snow.

"Two of our patrolmen tried to pick this guy up in front of his apartment," said the policeman as he hitched his utility belt up around his large waist. "Place is a flophouse. He tried to run. Our boys are down there now combing it over. We got an anonymous tip that the guy was flyering the neighborhood for some anti-Chelsea protest. He's got all kinds of crap up there, so he's at least going in the Dissent Registry."

"We've been expecting this for some time," said Eckart. He eyed his own fingertips as he grazed the walls of the station, his arm extended. "Chelsea and some of the other internment centers have been going to pieces. It's been the top story on Truth all week."

"Nationwide?" said the policeman.

"Yeah. It's getting almost as much coverage as the Purges. Savages – all of them. Burning down the only place they can afford to call home. What sense does that make?"

"You got me."

Eckart pushed his fingers forward off the wall as it went from painted plaster to cement. "Anything else we should know?"

"He won't tell us much," said the policeman. "Probably Muslim, but he won't admit it. For a troublemaker, he has awful tight lips now. You handle all the political ones, don't you?"

"We handle the Muslim ones, too."

The policeman chuckled and Eckart smiled.

"How much further is it?" said Blair.

"We're just about here," said the policeman. "I'm not sure how happy the two who collared him are with you being here. His ID said his name was Vincent Cabrisi." The policeman handed the small plastic card to Eckart, who eyed it suspiciously. "I had this feeling about him. You get that feeling with some of them, it's like you can tell – like it's in their eyes or something."

"Anyone detained for dissent is automatically in our jurisdiction anyway," said Eckart. "Even if you can't be sure, it's always better to let us know. You never can tell unless a proper interrogation is conducted – that's how crafty they can be. They think if they can meet the right people, a decent fake can fool anyone."

Eckart removed a small scanner from his pocket and ran the Cabrisi ID. The authenticator buzzed and turned green.

"This is a good one," said Eckart. "I still think it's bullshit."

The policeman reached out ahead and grabbed the knob to a door marked INTERVIEW, opening it.

"Right in here, gentlemen."

The policeman showed the Protection Servicemen a gray room with cement walls and a loose four-legged table in the center with two chairs on each side. The prisoner was sitting in one of the chairs, his arms resting on the table. He was in handcuffs and his dark hair hung down over his face, tangled and dripping wet. His clothing was ripped and his shirt was stained with blood. He raised his head fast, flipping his hair back to look at the three men. His face was bruised and puffy, shiny from sweat and swelling. He coughed loudly as Eckart walked towards him.

"We'll take it from here," said Eckart to the policeman. Eckart took off his coat, folded it at the waist, and placed it on the table. Blair leaned against the wall next to the door and crossed his arms. He looked on as Eckart sat next to his coat on the table facing the dissenter.

"Do you know who we are?" said Eckart with a prying smirk.

"You're an officer in the Protection Services," he said coldly. "Is that your junior partner over there?"

"What makes you so sure?" said Eckart.

"I can tell from how you're dressed. You've got the insignia of a ranking officer on your badge there, means you're important." The prisoner nodded his head towards Blair. "He doesn't have anything on his badge but the PS emblem, and he seems like he defers to you. Am I right so far?"

"If I were you, I'd be more worried about yourself than my partner."

"If you're so smart," said Blair, "then why are we here now?"

"That's a damn fine question. What's your name?"

"Vincent Cabrisi."

Eckart gripped the side of the table for leverage and punched the prisoner square in the jaw, sending him out of his seat and onto the cold cement floor. The jab was quick and it happened so fast that Blair didn't know what happened until Eckart had grabbed the prisoner by his hair and pulled him back into the flimsy chair.

"I'll ask you again," said Eckart. "What is your name?"

"You've got my ID…you know who I am." The prisoner was holding his jaw, wincing as he spoke.

"This is counterfeit."

"What makes you think it's a fake?"

"The police scanned it, they figured out it was phony by the time they sat you in this room. Why do you think we're here?"

"It's not fake!"

"Come on! We know how it works. You'd think a Brit would have some reverence for the country that takes him in after the outbreaks. Never heard an Italian with a British accent. I'm confused. English by way of Italy by way of where…Iraq? Syria? You look Saudi."

Blair fished around in his breast pocket for his pack of cigarettes. He struck his match against the booklet and took a long drag, waving the match out and tossing it on the ground. ProServ certainly had their benefits, Blair thought as he took the cigarette from his mouth and flicked a small amount of ash on the cement floor. Immunity from prosecution was at the top of the list. He could smoke wherever he wanted.

"So why don't you tell me the truth," said Eckart as he placed his hand on the prisoner's shoulder, "and just come clean to us. You want a cigarette?"

"Yeah."

"Blair, give him one."

Blair took the cigarette out of his mouth and passed it to the prisoner, returning to his spot against the gray wall. He watched as the prisoner took a long drag. Eckart took his hand from the man's shoulder.

"You know I looked at your ID card myself," said Eckart. "It's well made, for a fake. I bet even the biometrics match your fingerprints. I mean, they would have to for you to get around." Eckart moved in close to the prisoner's face and spoke with a soft but firm voice. "Why don't you tell us who made it for you? Maybe we let you walk away with a slap on the wrist."

"You people caught me and you know what I've got in my apartment," said the prisoner as he inhaled from the cigarette again, "what makes you think I'm going to cooperate with any of you? This is it for me, I know it." The words left his mouth with drifting white smoke, lingering around Eckart's face. "I'm a dissenter no matter what. What more can you do?"

Blair took another cigarette from his pack and placed it in

his mouth.

"That is not something you want to find out firsthand," said Eckart, baring his teeth close to the man's face. "This is your last chance. Tell us something we want to know, like your real name or where you got that ID card."

"No."

Eckart reached into his belt and pulled out a long blade with a serrated edge, stabbing it into the table. "Last chance – I mean it when I say it."

The man didn't budge.

Eckart grinned and calmly got up and walked to the far end of the table. "Do you know why I let you have that cigarette?" he said as he placed his right hand on his hip.

The man eyed Eckart nervously. "Why?"

"Because it's your last."

The muzzle flash lit up the room, blinding Blair for a moment. He dropped his lit match and cigarette to the floor before he realized Eckart had drawn his pistol and fired three shots into the prisoner's chest. The shots echoed through the room, and a ringing started in Blair's ears. The prisoner fell backwards in his chair, landing hard with a thud and nothing more.

"What the hell was that?" Blair's voice cracked. "I thought we were taking him in!"

Eckart placed his pistol back in its holster, folding the leather strap over the hand grip and snapping it in place. "He was a raghead hiding in plain sight. I could smell it all over him."

Blair couldn't keep his hands still; a slight shaking had taken him over. "But there was more he could have told us. What about where he got his ID?"

"Were you not paying attention? We weren't going to get anything useful out of him. He was unfit for trial, we would have put him

16

in Chelsea anyway. Why bother processing him? A dead unfit is more useful to us than a live one – less paperwork."

"You could have let me know you were going to shoot him," said Blair as he knelt to pick up his cigarette. The floor hurt his knee. "You scared the shit out of me." He nabbed the cig with clumsy shaking hands. Eckart made his way toward Blair, and as he stood up Eckart had lit his steel Zippo lighter for him.

"You should get one of these," said Eckart as he snapped it shut, "they're better than matches – nothing to throw away."

"I'll try to remember." As Blair drew in the smoke, his nerves began to calm. Plumes of white filled up the room again. The door flew open, a policeman storming in with his gun drawn. Eckart and Blair turned to face him.

"What happened here?"

"ProServ business," said Eckart as he flashed his SubCrimes ID. "We exercised our own judicial discretion. You aren't needed."

The policeman put his gun down, a sour look on his face. "I'll have someone come in here for the body then." He shut the door behind himself as he left.

"Now we can learn something useful," said Eckart as he removed his scanner from his trench coat pocket. "The flatfoots don't have this kind of tech." He took the scanner and put it against the dead man's fingertip after punching in his ID serial. As it dinged approvingly, Eckart picked up the dead man's hand and held his thumb. He started scratching lightly at the fingerprint and a thin film began to come off his thumb. "Look at this." Eckart ran the device on the clean print. An alarm buzzed on the device and the thing flashed IMPRINT MISMATCH…SCANNING GENISYS FILES.

"What's Genisys?" said Blair as he took another drag from his cigarette. "Haven't heard of that before."

"You wouldn't, Officer. It's General Information Systems.

Bunch of eggheads out of Cambridge, it's a tech company. They collect metadata. We contract with them; they've got files on everybody. You're all getting a tour soon." The scanner started beeping. "See? We've already got a match."

Eckart looked at the scanner screen and pulled up the matching DNA file of the man on the floor.

"Christ."

"What? Who the hell is he?"

"The DNA match came up for a file on an Abd al-Haqq. He's an unfit…"

"What?"

"Let's see if he's chipped." Eckart pulled the dead man's shirt sleeve up and scanned his arm. The scanner started beeping. Eckart read the scanner. "He's got an implant. The son of a bitch was interned in Chelsea three months ago."

"How did he get out?" Blair dropped his cigarette butt to the ground and stepped on it.

"I don't know. We're going to the Facility to find out. Let's get out of here." Eckart gathered his belongings. He adjusted his heavy coat collar before taking the knife out of the table. Blair stared at the dead man, a pool of blood collecting under him. "This isn't our problem anymore, Blair. Let the garbage men handle the garbage." Eckart led Blair out of the interrogation room. Blair turned back to close the door and looked through the blurred glass window. Before walking away, he took a glance at the word on the door. INTERVIEW.

CHAPTER II

Congressman Joe Grant slouched in the back of a black sedan, drinking a whiskey on the rocks as his driver navigated the Back Bay traffic. The ice clanged in his glass as he swirled it. He leaned closer to his driver as he spoke.

"How much longer?"

"Not more than a few minutes, Congressman. Not factoring the security checkpoint."

"We get waved through. They know we're coming."

"We'll be there shortly then."

"Good." Grant took a swig of the whiskey and spoke again. "Hey, where you from?"

"Hell's Kitchen, originally."

"Jesus. You lose anyone?"

"More than half my close family. Maybe one or two are still in the Brooklyn Quarantine Zone, in Red Hook. They're not great at record keeping so it's hard to know. Some of us came up here. It's where all the opportunity is supposed to be now."

"I'm sorry about that. We'll get them all one day. al-Mummit, Ikhwaan. All of them. Anything I may be able to do for you? Maybe I can put out feelers for you in Brooklyn."

"Not really. What's done is done. You know I don't know if we'll ever find the guy, honestly. Every time they think they have him he gives everybody the slip. Thank you though, sir. I appreciate the offer."

"I wouldn't be so sure. I'm hearing a lot about him popping up in Nigeria. We may be deploying there soon… Praetorian Global mission, I mean. They won the contract."

Grant finished the rest of his drink as the sedan pulled up to the front of Arbitrage Tower. ProServ had sentries patrolling the grounds and working security. The driver rolled the window down to speak to a guard.

"I've got Congressman Grant here for a meeting with Executive Vice President Mura."

Grant cracked the window and looked to the guard. The guard pulled a small scanner from his hip belt and ran the biometrics. When the database photo of Joseph Grant appeared in the small screen of the device, the guard looked up.

"Yes sir, Mr. Mura is expecting you Congressman. We can escort you to his office."

"Very good," said Grant. He turned to the driver. "I'm all set from here. What was your name, by the way?"

The driver turned back to face Grant.

"Tim, Congressman. Tim Vernon."

"Take care, Tim. Good meeting you."

Grant patted the driver on the shoulder and stepped out of the black sedan, buttoning his jacket before adjusting his tie. The guard was joined by another sentry, each with automatic weapons holstered to their body armor. Grant walked at a fast clip to avoid as much of the falling snow as he could. One rushed ahead up a few steps to open the door, and Grant stepped through without looking twice at the sentry. A young woman, pretty and heightened by her heels stood with a leather portfolio bound up in her arms. She tucked it under her arm as the Congressman approached her and extended her hand to shake his.

"Hello Congressman, Executive Vice President Mura is waiting for you upstairs. I'll be escorting you the rest of the way."

The woman waved the two escorts off, and Grant smiled as he

watched them walk back outside into the cold and the falling snow.

"We're all on a first name basis here, I hope: call me Joe. Please." Grant thought of her naked.

"My name is Anna. I'm Julian Mura's executive aide."

The two walked at a fast clip through the lobby littered with the many employees of Arbitrage Holdings and its countless subsidiaries and affiliates, past the check-in desk, and towards the bank of elevators.

"Mr. Mura is very happy that you could meet with him about new opportunities for business development. How was the traffic here?"

"A bit rough, but we made it. Very impressive work that Arbitrage is doing with the Back Bay. We could see all the cranes coming into the new downtown."

"When we're finished the old John Hancock will be dwarfed by the new Arbitrage Headquarters."

"I very nearly forgot this was the Hancock."

The elevator dinged as it opened in front of them. They stepped on and Anna pushed the button for the 60th floor. The elevator made its way up the shaft and towards Mura's top floor office.

"So, your boss is pretty much running the show here in Boston now, is that right Anna?"

"Yes sir. Mr. Mura oversees all new projects and operations in the Northeast, including the internment program and resettlement for British refugees. Prior to that, he led the consolidation of several private military contractors into Protection Services. He rarely grants meetings to those outside of Arbitrage and its subsidiaries unless we're making a buyout or opening up a new market."

Grant's ears popped as he watched the floor numbers move through the thirties, then forties and fifties. The elevator made its way to the top floor with incredible speed. The doors dinged and let them both out. Grant was surprised by a painting in the lobby area. It was oil on canvass: a king's feast taking place in a hall with oversized columns and a massive tower in the background. A panic had gripped the feast goers as the clouds parted and the heavens heaved with anger. He didn't immediately notice Julian Mura standing outside the doors of his office.

"Impressive, isn't it? John Martin painting. *Belshazzar's Feast.*"

"Knowing you, that must be the original." Grant extended his hand, shaking Mura's as they smiled.

"This? No. I don't think it is, actually." Mura bared his teeth, and Joe noticed the subtle sharpness of Mura's incisors. "Not to worry...I have many, many more."

"Good to see you, Mr. Mura."

"Come into my office for a drink."

*   *   *

Blair and Eckart were cruising through the streets of Chelsea, part of a convoy of ProServ Humvees. They were in the middle vehicle, sandwiched at both ends by Tactical Division squads armed with automatic weapons and manned machine gun turrets. Blair and Eckart were sitting in the backseat, Eckart talking on his phone as Blair stared out the window. The whole place looked washed out, like a warzone on the other side of the world. They zoomed past buildings set ablaze and endless rubble. The smell of smoke was thick in the air and he could hear gunfire in the distance on and off.

"That's right," said Eckart. "We're on our way now. Be ready and waiting outside."

Eckart hung up the phone and turned to Blair.

"We're going to meet with an informant of ours – a member of the Chelsea Council."

"They let them have cell phones in here?"

"Not exactly."

The convoy came to a hard stop. "Stay here," said the driver.

"The rioting is winding down, but we don't wanna take any chances. He's being ushered out now."

A tall and slender man in a long wool coat with dark hair and features hurried himself into the middle Humvee. As quickly as the convoy had stopped, it started moving again as the man in the wool coat climbed over Blair to sit in the middle seat between him and Eckart.

"Hello Lieutenant. Who's your partner? Name's Dhananjay." Dan extended his hand to Blair to shake.

"How are the Pakis faring in here, Dan?" Eckart pulled his scanner out and showed him a picture of Abd al-Haqq. "Where does he live?"

"Couldn't tell you. I'm Indian," said Dan.

"I could give a shit."

Dan sighed and threw a look at Blair before he turned back to Eckart. "His name is al-Haqq – he's been a pain in the ass for us. He was involved with a lot of the unfits trying to start rebellion on this side of the Wall. He was a real activist, but he went off the grid a while back. The last I heard he was squatting in some place near Malone Park on Lafayette."

"You're sure of this?"

"Positive." Dan smiled uneasily as Eckart stared at him.

Eckart turned to the driver. "You heard him. Head to Malone Park."

Blair continued to look at the buildings and street corners as the snow fell and unfits huddled themselves around burning trash cans and makeshift pyres. They weren't menacing looking like in the posters or in the training videos. They mostly just looked defeated. Usually Chelsea bustled and just looked like some overpopulated slum. It was a curious place, a transplanted township from a third world country just five minutes outside Boston. Today it felt different.

Skirmishes with rebels and the deployed ProServ tactical units were breaking out in spurts. Blair could see it in most their faces: nobody wanted any part of this violence. Most of them seemed to be interned by a quirk of fate. One global catastrophe lead to another until a few hundred thousand people deemed unfit for trial called the tattered remains of a once proud city their home. Blair was surprised when the convoy came to another stop, nearly sending him out the front window of the Humvee.

"Stay sharp, everybody," said Eckart. "We have aerial support coming in fast. Let's roll."

Protection Servicemen clad in full body armor and urban camouflage swarmed the outside of the convoy. The ones manning the machine gun turrets readied themselves: one pointed at a shanty settlement made of corrugated plastic and metal sheets and trash set up in Malone Park, the other pointed squarely at a brick apartment building.

The whirring of a helicopter grew steadily louder until it was on top of them. It hovered over the target building and two ropes descended from the chopper followed by commandos rappelling down to the roof. They readied their machine guns, scrambling to secure the area. A voice came over the radio in the Humvee.

"Roof is secure. Assessing the street from the top. It's a go."

"Alright, let's move out," said Eckart. "Blair, come with me."

"What do I do now?" said Dan.

"Enjoy the show." Eckart tapped the driver of the Humvee on the shoulder. "Watch him."

"Yes, sir," said the driver as he took the gun from his holster, keeping it on his lap.

The ProServ commandos moved into the red brick building with Eckart and Blair following close. Eckart drew his pistol from his holster and Blair followed suit, keeping it low and pointed at the ground. Blair pounded his left fist on his body armor, a ritual that gave him some piece of mind. His adrenaline was going. Blair never sought out the kind of action that most Service grunts prayed for daily, but now it was on top of him and it had him feeling he could sprint at light speed.

The halls of the place were a blur, commandos kicking in each door and securing rooms of screaming women and ragged children huddling for warmth. Just when Blair thought the place was coming up empty, he heard muffled music that seemed to make the whole place throb. As two commandos rushed ahead of Eckart and Blair and up a flight of stairs at the end of the hall, machine gun fire broke out and a commando fell backwards. He was a tangled mess on the staircase, covered in his own blood.

"Second floor! Second floor! Get here now!" yelled Eckart to the other commandos still clearing rooms.

Massive booms made Blair cover his ears and duck into a corner before the stairs. The machine gun turret was ripping apart the second floor, blasting out windows and taking chunks of brick off the building. A commando radioed for the Humvees to hold fire as more ProServ grunts made it down from the roof to the third floor. Blair made a dash up the stairs after the commandos rushed the second floor and lit the place up with muzzle flash. The shooting stopped as two commandos, followed close by Eckart and then Blair, nimbly made their way into one of the apartments. They stepped over an unfit riddled with bullets and coughing blood bubbles strewn out on the floor, an AK-47 just inches from his outstretched arm. Eckart kicked the Kalashnikov away from him, pointing his pistol at his face. He fired a shot, killing the man instantly.

The music was still loud, the only thing that could be heard in the apartment. Eckart turned to Blair to mouth something but Blair could barely hear him as the two commandos disappeared into another room. It's *The Clash*, Blair thought listening to the pounding music. An album he liked to listen to as a kid. Blair blinked. He was staring down the barrel of his pistol as it smoked. He looked around and saw hot shell casings and a dead man who had fallen backwards into the bathroom. The man landed in a tub covered in his own blood. The music stopped.

"Blair," said Eckart softly. "Blair, put the gun down. Put it back in your holster, alright? We're good here."

Blair stood stupid, his mouth hanging open slightly.

"You good?" said Eckart with a chuckle as he patted Blair on the shoulder. "I didn't think you had it in you."

Blair let Eckart lower his arm and the gun seemed to go back into its holster on its own. He rubbed his own neck slowly. An unfit had jumped out of the bathroom from behind the wall and was about to spray bullets at Eckart and himself, and then the training and everything his brother Stephen had ever taught him had taken over.

"Lieutenant Eckart, come and take a look at this!" yelled a commando from the bedroom. Eckart put his hand on Blair's shoulder and ushered him into the room. He smiled ear to ear when he saw what was inside the closet: an entire cache of automatic weapons, submachine guns, and assault rifles.

"This kind of thing makes careers," said Eckart.

Blair went into his pocket for a cigarette. He took a long drag and sat down at the edge of the bed as a commando holstered his machine gun to his chest and started rummaging through the weapons.

"Everything we've been taking off the streets, it's all right here."

Blair watched as Eckart made his way to a bureau to pick up a framed picture, three men all smiling and with their arms around each other's shoulders. Two of them were strewn out dead on the floor of the apartment. The third was Abd al-Haqq. Blair took the photo from Eckart and began to examine it, flipping it over. It read HOSNI, SABRI, ABD. HAJJ TO MECCA.

"We did good today, Blair. Very good."

*　*　*

Joe Grant was laughing with Mura in his office as they drank. The place was all cold steel, large windows and sleek furniture. Spotless marble floors were black and veiny. The telephone rang.

"Pardon me, will you?" Mura asked.

"Of course."

Mura made his way to his desk, away from his drinks cart and picked up the line. Joe looked out the windows, extending from floor to ceiling and offering views for miles around. He saw faint smoke drifting up from Chelsea as he took a long swig, swishing the ice cubes around. He bit his lip slightly as Mura put the phone back on the hook.

"Good news?" said Joe.

"Good for you, yes."

"How so?"

"Why don't we have a seat?" The two made their way over to Mura's standalone desk. Joe eased himself into the seat across from Mura. "Before I get into that, we want you to know how much we appreciate the work you're doing for us on the Hill. Your advocacy, support, what have you. I know these last few years haven't been easy."

"My pleasure, Julian. The work that goes on here is too important. I mean it."

"ProServ just uncovered a significant cache of weapons in Chelsea. They think it's the supply for the unfits responsible for the attacks." Mura put his glass down.

"Is that so," said Grant. He realized Mura had sipped very little of his drink.

"We're trying like hell to regain control. We're parting ways with the current leadership team. How they let this deteriorate as badly as they did, I'll never understand…"

"I thought the Chancellor was close with Leader Wright. Particularly here."

"He was. Now, it seems there's some rift. He'll be on trial in DC by the end of the month, along with a few deputies."

"Good Lord."

"That means there's an opening, Joe." Mura picked up his glass and took a small swig. "We're in the market for a new Chancellor to run the internment program here at Chelsea. We'd like it to be you."

"I don't know what to say. Thank you, Julian."

"Moments like this I'd prefer you say yes." Mura took his drink and raised it to Grant. "Congratulations."

The two took long swigs and Joe emptied his glass. Mura picked up a remote and pointed it towards a large wall. After clicking it, a massive display screen unfolded with a map of Chelsea, with highlighted zones.

"As you know, Arbitrage won federal contracts to detain suspected terrorists and political dissidents due to ongoing conflicts worldwide. We've struggled with developing models for detainment, currently 35 million nationwide with several million in New England alone. However, after your legislation and cooperation with several of our affiliate companies, Chelsea along with other…what did you used to call them?"

"Gateway Cities."

"Right…cute. Some of these Gateway Cities were effectively condemned and transformed into internment centers. We've had such good fortune we've begun replicating the model nationwide. We want you to run Chelsea on a day-to-day basis. I know the program technically constitutes several facilities, but we're already in the process of decommissioning many smaller internment zones and shipping the unfits to Chelsea, or our new Camp Birch Tree, near Amherst. Chelsea is the big show. That means providing food, shelter, clothing, policing strategies, effectively a place to warehouse those inside these facilities while we search for a more permanent solution to the Unfit Question."

"You know I don't even have the clearance to know exactly what's going on with the program."

"Quarters are becoming cramped for the unfits. We initially planned on 50,000 more moving in by the end of the year from our smaller facility in Lawrence and the Mattapan Processing Center, but we've already encountered rioting in certain sections. We're hoping it's coming to an end. With the most recent operation in Malone Park, we think that things will be a bit quieter in the future."

"Here's hoping." Joe drank the melting ice.

"You know officially that the internment program exists as a precautionary measure to help prevent future attacks on par with Black Friday: nuclear, radiological, chemical, or biological as we suspect in the British Isles. Our private military contractors – under ideal circumstances – cast a judicious net and detain those who fit a specific profile. We do have fears that Leader Wright and his most loyal followers are relishing in the opportunity a bit too much. Increasingly, we find newly declared unfits to be little more than what the Leader deems to be personal political opponents, and new private military recruits seem to be taking on a more radical ideological bent. But the government continues to pay for every person interned at the rates we set." Mura smiled. "Good business while it lasts."

"I know what you mean."

"We want to make sure it all goes as well as it possibly can, given the circumstances. Personally, I don't think I'd trust anybody else with this responsibility." Mura fetched more whiskey and sat at the edge of his table to pour Joe another. "You understand the importance. You've built the template: we're expanding our facilities in California and Texas, all over. You're the innovator here. How do you think that'll serve you politically in years to come?"

"I have no intentions of seeking higher office."

"Sure you do." Mura stood up and patted Grant on the back. "You're built for it, clearly. Governor's out after this term. Perhaps a cabinet post could be in your future as well, should you serve the Leader well here – and even he can't live forever. While your friends in Congress twiddle their thumbs and debate how many stars should be added to the flag after the Caribbean incursions, you'll have been doing serious work securing the future of the American people. Regardless, we're prepared to offer you an employment package today.

"What are the terms?"

"$40 million over five years."

Grant choked a bit on his drink and cleared his throat.

"That includes benefits and equity in Protection Services, which is the subsidiary in charge of this sector. Depending on the success of your tenure, we may renew your contract. Whether or not you continue in that capacity, you will have a significant stake in ProServ at a time when it's primed for rapid growth at home and abroad."

"I'm truly honored by all of this. But you do understand that I'm going to want to run Chelsea as I want to run it, right?"

"I couldn't imagine any other arrangement. Just as you understand your performance will be closely monitored."

"I get it, I can appreciate that."

"You dismissed your driver as instructed?"

"I did."

"Good. In a few moments we'll have a chopper waiting for you on the helipad on the roof. You'll get a full aerial tour of the Chelsea Facility."

"Excellent. Any paperwork I need to sign?"

"We'll send everything to your office. Congratulations again, Joe. We know you're the only man for the job. Our only catch is we would like to start you on a provisional basis as soon as possible."

"Hmm, that could be tricky. I'll make it work."

Mura stood up and raised his glass. "To the future, Joe. Yours and ours."

Grant stood as well. "To the future."

CHAPTER III

"This is the Truth – an Arbitrage Media Partner. A breaking story on the Homefront: Protection Services executed a daring raid inside the Chelsea Internment Facility yesterday, killing several terrorist unfits and uncovering large stockpiles of automatic weapons. For the fourth consecutive day now, fighting has erupted in the Facility designated for suspected enemy combatants and others deemed potential security risks – however with recent ProServ successes it is estimated that such violence should be coming to an end. Three of the unfits, identified as brothers of Arab descent, are thought to be agents of the Ikhwaan terrorist organization responsible for the events of Black Friday in New York. In other news, Volkstaat forces continued their siege of Cape Town with American and French naval vessels assisting the sea blockade…"

Harold Maguire listened to the Truth as it tumbled out of his clock radio, his face buried in his pillow. They commandeered the airwaves at the top of every hour on most TV, radio stations, and streaming services for a few minutes every day – in addition to their own 24-hour networks. He moved his head to the side and stared at the ash tray on his bedside table as the newscaster muttered something about radiation levels spiking in the Mid-Atlantic States. Harold reached for his lighter, then gingerly picked up what was left of his joint from the night before and brought it to his lips, lighting it at the end. He took a long drag and held it in his lungs for a few seconds before letting the smoke drift out of his nose and mouth.

His phone rang. The number was one he didn't recognize so he let it sit buzzing on the bedside table. The sheets drifted off Harold as he sat himself up, still smoking. The phone vibrated again, and a voicemail icon appeared on the screen. Harold picked it up.

"Hi Harold, this is Hannah from Congressman Joe Grant's office. We wanted to let you know that Joe is interested in sitting down with you sometime soon to discuss a few personal and professional matters. Please give us a call at your earliest convenience. Thank you and have a good day."

Fucking tool, Harold thought as he dialed Grant's office. We've known each other since college and he still has an assistant call me? Because he's such a big swinging dick? Asshole.

"Good morning, Office of Congressman Joe Grant. How may I help you?"

"Hi, Hannah?"

"Yes"

"Harold Maguire here. You just called."

"Hi Harold! How's everything going?"

"Good enough."

"And Aiden?"

"She's coming back from school soon. I'm meeting the boyfriend as well, so that should be good for some entertainment…"

"Oh, that's rich! Joe wanted me to get in touch with you about meeting with him soon; do you have time in your schedule today? He's all clear for a window between two and four in the afternoon."

"I think I can sneak away today."

"Shall we send a car for you?"

"That would be fine."

"How does two o'clock sound?"

"Let's do it. I'll be at the house. Thanks, Hannah."

Harold hung up. Of course I can sneak away, Harold thought. I don't have a real job. Harold made his way to the shower in the bathroom down the short hall of his upstairs, pulling the curtains back and turning the faucet. He turned it completely to the other side, as hot as it could go. As the steam of the shower lingered into his bathroom and fogged his window and vanity mirror, he stepped in. The water warmed him to the bone after a night of power failures. The whole country's grid was falling apart, and oftentimes the power company would brown out the poorer living quarters to ensure a constant flow to areas designated a priority by the utility companies. He had gotten used to it.

He stepped in and leaned against the shower wall, letting the water fall on his hair and neck. It ran down his back, thawing him out from the past night's sleep. He had begun to close his eyes, wishing he could fall asleep again standing right there. The thought was interrupted when the shower sprayed him with icy cold water, shocking Harold out of his stupor. He slammed his right hand against the wall. "FUCK!" As Harold's teeth began to chatter, he soaped up, rinsed off, and got out. It was only until he stepped out of the shower and reached for his bath towel that Harold realized the lights had dimmed in the bathroom. Another brownout had been initiated. They were happening more than usual. Maybe Joe could fill him in.

*   *   *

Harold wound his way through the taupe walls and bland décor of Joe Grant's district office lobby. When he reached Joe's office, an eager looking young man smiled and buzzed him in.

"Hi, are you Harold Maguire?"

"That's me."

"Have a seat, Mr. Maguire! The Congressman will see you shortly."

The young man went off with haste into the office space behind him, making his way through cubicle-partitioned halls. Poor kid, Harold thought. He probably thinks he has a future in this. Harold has thought that, once.

Joe appeared before him. "There he is! How's it going Harold?" Joe Grant reached around Harold and gave him a back-slapping sort of hug. Harold forced a smile.

"Good to see you again, Congressman."

"Come on, Harold. Call me Joe. Come with me to my office. You want anything, coffee or a snack?"

He spoke with a natural smile that Harold knew was little more than a trained response to the constant wave of beggars in expensive suits and bottomless appetites. They made their way back to Grant's office, the Congressman closing the door behind them.

"Have a seat," said Grant as he sat down behind his desk facing Harold. "It's good to see you again Harry. What's new?"

"Not much. Aiden's coming back from school."

"I can't believe she's already in college. That's unbelievable! How does she like UMass?"

"So far so good. Although I think she may be a bit too much like us at that age…"

"Hmm…I'll keep that in mind. I can call the dean; make sure she doesn't end up in the Dissent Registry or something. You know how that can be."

"Sadly, yes. Nice kid you have out front there."

"He's an idiot," said Grant. "Some intern, big-time donor's son. We'll be letting him go soon. Nothing like Janet. Your wife made this office hum. We're all still feeling it. We miss her so much; I can't even begin to imagine how you feel."

"You knew that before you hired her, though."

"Some days I really miss our time as the campus rabble rousers." Grant chuckled as he opened his desk drawer. He pulled a bottle of scotch and two glasses from the desk and started pouring. "Aged 30 years. You want a glass?"

"Sure, why not."

"Here you go."

Harold took the glass in his hand and took a swig.

"That's excellent; very smooth, Joe."

"I wanted to invite you in to catch up on things. This isn't public knowledge yet: there's going to be a lot of press in the next few days, but I wanted to tell you personally that I'm going to be resigning my seat in Congress. Arbitrage wants me to oversee internment here, which as you might know is mostly based out of Chelsea at this point."

Harold stared at the glass and took another sip. "Congratulations. That's a big deal."

"It's the right move to make at this point in time," said Grant. He started stroking his hair in the direction it was combed, bringing his hand back to his chin as he continued. "I think to myself all the time about the state of the world we're living in…"

Grant droned on. Harold drank more of the aged scotch and considered how completely full of shit the man sitting behind his desk was. Grant kept on about how he would revamp security measures for the country, about his obligation to the Party and the people of Boston to do everything in his power to keep them safe. Grant's ability to bullshit was his greatest strength. But that strength, that capacity to lie convincingly, was his greatness weakness as well. Grant had the ability to bullshit himself.

"I brought you in today, Harold, because I want you to have some involvement with what's happening."

"You're serious?"

"I know your politics, Harold. You're a reasonable guy and it's why I respect you. For all the shit that's going on in these places, we need someone who can temper the violence and resentment that the unfits have for us. There's no hope in there. We need someone who can oversee outreach with the unfit populations. You'd be coordinating with their internal councils and figure out a way to improve quality of life with the limited resources we have for them. I think you have that capacity, and I'm choosing to put my faith in you."

If he were serious about improving the lives of unfits, Harold thought, he'd open the gates and let them all go free. Now this man, feigning interest in their horrible lives, wants to ride in like a white knight and make everyone love him. Unfits included. People who lived in shacks made of refuse and lived on scraps. People who huddled over open flames to keep warm and did God knows what just to survive day to day. He expected to be adored by the emaciated and the distraught because he would be the one to make their lives just a little bit better. This man was rotten to his core.

"So what do you think, Harold? Are you up to it?"

"What would this job even look like?"

Joe Grant smiled. "God…that's you in a nutshell. I'm giving you an opportunity here and you're trying to talk me out of it."

Harold smirked back. "Don't get me wrong." He leaned forward and put the glass on Grant's desk. "I'm interested. What would I need to do? What does it mean, exactly?"

"Well, it would mean Party membership for one – and I don't mean standard cookie-cutter card carrying either. This position would put you on the track to be a real leader in this part of the country. I mean if you wanted to be."

"Really?"

"As long as you don't fuck it up." Grant laughed. "Honestly, I'm amazed you didn't take a crack at running for office yourself. We could have really mixed it up, you and me. Maybe this way is better."

"I wouldn't want to get you into trouble out of the gate."

"These unfits wouldn't be burning Chelsea to the ground and making everyone nervous if they had enough food to eat or better living conditions. It's why Hartford basically went up in flames not long ago and it's why they're trying to close out the Lawrence Facility. I know you know that. This is your chance to make the big, meaningful difference I know you're aching for. Let me tell you something, too." Grant leaned in closer as he spoke in hushed tones. "There's a lot of bad stuff going on in the Party right now, Wright is totally paranoid, and he thinks the bottom is falling out from under him. If you join me – let's just say there are a lot more people hovering around who think like us as opposed to Dear Leader and his true believers." Harold nodded as Grant leaned back into his chair and returned to his normal volume. "Plus, with what I'm hearing about with mortgaged properties in Metro North right now, it might be the best thing for you to join up."

"I wanted to talk to you about that, Joe. What's going on with these foreclosure threats? I pay every cent of the mortgage on time every month. It's scaring the shit out of my tenants."

"It's where your properties are located. It's prime territory for redevelopment. It's not personal. Like I was saying, Keiser Blackstone is consolidating all the banks up there, they're Arbitrage-backed. My hands are tied. Look, I know it's a bad situation. That's why I'm giving you this opportunity. Don't get me wrong, you're the best guy for this job – but think of it as added incentive. Better to have the banksters be cutting your checks than trying to collect."

"How would I apply for Party membership?"

"It's easy. We can take care of that for you, we'll get you fast tracked through the whole process. All it would really take is your saying yes, Harold. We can handle anything else that might creep up. I'm telling you that this is where you need to be. It'll certainly raise your standard of living. You won't have to worry about how you're going to pay for Aiden's school. Who knows? You do this for a while and you may be sitting where I am now, if that bug ever does strike you like it did me."

Harold looked down at his scotch, swirled it around in his glass and took a long gulp. He raised the empty glass to Grant. "Let me think on it."

Grant smiled. It was all small talk for the two and more scotch was poured as if Harold had already agreed. They reminisced more about their college days and shared laughs.

"What's on the agenda for you after I walk out?" said Harold.

"Slow day, just winding down now. Not much to do when you're a lame duck. I've got some ProServ guys coming in soon. I'm giving them a commendation."

"Was that for the raid yesterday? In Chelsea? That seems fast."

"They spearheaded the whole operation so I figured it would be nice to have them come in and congratulate them. Good way to kick off the new gig, win some friends in low places. Then you sit back and watch the word spread."

"Always an angle," said Harold with a laugh.

"You know it, brother."

A knock came at the door and the plucky young man from the front desk stuck his head through the doorway.

"Congressman, the ProServ officers are here to see you."

"Tell them one minute, I'm just finishing up in here."

Harold extended his hand to Joe Grant and they shook.

"I want you to let us know as soon as possible. Give me a call anytime, Harold."

"Thanks Joe. Thanks for everything."

"Let me walk you out."

They made their way through the partitioned halls and back to the front office and saw the two Servicemen sitting on the lobby couch.

"Good talk, Harold. Take care."

"See you soon," said Harold. As he left, he nodded to the two Servicemen who stood for Grant as he appeared. "Thank you for your service." The older of the two dismissed him but the younger said thank you. As Harold opened the door to leave, he overheard Grant making his introduction.

"How are you boys doing? Officer Blair and Lieutenant Eckart if I'm not mistaken?"

CHAPTER IV

Eckart and Blair were headed to the other side of the Containment Wall again. It was dark out and the weather was unseasonable – the snow was melting, and it was balmy in the open air. Eckart had rounded up a few more Servicemen for a night out. They were parked at the McArdle Bridge Checkpoint, waiting for clearance to come through. The bridge was fenced at several points with barbed wire and constant spotlight passes at night, creating security compartments along the way. ProServ officers armed with assault rifles monitored the gates from watchtowers. All were clad in urban camouflage, helmeted and ready for the next riot. Blair exhaled and smoke filled the air around him as he flicked cigarette ash out the passenger window.

"How's it looking inside now?" said Eckart.

"Got quiet real fast after you boys rolled through." The gatekeeper's headset buzzed and he reached for his ear to hear his orders. "You guys are cleared. Have fun."

The ProServ Humvee rolled down the McArdle Bridge as gates opened for their entry. As the last gate closed, they zig zagged around fenced partitions until they stopped in front of another large gate. After a minute or two of slow going, the second thick iron gate built into the tall concrete walls of the Facility lumbered and screeched open. The gate was half rust and dense, some unholy bellowing monster stretching its jaws and unleashing a guttural moan. The gate was finally open, and they sped off into the streets of Chelsea.

"It's eerie how quiet it is now. I don't even see that many people in the streets anymore." Blair took a long drag and blew smoke that danced out of the window. "What are we going to do about that guy?"

"What guy?" said Eckart.

"The one we interrogated the other day. The one who managed to get out of this place."

"We're here to have a good time, Blair. Don't think about it right now. I've got something planned here."

But that was a useless thing to say, Blair thought. It was all he could think about. The Humvee came to a halt outside a three story red brick building in the shape of a vamp. By the looks of the place you wouldn't know you were in Chelsea, Blair thought. The Chelsea electric grid alternated between nonfunctioning and a bad joke, but this place was juiced just fine. Neon signs lit up the windows and he saw unfits ranging from the kind of goons who would otherwise be hired muscle to women barely dressed laughing and kissing and smoking and dancing. They all mingled with the Servicemen who were already there. This was it, Blair thought. The Joy Division.

"Move out, gents," said Eckart.

The place was filled with smoke and loud music a few decades old. Blair was overwhelmed by the distinct smell of sex, growing more potent as the four men made their way to a round old wooden table stained with cheap beer. Eckart motioned to a call girl working the room to come over. She was a Spanish girl in a miniskirt and tank top.

"Bring us a bottle of something and send some talent over this way, would you?"

"Vodka!" yelled Clark, one of the Servicemen who had joined them. "We'll treat you right my love, don't worry."

The girl smiled nervously and spoke with a thick accent. She gripped the back of her neck with one hand as she spoke. "Vodka and girls. Yes, thank you sirs." She walked away and Clark looked over to

Blair and Eckart.

"A newcomer to our shores, no doubt. I could tax that for all it's worth."

"Which division are you in, Clark?" Blair yelled over the music.

"Sex Crimes." Clark's eyes wandered to the stage where a woman was working her way around a dance pole.

"How's that going?"

Clark leaned towards Blair. "I'm supposed to investigate top Party members for irregular activities and dissenting sexual conduct. So I've got free time on my hands."

Clouds of cigarette smoke and artificial fog filled up the place. The clouds bent the neon light coming from the performance stages and light fixtures hanging in the windows and decorating the interior. The women dancing were dark-skinned but they were fine women, Blair thought. Clark took a little plastic baggie with two small tablets in it out of his shirt pocket. The girl came back with a bottle of vodka and four glasses, poured, and left the table. Eckart raised his glass.

"To Blair and the takedown that made this shithole a little more bearable. And to doing what it takes."

As they drank, Clark put the two tablets in his mouth and chased them with the vodka.

"You wanna roll, Blair?"

"I'll stick with the booze. Am I the only one who hasn't been here before?"

"I think so, bro!" Yelled Jansen, the fourth at the table. He was an idiot. Blair went through training with Jansen much like the other grunts; he learned to tune them out when they started speaking nonsense. That was usually what came out whenever they opened their mouths.

"You'll have a good time Blair," said Eckart. " Unless you catch something. Though even that was good for Clark; he put it on his resume and ended up in Sex Crimes."

"Fearless leader and funnyman," said Clark as he flipped Eckart off. "You get called up for riot duty for the protests coming up?"

"I got my notice today," said Blair.

"I'll be there," said Eckart.

"Fine way to spend Christmas," said Clark. "At least we're getting overtime pay. Supposed to be cake from what I heard – it's all rich kids and snowflakes making noise. The lion's share won't even end up in the Registry."

"That's always the way," said Eckart. "The ones who take the biggest risks are the ones who don't understand them. They shout and then they hide behind Mommy and Daddy. Spoiled rotten and living in a bubble, crying for the people who'd obliterate them if they had the chance."

Blair felt a hand on his shoulder. He looked up and saw the face of a woman with light brown skin and soft features. She had dark eyes and he stared directly at her as she pressed her lips against his, her tongue already in his mouth. She grabbed his hair and pulled it slightly and Blair found himself reach up to grip hers. He pulled back to take a better look at her and she spoke. "I hear you're the man of the hour. I'm yours for as long as you want."

Blair looked around at the table, each one of his fellow officers smiling at him. "Compliments of the house," said Eckart. "Our treat."

"You're serious?" said Blair. He raised his drink to his lips and finished it. He scanned the room and noticed at the far end of the bar a cabal of men staring at him. Probably the ones who provided the girl. They had the look of the Chelsea Auxiliary Force, the band of a few thousand unfits handpicked by the Council to handle security in the Chelsea Ghetto. The majority were gangsters – thugs and criminals meant to keep the peace in exchange for better treatment while they were interned. Many were transferred from state prisons for budget reasons. They were really the only human beings that deserved to be locked up forever in this place, Blair thought. They stared as he followed the woman through the writhing crowd, under the hanging smoke.

The table and the rest of the men sitting at it were tinged by the neon light and Blair saw that some other girls were crowding around them. Clark was stroking one's arm and Eckart was grabbing at another. Blair lost sight of them and followed his girl behind thick curtains and up a flight of creaking wooden stairs where the smell of garbage grew stronger. He watched her from behind as she climbed the stairs, and her figure swayed back and forth.

Blair found himself in a room that was all mood lighting and shades of bold red, this woman standing in front of him peeling off her clothes. The window was open, and Blair welcomed the cool breeze. Blair was thinking of the million things he wanted to do as he moved toward the dark, shapely woman naked in front of him.

*   *   *

"What's your name?" said Blair as he lay holding the woman on the rickety bed. They were lying above the covers, and as Blair looked around at the place, he was less impressed with the surroundings. The carpet was more filth than fiber and he had realized that the window was kept open out of necessity because of the stink coming from everywhere. "I mean your real name."

"Asiyah."

"I enjoyed that, Asiyah. It was good."

Asiyah got up and started putting on her clothes. Blair sat himself up in the bed and leaned against the headboard. His mind was clear now. "So…how does all this work for you?"

"What do you mean?"

"I mean, I imagine that you sort of do this as your living. Right?"

"There aren't really jobs in this place. It's just how things play out. Most of us get forced into what we do, or how we live." Asiyah pulled her skirt over her shoulders and let it slide down her body moving slow over her hips and thighs. "How long have you been in ProServ?" She pulled the bottom of the dress down to the halfway point between her knees and waist.

"Not long at all. Months. My brother was in the Army before he went private. Special Forces. He showed me a lot, so I guess I beat the learning curve with some stuff."

"Well from what I've heard, you're someone to watch. The shootout in Malone Park has everyone talking."

"I'll choose to take that as a compliment."

"It was."

"Were those guys at the bar downstairs your handlers? They looked like Auxiliaries."

"They were watching me. I have a deal that if I keep doing this, they'll let me free. They work for Raikenov."

"Head of the Chelsea Council?"

"I don't even know how he ended up in here, he was supposed to be some kind of big-time gangster in town before he was declared an unfit."

"Wrong place at the wrong time?"

"I don't really know."

"Have you ever heard anything about a way out of Chelsea? Like a gap in security that unfits could take advantage of. A way to smuggle things in or people out."

"No one's ever escaped Chelsea. I've never heard of anyone getting out that ProServ didn't want out."

Blair made for his pack and lit a cigarette as he spoke. "You know that raid in Malone Park? We found out about that weapons cache because the police picked someone up in Malden who was supposed to be in detention here."

"How do you know for sure?"

"He was tagged. He was interned months ago. Now there's a connection between the demonstrations in the next few days and the uprisings in Chelsea. He had all kinds of Free Chelsea literature in his apartment."

"You're the hero, Mr. Blair." Asiyah leaned over and kissed him on the lips. "I'm sure you'll figure it out."

"Raikenov promised you that you'd be free if you kept doing this?"

"He said that if I did this long enough, they'd move me out of Chelsea. I just hope he doesn't promise me to someone."

"I wish I could take you with me."

"You're sweet. You don't belong in that uniform, you know. Come back and see me again. Maybe I'll know more about what you're talking about then." Asiyah unbolted the door and turned around before leaving. "You know…if you know the right people in here, you don't have to look very hard to meet someone who works with you people to offer a little help. Maybe start there."

Blair stared at her for some time. "Like who?"

"I don't know personally. But if you ask around, I'm sure you'll figure something out."

Asiyah closed the door behind herself and left Blair blowing smoke on the bed. He finished his cigarette and got up, putting his pants back on and then his shirt. He laced up his shoes and then grabbed his jacket, leaving the soiled room behind.

The halls of the second floor were filled with empty bottles of liquor and unclaimed articles of clothing. The lights were dim yellow, and they flickered and the walls were cheap and paint was peeling off. Everything had the quality of dinginess to it and Blair touched nothing, even going so far as to use his sleeve to cover his hand as he opened doors. Blair saw Clark at the end of the hall, his arms around one of the girls as he felt her up and down. Blair had to walk past them to get back downstairs.

"Eckart says he's got a surprise for us when we come down," said Clark, still groping the girl. "He's out front with Jansen now."

"I'll see what it's about."

Blair was quick down the creaking stairs and out the back exit. He walked through puddles of melted snow around the building, past ProServ officers smoking joints and Auxiliaries drinking outside and keeping watch. He saw Eckart and Jansen tying something to the rear bumper. Blair gagged as the stench of death. He had to back up and lean against the building as he spit up. He looked up at the pile behind the Humvee and his chest sank into the pit of his stomach as Eckart smiled at him. Blair clenched his fist and held his tongue as best he could. He was staring at the bodies of the two unfits he killed in the Malone Park raid.

"They were al-Haqq's brothers." Eckart looked to Blair as he stood back up. "You want to make sure there isn't a full-scale rebellion? We'll make an example of the ones who cause the most trouble. Sack up and get in the driver's side, Blair."

"What are you thinking?" Blair continued to retch slightly.

"We're gonna go for a ride. Chelsea's a lot smaller than you think. We're going to teach all the unfits a good lesson." Eckart turned to Jansen "How's it looking?"

"Good to go!"

Blair climbed into the drivers' side of the Humvee, feeling drained completely of his decency. Eckart sat down next to him and Jansen climbed into the gun turret with a stupid look on his face. Clark climbed into the backseat just as Eckart got on the loudspeaker system built into the Humvee.

"Attention! Unfits! Protection Services keeps you safe – and there is zero tolerance for acts of terror! This is what happens when you shoot at us!" Eckart got off the speaker and looked at Blair. "Drive."

Blair let his foot off the brakes and started rolling down the open avenue. He eased onto the accelerator and the Humvee picked up speed.

He looked in his rear mirror and saw the stunned faces of Servicemen and Auxiliaries, and the few nameless rabble that still lined the streets and whose faces dotted unlit and broken windows. He saw the blood of the corpses staining the streets. Then Blair peered up at one of the rooms in The Joy Division and swore he saw Asiyah in the instant before curtains were rushed over the window.

CHAPTER V

Harold Maguire walked briskly past the stream of T riders getting off and on buses or heading for the subway at Malden Center. The weatherproof security cameras dripped with melting snow and a few ProServ sentries stood watch with their machine guns. One had a German Shepherd on a leash that was sniffing at everyone passing him. The dog got to Harold and shoved his snout into the side of his leg and then tried to get at his shoe, but Harold moved just in time. He instinctively pulled his flowers away from the dog. The ProServ grunt gave Harold a look that he couldn't give back. It was enough to anger him and then unnerve him but was in and out of his mind and soon as he set eyes on his girl making her way through the crowd. Aiden ran up to her father with a giant smile and squeezed him with everything she had.

"Hi!"

"Oh, it's good to see you, sweetheart."

"Good to see you, too. I missed you."

Harold put his hand on her shoulder and gave her a squeeze as he handed her the flowers, neatly wrapped. "How was the trip from Amherst?"

"Dad, you didn't have to get me these. They're beautiful! The trip was awful. The rent-a-cops at North Station we-"

"Sweetheart, tell me in the car." Harold interrupted. "Let's get out of here. Give me some of your bags."

Aiden walked with her father, past the armed guards and buses parked in front of the station and up the long ugly concrete walkway to the city streets. The loudspeakers were babbling about biometric scanners and having your ID ready for inspection, but the announcement faded into the distance. The largest digital poster at Malden Center was a series on WMD. The one on display as Harold and Aiden passed by showed victims from the UK: their skin looked grotesque and loose and turned to mush, their eyes blood red with gaping mouths screaming in agony. The image ran with bold text that read DON'T LET IT HAPPEN HERE... SEE SOMETHING, SAY SOMETHING. As the crowd streaming up the walkway and down the streets thinned out Aiden looked to her father.

"I can't remember the last time it was almost 60 degrees at Christmas."

Harold took a look around and in the distance saw blue skies dotted with swirling orange clouds of midday winter. He unzipped his coat as he felt the sun on him. "It is strange, isn't it, sweets? New normal I suppose. What can be done about it?"

"The time to have done something was thirty years ago. Now we get to brace for impact. I'm actually sweating."

God, Harold thought. She's already started and she's not even home yet. Harold popped the trunk to his rickety sedan, rearranging Aiden's baggage until the trunk could close. He pushed down on one bag hard three or four times before it finally jammed in and Harold nearly bashed his forehead against the open trunk.

Aiden laughed at him. "Don't hurt yourself."

"Get in the car, will you?" Harold had to hold back from laughing himself. As Harold started the ignition, Aiden was finishing her story.

"I got held up for ten minutes because some doofus just had to check my ID. My ID was fine. It is fine. Eventually he comes back to clear me just in time for me to miss the bus. It's ludicrous that these mouth-breathers get paid to be this incompetent."

Harold turned up the radio and rolled the window down on his side. He was tapping his hands on the steering wheel and mouthing the words to the song.

"Are you even listening to me?"

"I'm listening to you," said Harold. "But I'm listening to Phoenix, too."

"Really?"

"This band was big when you were a little girl. Your mother and I went to see them when they came to town 20 years ago. They were a secondary act for some weird front group. I forget their name, something to do with hot dogs or cars. I remember it because we got to see this band before they really blew up. A couple years later they were all over the radio and playing these sold-out shows. You came on the scene sometime around then."

"They're a bit dated."

"You used to start bobbing your head in your highchair when I put this album on when you were a baby. Now that I'm thinking, you may have been conceived the night of that concert."

"Thanks for that."

"Speaking of which…what's the story with your boyfriend?"

"He's nice. You'll like him. I told him to come over for Christmas, we could have dinner then. He's British."

"British?"

"Yeah, he came over here after it happened."

"Did he get sick?"

"Dad come on! He wouldn't be here if he were. He went through Resettlement Services; he even got his medical discharge papers framed and hanging in his dorm room."

"Well who knows? He could be a carrier. They don't seem sick, but they can give it to you. More than 10 million people are still being treated in the UK; they still don't know what all the signs of infection are. They just know the result. We're lucky we could quarantine the damn place before it got here."

"They used to say the same shit about HIV and AIDS. He's perfectly fine. You'll like him, just wait. Plus, if he infected me with something, I'd have figured it out by now."

"What does that mean?"

"Between tiddlywinks and hopscotch, I'm sure he may have pecked me on the cheek once."

"Such a smartass…"

"I learned from the best."

"I just hope you have enough sense to make him put something on when you…"

"Alright, that's enough. Unlike you, I don't feel compelled to share my sexual exploits with family members." Aiden paused. "I'm not dumb, you know."

"I know you're not." Harold made a goofy face and reached over to his daughter to pinch her cheek. "But you're my little girl."

Aiden recoiled in mock disgust, laughing. "I told him he should come over for dinner on Christmas at around three."

"I got a roast. It's well-cut – Joe Grant sent it over as a gift."

"That was nice of him."

"It was, I thought. You know he's taking a new job."

"He's leaving Congress?"

"He's gonna be the new Chancellor for the internment program here."

"Are you kidding me?"

"I am not."

Aiden shook her head. "Absolute scumbag. Just when I thought he couldn't sink any lower and he takes a job for his corporate masters as the face of Chelsea. He makes me sick."

"You really feel that way? You know, before he was just an empty suit, he used to have some radical ideas. Grant was practically a socialist in the old days. Back when we were at college, we used to go to all the demonstrations. He'd even jump on the microphone and give speeches about fighting tuition increases or ending the wars."

"That makes him even worse! That just means he knows exactly how full of shit he is and he's either too cowardly or too conniving to care. It makes me hope that there's a special place in hell for people like that."

"He was always sort of opportunistic, but he's not all bad. He pulled strings to get you into college and he's always been there for us after your mother passed. Sure, his politics aren't great, but he's been good to us."

"Yeah, but if we were from Indonesia or one of occupied countries, he'd be treating us like trash. He helped push all that through Congress and now he's literally profiting from commodified misery."

"Maybe he's taking on the job to make things a little better for them. Realistically, sweetheart, if any one elected official came out swinging against Leader Wright, they'd end up in one of his kangaroo courts. You know how erratic he is. This could be an incremental change to the system."

"The system doesn't need incremental change. It needs people taking sledgehammers to it."

"I hope you don't talk like that in front of people you don't know. It keeps me up at night, thinking about what could happen to you. I know just as well as you how bad things are. Believe me, I know it better. But I'm not out on the quad every other day when I know that it could land me in the Registry. Or worse, Chelsea."

"I don't care." Aiden stared coldly out the window, clenching her fists. "I'm not afraid of them."

The car slowed as Harold and Aiden approached the house and pulled up into the driveway. "That's your problem, Aiden. Maybe you should be. You should take it more seriously; this isn't a game. They don't care if this is a phase you're going through, you'll suffer the consequences regardless." The car came to a stop in the driveway. "Sweetheart, Grant offered me a job with his office, with Protection Services. I think I'm going to take it." Harold noticed Aiden darted her eyes at him, her face contorting slightly. "I would oversee outreach to the unfits, be in charge of figuring out how to make their lives better. I'd be sworn in as a Party member and it means we'll finally have some financial security. We can move out of this place, and you won't have to take out loans to go to school anymore. Maybe we can get the loans forgiven and-"

Aiden slapped her father across the face, tears in her eyes. She got out of the car, slamming the door behind her, and was in the house before Harold had time to react.

Harold sat in the driver's seat for a moment, gripping the wheel and gritting his teeth. He wanted to rip the steering wheel off the console and bash the interior of his car. In that moment he could have told Grant to take his job and his bullshit and said to hell with it all. Harold had held out hope that Aiden would be even slightly understanding about his new career opportunity up until this moment. Now he knew for sure what shouldn't have been a surprise. She would hate him for it.

Harold slunk out of the car and up his front steps and into the house. The stairs up to Aiden's room were impossible. After a few knocks, he opened her door to see his daughter sitting up on her bed, holding the plastic wrapped flowers. They gave her an ethereal glow, all reds and yellows and oranges that lit her up even as she sat stewing in righteous indignation. He sat down next to her on the edge of her bed, reaching his arm over her as she caressed the petals of the flowers.

"Please don't hate me, Aiden."

"I don't care how much money they're offering you. What's happening there isn't right and you won't change anything."

"I have to protect us. You're all I have left, Aiden. If I lose you...I don't know what I would do. It would be the end of my life. It nearly broke me when your mother died at Orient Heights, and I know it nearly broke you, too."

"You doing this feels like you're turning your back on everything I believe in. Everything you believe in."

"When I was your age, I felt like screaming at people to wake up to what was going on. But you as an individual can't change the world. You can't be the outlier or at least you can't let people know that you are. There's something to be said about making your peace with the establishment. Aiden, I'm tired of us being on the rotten side of the coin. This is going to be a good thing. This is our way out of here and this is how I make sure that you're going to have a good life. Sooner or later you're going to have to figure out how to learn to live with the way things are. It's something everyone does."

"I can't do that, Dad. Not now. Not when we're this close to losing everything. I'd like to know what it's like in a world where people have rights, where they don't live in constant fear. I can't accept the way things are now." Aiden picked a budding deep blue rose from the flowers. She raised it to her nose and sniffed it. "How did this get in there?"

"I don't know. I've never seen a blue rose before in my life. I didn't know they exist."

"No, they do. After the Indo-Pakistan Exchange a few years ago, they started growing in the Swat Valley."

"Where'd you hear that?"

Aiden eyed her father and spoke in a mock monotone. "From someone screaming on the quad about nuclear proliferation."

Harold smirked. "Funny."

She put the flower in her lapel. "I like it."

"I hope it lasts for you."

"Who knows if it will. But it's a beautiful thing."

"I love you Aiden."

"I love you too, Dad."

*   *   *

"General Information Systems began as a startup in Cambridge," said Stewart Andre Carmichael, standing before a gaggle of fresh ProServ officers. Blair was front and center with his arms crossed and his eyebrow half-raised, standing near Jansen. Carmichael was a salt-and-pepper-haired multibillionaire with a speech affectation that gave the impression that his brain was moving too fast for his mouth. His words sounded like a wall-to-wall slurry. "Today we employ over 200,000 people in data fusion and intelligence gathering centers dotted around the country, and we plan on expanding Genisys in Liberated States throughout the world. Our most recent contracting with Protection Services will afford many of you access to technology and logistical support that would have been unimaginable even five years ago. We've gone from selling advertising space and political consulting to tapping into the veins of human existence, and our new predictive software patches..."

Blair was starting to tune in and out. The mumbo-jumbo this perennial entrepreneur was spouting just put it over the top. Blair was overwhelmed, looking around through the all glass-and-steel Genisys Analytics HQ in the Seaport. Carmichael didn't need to do this – what could have easily been a "thank you for your service" was turning into an in-depth discussion of an invasive surveillance apparatus that was totally out of the realm of understanding of the men Blair served with. Interesting and provocative, yes. Critical for the average ProServ grunt's job performance? Not exactly. Sometimes Blair thought his own ability to think critically put him at odds with the people he served with.

Carmichael's chatter had become a walking tour through a maze of open-air offices full of young tech geeks chatting about anything other than work, their conversations ranging from bingeworthy TV to microbrews. I missed my calling, Blair thought. He wondered how any of these employees would respond if their boss told them to drive a Humvee dragging the bodies of dead unfits through an internment zone. He felt a pat on the shoulder.

"David Blair! You've got to be kidding me."

Blair turned to face his old friend from the neighborhood he'd left behind as a teenager. "Carlos Contreras! How are you?"

A nervous smile crept on to his friend's face "Hey listen, name's Carl Carver now," said his old friend leaning close into him. "You know how it is. I'm doing good, working here now at Genisys. I'm coordinating with ProServ stuff now, doing data and threat analysis for the fusion center here. Beats the hell out of Nigeria, you know?"

"You served?"

"I was in the Marines before the scale-down, did some contracting with ProServ overseas. They ended up transferring me to the tech side, and then I ended up here."

"God damn, dude. That's great."

"If you stick with it, you can do it too, man. You've just got to keep a good head. You can turn this thing into something that ends up working for you."

"I'm basically just starting out, figured it beats minimum wage."

"Listen, you want the real tour? Come with me; I'll show you around." Carver waved to his boss, who nodded the two away. Blair gave Jansen a weak smile as he left. Passing the open-concept desks and offices with employees glued to headsets and monitors as they crunched code and scanned spreadsheets, the two made for the elevators. "Once Carmichael gets going, he doesn't stop. The guy has grandiosity in his DNA. Those poor bastards are going to be stuck with him for at least an hour. This way, you'll see what really matters around here."

"He was starting to grate on me."

"No worries my friend. I was literally in and out to check on a software conversion in-house, can't believe I caught you. Merry Christmas Eve, by the way."

"Just how I wanted to spend it."

"It's tough for all of us starting out. It gets better."

The two climbed into the elevator, sending them to the tenth floor. Blair remembered Carlos Contreras young, taller than everyone for the longest time until Blair and other kids in the neighborhood caught up or outgrew him. He was a few years ahead of a lot of them, but he would always watch out for Blair. Carlos was easygoing most times, except when he bounced someone's head off of a sidewalk once for trying to steal his bike. Blair never saw anyone run so fast. In one deft move he grabbed the thief by his shirt collar, lifted him off the seat, and chucked him to the ground head-first. Nobody ever forgot that story and Carlos never had to do anything like it again.

"I barely recognized you." Blair was counting the numbers going up.

"We'll talk later." Carver stared for a few beats longer than felt comfortable, then pivoted to tour guide again. "You're about to see one of the most powerful supercomputers in the world. Genisys is a company, but this thing is really what makes it what it is. Any search engine or algorithm-powered computing is dwarfed by our capabilities." The elevator came to a stop, and Carver flashed his ID badge over a keypad to open the doors. "The next three floors belong exclusively to mainframes and fiber optics. This is what it's all about here – everything you've ever searched for, said on a phone call, sent in a text, or follow on social media. We've got files on 3.8 billion people so far…and we've barely started."

"I can't believe I've never heard of this."

"That's essentially how we like it. We've retained more federal contract dollars than all the private military and security companies combined, and the average person has no clue. The Pentagon, the NSA, CIA, all of it: they're just buildings and names at this point. They send all their work to us these days." The two kept walking through corridors and hallways of mainframes, all lined perfectly and lit up. "We can access these mainframes remotely, as long as our programming is installed on any computer, tablet, or smartphone with internet or data enabled. We even get live CCTV camera feeds almost anywhere in the city they're set up." They made their way around to another bank of elevators on the far side of the floor. "More importantly – you hungry?"

Blair's cell phone dinged, and he checked his messages. "Shit, I need to get back down there. Can you take me back?"

"Yeah, of course."

"I appreciate it – it was good to see you."

"What are you up to for Christmas?"

"Probably psyching myself up for riot duty the next day."

"Jesus, really? You got sucked into that, huh?"

"Oh yeah."

"Why don't you and I meet up after, grab some drinks. There isn't anything you're about to do that I haven't done already. Maybe it'll help."

CHAPTER VI

The snow had melted and Harold was enjoying Christmas Day with Aiden. They reminisced in front of the fireplace filled with scavenged bits of wood that crackled, the glowing orange embers creating enough warmth for them both. There were Christmas specials on, but neither of them felt inclined to turn on the television for fear of getting sucked into an argument or some awful bit of news. Instead, they alternated between lounging and making the house ready for dinner and Aiden's boyfriend. Before long, there was a knock at the door and Aiden greeted him with a big smile and a peck on the cheek before letting him into the house. Harold appeared from the kitchen wiping his hands on a cloth and putting on his best poker face.

"Dad, this is Nigel."

"Good to meet you, Mr. Maguire. Happy Christmas." Nigel Whitmore extended a hand to Harold and they shook. The boy had a good grip and gave Harold an easy-looking smile.

"Oh, come on, call me Harry or Harold or something. Make me feel like my father. Why don't you have a seat at the table, dinner's almost set. Aiden, will you help me in the kitchen?"

Aiden showed him to a seat and made her way into the kitchen and saw her father washing his hands.

"Really, Dad?"

"What? Grab the potatoes and bring them out."

Aiden came in close to her father. "Do not embarrass me in

front of him. He is fine."

Harold turned the water off and dried his hands on a dish towel. "All I'm doing is washing my hands. I didn't mean anything by it." He put his hands on his daughter's head and kissed her forehead. "I'm looking forward to getting to know the young man. What's he like?"

"Why don't you take the roast out with me and get to know him yourself…"

The two made their way into the dining room area and the meal began to take shape on the dinner table.

"Do either of you need a hand? I'd be happy to help."

"Not necessary, stay right there. You like roast, don't you Nigel?"

"Yes, I do."

"Good, that's what Aiden told me. Are you a man of faith?"

"Uh, of course. Perhaps we could say grace."

Aiden sat down and looked to her father. "Eww. Don't pay attention to him, Nigel. He's screwing with you."

Harold laughed at Nigel. "You looked like you had gone pale for a bit there. Did I really strike you as the religious type?"

Nigel rubbed one of his palms deliberately. "I've got a policy about keeping 100 feet between myself and religious institutions. I just don't get it, really…"

"Not much to get," said Aiden as she cut up her slice of the roast.

"I remember when the last of my grandparents died," said Harold as he scooped mashed potatoes onto his plate. "This was when I was a child, maybe the 1990s. My mother told me I didn't have to do that shit anymore. Can you believe that? All this time I'm going to Sunday school and regular services and getting ready for my first communion, and as soon as my grandparents are out of the picture my parents just stop it all dead in its tracks. I was relieved – it was just enough to fuck me up for the rest of my life. Maybe that's unfair. I don't have anything against people who have religious convictions, but I really can't stand the proselytizing, or the way people use it to control each other."

"Well that's exactly what it is," said Aiden. "That's all it's ever been. God was watching us before Big Brother ever did. The eye in the sky was cheaper and more conniving than a state-of-the-art mass surveillance system."

"Then it's settled," said Nigel. "We're all heathens."

"What exactly did my daughter tell you about me, Nigel?"

"Well, she said you would probably start tormenting me as soon as I walked through the door."

"You're such a brat," Harold said to his daughter, laughing. "I'm not that bad, am I?"

Nigel said, "I don't think so. The food is good and I saw that you've got about a wall's worth of records in your front room. That's a good sign."

"I've been amassing that for just about my whole life. There was a good base collection that came from my parents, and then I started buying one or two every month when I was a teenager. When you do that for more than 20 years they start to add up."

"It's the largest part of my inheritance when Daddy dearest kicks the bucket."

"I'm a little offended that you're counting the days."

"Objectively, it's a great collection."

"You can borrow ones you like," said Harold. "You just need to bring them back in a week or so. I want to listen to them more the further away they are."

The three carried on with the meal spread out before them. Roast and mashed potatoes and a few vegetables. Few people in his neighborhood would eat this well tonight. Harold uncorked the bottle of wine, a gift from Nigel. Harold passed the bottle over to Nigel as he swirled the wine in his own glass.

"I'm very sorry Nigel. It couldn't have been easy for you."

Nigel poured Aiden's glass and then his own. "It's not. I still can't get over how sudden it was. My mother getting it and then losing track of my father and my brother and sister: I can see now that I was lucky, but I didn't feel that way when it was happening. If there was hope that anyone got out, it was my sister. She might be in Norway or Sweden, and the way things went I doubt she'll ever try to leave." Nigel moved to take Aiden's hand under the table and gave a timid grin.

Aiden raised their hands from her lap, in Harold's view. She placed his gently on the dining room table. "You'll get to see her again, sweets. One day. I'm sure of it. This can't go on like this forever."

Harold took a sip of his wine. "I used to call her mother sweets." He gestured to the two of them. "She got that from me."

"The last I remember seeing her was making it through the checkpoint," said Nigel. "We got separated: she was marshalled off through the Nordic-controlled line and I end up with most of the others with some private company working with NATO. Security Solutions." He took a bite of the broccoli on his plate. "They practically run the country now...what's left of it."

Harold put his glass down. "I didn't mean to make you rehash it all."

"I don't mind," said Nigel. "I'm studying it now, Aiden and I met in a class where we talk about it."

"I should have known," said Harold.

"It's a 400 level class," said Aiden. "Nigel's a sophomore."

"I thought you were old enough to buy the wine," said Harold.

"I am. I didn't go to college right away after I came to Boston. I worked at a nonprofit that dealt with refugees before I applied to UMass."

"Interesting," said Harold. "What program?"

"Sociology – I'd like to go for a Ph.D. I'm focusing a lot on displaced peoples, state repression."

"That's how we met." Aiden picked up the bottle of wine and

poured a glass for herself.

Harold eyed his daughter as she took a sip. "I thought that was a political science class?"

"I lobbied my academic advisor to count it towards my course requirements, so it goes both ways. Plus, there's a lot of applicable stuff in that class. A lot of those sociology classes."

"If you listen to Arbitrage," said Nigel, "Great Britain was a failed state when the virus broke out. They've effectively indebted the government by enforcing a quarantine on its behalf. Same thing with resettlement. There's nothing here waiting for a lot of immigrants. It's why a lot of them are ending up in the internment centers in America. They're charging you a fortune to run them and keep those private armies on the streets."

"Is that something you've learned at school?" said Harold. He took another bite of his roast.

"That and other places," said Aiden. "We've been getting more involved on campus."

Harold spoke through a mouthful of food. "We honestly can't get through one meal without this shit coming up?" He took a sip of wine and forced a hard swallow. "I'd love to learn more about Nigel as a person before we get into the utterly fucked nature of human existence."

"I really hate to say it, but the two are a bit commingled." Nigel took a bit of his potatoes.

"You know, when I was your age, I really couldn't get away from it either. I was an activist. At least I wanted to be." Harold looked at his daughter. "I was involved on campus, too. Sometimes I thought it was a little dicey when I was younger, but it's worse now. All I ever had to worry about was being taken seriously, or if people would listen. That's the least of your concerns now. You've both got to try and be a bit reasonable. When you're older, you'll eventually realize that there's no benefit in being the one who falls on their sword to make the world right again. That's the downside in being a martyr, even for a good cause. You have to die."

"You don't have things in your life you'd die for, Dad? Things you feel strongly about, even now?"

"I'd die for you, kiddo. In a heartbeat."

*   *   *

Asiyah walked down Broadway in Chelsea, dodging gaping potholes and the sea of people crowding the major roadway. She pulled up on the collar of her overcoat and shoved her hands back into her pockets as she passed shanties set up in Winnisimmet Park and the gaunt faces wandering aimlessly. The winds had begun to whip up around her as she looked off past some of the red brick buildings, each alternately slouching or with boarded windows, and saw the Containment Wall reach nearly as high as where Route One met the Tobin Bridge. Asiyah jostled passed someone stumbling and falling into people. The man begged for food in the long, drawn-out guttural pitch of a heroin addict. He fell almost effortlessly to the ground as she sidestepped him.

Asiyah ducked into an emptied-out alleyway lined with graffiti and refuse and came upon a man and a woman covered in rags. The two were sitting next to a dumpster with their faces buried in their crossed arms. As Asiyah's footsteps drew closer to them, they looked up. The man got to his feet and looked up and down the alley. He took a few steps and gave Asiyah and the woman some room, then he slowly removed a pistol from his jeans waistband. He kept it low and out of sight as he continually scanned the area.

"How are you, Asiyah?" said the woman.

"We've got a problem, Leona."

Leona stood up and took off her hood, revealing a small black halo of coiled curls. "I heard about al-Haqq. It's not ideal."

"They know about us."

"They're grasping at straws, they don't know exactly what's going on." Leona walked closer to Asiyah. "Who's been asking?"

"ProServ."

"Who?"

"His name is David Blair. He's young."

"Was he any good?" Leona smirked.

"Fuck yourself!" Asiyah gritted her teeth. "He'd be all over you if I didn't feed him some bullshit about al-Haqq paying off ProServ to get out."

"I'm sorry." Leona stroked Asiyah's cheek. "I shouldn't have said that. You're an important part of all this."

"You screwed up." Asiyah pointed in Leona's face, then pointed at herself. "I didn't. Understand?"

"We told Abd not to move. He moved. He wanted to help with the Dissenter's March before we got him to Quebec. He couldn't help himself. He got his own brothers killed in here and believe me when I say it: I would trade ten Abd's for one of his brothers."

"Maybe you should all stick to killing mercenaries and blowing up buildings. This whole supply chain thing isn't really working out the way it was advertised to me."

"We have other avenues. We always do."

"Like what?"

"You should know better than to ask."

"So then you have what I came for?"

Leona walked over to a shopping carriage covered in rough gray blankets. She peeled one of them back to show what lay underneath. "You've got first aid, field surgery equipment, some intravenous fluids."

"What about the midwife kit?"

The blanket covered the materials. "It's all there. As promised."

"And you weren't followed?"

"Not a chance."

"OK." Asiyah took the carriage and spun it around, taking it by the handle.

"I'll put some feelers out for a David Blair. That's good intel – and as long as you have more of it, we'll have more supplies for you."

"I'd ask you to get me out, but it doesn't seem like your strong suit."

"Do as much as the al-Haqq brothers did for us, and maybe we can talk." Leona met the man standing some distance away from them. "Fenster – let's go."

The pair huddled themselves in ragged overcoats and pulled sweatshirt hoods over their heads before they disappeared down the alley. Asiyah went in the opposite direction with her cart and did the same.

*   *   *

"It's now nearly five years on from the Exchange, and we visit the city of Karachi, Pakistan. Once home to nearly 16 million, the greatly diminished population deals with the after effects of radiation and attempts to rebuild. In Mumbai, India, the same fate. This being the end result of a standoff among regional powers that ended in nuclear stalemate. It is now known that the collapse of these countries allowed Pakistani General Khaled Murad al-Mummit to disappear with the nuclear material used in the Black Friday attack in New York City. He now lives as a coward on the run, still in charge of the terrorist organization Ikhwaan. Leader Wright himself attended a Christmas Day ceremony in Queens to commemorate-"

Harold clicked the television off, looking towards Aiden and Nigel on his couch. Images of radiation victims, ruined landscapes, and the borough of Manhattan devoid of human beings were burned into his memory. "This is what I get for trying to watch the Charlie Brown Christmas Special." Harold sat up more, looking pensive.

"I can't believe we were that close to nuclear winter." Nigel crossed his arms.

"The radiation spikes are bad enough," said Aiden.

Harold looked at the blue rose on her lapel. "Well I guess something worthwhile came out of it."

"I'd give the flower back for a disarmament treaty. Or for Nigel to have his country back. That's part of what tomorrow's about, right? Trying to set things right?"

"Sweetheart." Harold leaned forward in his chair. "You can't do it."

"We're going, Dad. We have to. It's the only way things are going to change. If we sit here and recognize how horrible it is and then do nothing..."

"Well some of this was thrust onto us, all of us," interrupted Harold. "I don't think anyone could have predicted Black Friday or what happened in the UK or the Exchange. I'd say all the above warrants something. But what else can we do? Can we take chances in a world where the stakes are this high? They don't know if al-Mummit still has nuclear capability, or if they were able to secure the UK after the Hackney Virus."

"Jesus Christ, Dad. You sound just like them. You want to start calling England the Sick Man of Europe now?"

"Very cute of the Truth to come up with that nickname," said Nigel.

Aiden leaned forward herself. "Do you really think that merits what interned people are going through right now?"

"Unfits?" said Harold. "Look, I want better conditions. A lot of people do. But all I'm saying is this didn't come out of nowhere."

"Interned people, Dad. They're human beings. Somehow we forget along the way?"

"What happens if you do go tomorrow?"

"When we go."

Nigel looked to Harold, and then Aiden. "Why don't we try to ease up-"

"What happens when you all get on your soapbox at Chelsea?" Harold stood up. "I know that you're young and you think that you can handle what comes, but you don't have any idea what you're getting into. Look at all this, for God's sake! You're right about everything. It's government collusion with big business, it's racism for profit, it's slum conversion into open air prisons, all of the above. It's all true. So doesn't it stand to reason that if they're capable of all that, they're more than capable of putting a permanent target on your back? You need to stop this, Aiden. Stop before you ruin your whole life for things you can't change anyway."

"Don't talk to me like that just because you don't have the heart to do something about it!" Aiden stood up and walked over to her father. "You could have helped your tenants escape when Wright issued the internment orders and his fucked-up minions were rounding people up in the middle of the night. But you didn't. You told me that it was precautionary, and it wasn't permanent, and things would change, and Wira and his family would be fine. Now it's two years later and they could be dead or worse. People aren't going to take this anymore and they're looking for a way to fight it."

"You're not going tomorrow." Harold backed up a bit from Aiden and pointed towards Nigel. "You won't either if you have any sense. It's not going to end well for anyone there."

"They're expecting over 20,000 people," said Nigel. "They don't have the resources to detain 20,000 people all at once."

"No." Harold put his hands on his hips as he paced somewhat in his living room. "They have the resources to detain tens of millions of people and the number grows every day. You two can't afford to be this naïve."

"It only worked to begin with because people were too afraid to say anything." Nigel made his way to Aiden on the other side of the living room. "But now people are speaking up, they can see how bad things have become. They want to dissolve the Nats and have new elections. More than anything, they want places like Chelsea shut down."

"Do you think that having some family member high up in the Party is going to save you, Nigel? I can appreciate that losing your family is hard, but you've been doing pretty well for yourself since you landed stateside. I know all about your uncle. The one who put you up. The commodities trader."

"How did you know that?" said Aiden.

"I've got my sources." Harold began gesturing to Nigel with one hand still on his hip. "You're just another rich kid playing working class hero. You have people who could save your ass in a heartbeat. So don't put my daughter at risk for your idealistic bullshit!"

"It's my decision!" said Aiden. "I'm going tomorrow and that's it. You and your buddy Joe Grant can laugh at us; I don't care. We're going to do something you've become too much of a coward to do yourself."

Aiden went upstairs to her room. Harold felt the urge to smash his coffee table and give Nigel a beating. He might have done it, had Nigel been quiet.

"Harold, I'm sorry about all this. I didn't mean to start anything here. We carry on and say hurtful things to each other."

"I shouldn't have said what I did." Harold squeezed the bridge of his nose with his eyes shut tight for a moment before looking up at Nigel. He took a deep breath. "You've been through enough. I'm sorry."

"What are you doing for New Year?" Nigel smiled wryly.

Harold chuckled lightly, not enough to ease the tension he was feeling. "You should have seen the 4th of July a few years ago when she was in high school; she tried to organize spoken word performances. She wanted to do Frederick Douglass readings."

"*What to the Slave is the Fourth of July?*"

"Can you imagine how that would have turned out?"

"She's an adult."

"She's my daughter, Nigel. You might think it's romantic to do these things but she's all I've got. I can't let her destroy her life. You've got to talk her out of it."

"Aiden is the one who talked me into it. Her mind is made up."

"She's upset at me because I'm thinking about taking a job with them, Protection Services. I'm going to be working for Joe Grant."

"She told me about that. I'm honestly sorry to hear that."

"I'll make a wager with you. You go to the Dissenter's March in Chelsea tomorrow and do your protesting. Hell, do it every day for a year. I'll take that job. Then come meet up with me and we can weigh how much each of us actually accomplished against the other."

"That's pretty cynical, Harold." Nigel stood looking around in the living room.

"It's true."

"Your window here is cracked pretty well."

"Neighborhood kids. I've been meaning to fix that."

"Let me know if you want any help to do that."

"I don't know if that's necessary."

"I'll do what I can to change her mind, but I don't think it's going to be much use. Remember that you're not the only one looking out for her, too. Can I give you my phone number? In case you'd like to reach us in a real emergency?"

"That's probably not the worst idea."

The two exchanged information as Aiden made her way downstairs with a packed bag slung over her shoulder.

"I'm staying with Nigel tonight," she said.

"What?" said Harold.

"You heard me. I'm not staying here tonight."

"Sweetheart, don't do this." Harold moved toward the front door, putting his back to it to face his daughter.

"I have to." Aiden tightened the grip she had over the strap of her backpack. "If you don't get out of the way I'll go out the back."

"Aiden," said Nigel. "Maybe we should stay. At least for a little while?"

"If I don't do this now," said Aiden, "I don't know if I can live with myself." Her eyes began to water. "I really don't."

Harold went towards Aiden and hugged her, putting his chin on her shoulder. "Just stay. Please stay." He felt his daughter squeeze back before he got a kiss on the cheek. When he turned around Aiden was standing in the doorway on the front porch.

"Goodbye, Dad."

"It was good to meet you, Harold." Nigel extended his hand to shake Harold's and felt awkward when Harold did not. Aiden and Nigel walked out, leaving Harold with his soul tied up in knots.

* * *

"I can't believe they didn't give you guys Christmas Eve off," said Carver. He sat across from Blair in the booth of a sparsely crowded Charlestown pub.

"No heavy lifting, just that visit before they cut us loose. No real family to have the season with anyway."

Carver raised his pint glass to Blair's bottle. "Well then, Merry Christmas to you."

"Thanks." Blair took a long swig of the cheap beer and put his bottle back down on the table. "You got to tell me something. What's with Carl Carver?"

"I'm Dominican."

"Seriously? I thought you were from Spain. You're white."

"Don't make me scream it."

"I must have forgotten that."

"Well it wouldn't have come up when we knew each other,

anyway. It only recently became relevant."

"That is true."

"They're letting a lot of people change their names. It's a sign of good faith. Part of the Restoration. 'America for Americans' and all that shit. I'd rather lose my name than my life, you know what I mean? Plus, I served so they cut me a lot of slack. That's American History 101. The definition of whiteness bends to whatever white people need it to be. Or want it to be."

Blair took another swig of his beer. "Well, when you put it like that it makes sense. It just confused me when you said it to me earlier."

"It's still something I don't need people knowing outside of certain circles, you know?"

"Your quasi-secret is safe with me."

"Thanks, dude."

"Now that you mention it, you had a thicker accent when you were younger."

"I worked on it."

"Well, whatever."

Carver finished his beer and put the empty pint glass on the table in front of him. "How are you feeling about tomorrow?"

"Not great. It is what it is."

"Do you think you're going to catch any heat? I've been going over reams of data, everything seems like it's going to be fine."

"You're starting to swear by that supercomputer shit, aren't you?"

"It's a very powerful tool in the right hands."

"I still have a bad feeling." Blair finished the rest of his beer and waived the waiter over to their corner table. The music kicked up and he had to yell his order over Billy Squier.

"What makes you feel like that?"

"It's just a feeling. I don't want to kill anyone."

"It was justified. Some towelhead pulled a gun on you."

"It's not that. We went in again, after pacification. Eckart had the bodies dragged through the streets behind a Humvee. He made me drive."

"Jesus Christ."

Blair pulled his pack of cigarettes from his coat pocket and put it in his mouth.

"You want people to know you're ProServ?"

"Does it bother you? I mean, I'll go outside if it bothers you."

"By all means, go for it. I guess we're past the point of low profile."

The waiter came back with a beer for Blair, who lit his cigarette and blew smoke in the waiter's direction. He pulled his jacket back and revealed his badge, and the waiter made himself scarce. "I had a dream last night I was in Chelsea, just running. Then they all found me. First it was just a few unfits, and then it was hundreds. They caught me and they tore me apart. I woke up screaming."

Carver spoke in hushed tones. "Eckart's gone off the deep end. He's losing his mind. Part of the job is dealing rough with them, but that's beyond the pale."

"Then why isn't someone doing something about it? I've known him long enough – he sprawls out and no one does anything. He moves up in the ranks."

"Things are difficult right now. The Leader's got a stranglehold on everything, everyone I know is terrified of him or is ready to follow him off the deep end."

"Can you imagine having this conversation with anyone else?"

"Honestly? Not really. I can think of very few people who would be receptive to what we're saying, at least in your world. The open secret is that this country is filled with white liberals who love talking shit and didn't do anything when it got real."

"I never really thought of myself as a political guy."

"Well, you are whether you know it or not."

"My brother Stephen and Eckart were tight – they still are. I thought I wanted this life. There's honor here. I feel like my life means something when I go to work. I even got to pull the trigger, just like I knew I could when the time came. That's what's fucking me up. I thought it would be hard. I didn't know if I could kill someone. But it was easy. And I can't remember doing it. But I know he's dead because I killed him, and now I can't stop thinking about it. In my dream, right before they got to me, he was face to face with me. He was bleeding from the bullet in his forehead and he wouldn't stop staring me down." Blair drank his beer. "In my mind, I look in the rearview mirror and I see trails of blood. I didn't want to do it, but I knew that Eckart would make my life hell if I fought him. I could have said no, but I didn't. I caved."

"Blair, you didn't have a choice."

"We all have a choice." Blair took a drag of his cigarette. Smoke filled the air around him. "Something terrible is going to happen tomorrow."

CHAPTER VII

Joe Grant had been sealed in his office at the top floor of the Chelsea Internment Command Center since before sunrise, his staff buzzing around him as he stood looking down at the streets below. He had the vantage point that allowed him to see some of the taller buildings inside Chelsea across the river and over the Containment Wall, as well as some of the streets of East Boston. The skies were gray and intense. Chelsea was still smoldering in parts and it seemed that the fading trails of smoke blotted out the sun. On the whole, Chelsea had calmed down since the last few weeks of turmoil. It didn't stop Grant's nervousness. His aide Ed McGonagall, a tall thirty-something man with dull pale skin and beady eyes sidled up to him.

"I wanted to show you the chatter we've picked up through Genisys." McGonagall handed Grant a tablet. "Over the past week there's been a substantial increase in positive speak about the demonstrations. But the announcement of your tenure here has increased the approval of the general public about the internment policy. It's a crapshoot overall – people don't know what to make of it yet. The Truth is on our side no matter how things turn out and they'll help us wage the media war. However we want to spin this, we can."

"You forget that there are going to be college students, twenty somethings who show up to this thing, right at our front door. Party members. White kids. How do you think it's going to look if some Arbitrage executive's son gets his head bashed in? This is different; the tide could be turning against us – all of us."

"This demonstration is being talked about as treason. There are people out there who think it's the beginning of a revolution. I've spoken with Arbitrage employees who are ready to write their own children off if they show up here. It's nationwide. Leader Wright is monitoring the situation personally and he is prepared to do whatever is necessary. If you want my opinion you should let them all have it. Just open fire – non-lethal rounds – and end this today before it gets worse."

"No. I want ProServ to behave. The gloves stay on – we start firing only if they get violent. Tear gas, pepper spray, and rubber bullets if they don't disperse. Nothing experimental and nothing meant to kill. We want people to think that we were as easy on them as we could possibly be."

"What about contingencies? What if the crowd gets violent?"

"It's a protest, Ed. I'm not ready to see people die over this place. Not on my watch. We're supposed to be the new face around here. That's how we want to set the tone? Make the call already, will you?" Joe Grant stopped his pacing so that he could face his staff. "That goes for all of you! The message today will be that these demonstrations were dismantled peacefully. They came here, they had their say, and the ones who needed disciplining got it. We want to have everything in place when people start getting detained. There won't be violence on our watch if we can help it… and all of this is on your shoulders! If I am disobeyed or if my orders are not carried out, you better believe heads are rolling!" Grant was barking mad now, cupping his face and casting terrible looks at his employees.

"Joe, come with me." McGonagall guided his boss to the executive bathroom. He slowly and quietly closed the door as Joe Grant removed a small bottle of pills from his pants pocket. He metered out three and dry swallowed them in one gulp.

"We need you level, not catatonic." McGonagall shoved his hands into his pants pockets.

"Shut up." Grant shoved his face into the faucet and turned the cold water on to wash the pills down, lapping up the tap. He wiped his mouth and fixed his hair in the mirror before turning to McGonagall. "When I tell you to do something, I expect it done. Don't second guess me."

"I understand."

"Call the ProServ nitwits and tell them what I said."

Ed stared at Joe Grant blankly.

"Go do it!"

Ed McGonagall hurried himself out of the bathroom, leaving Joe Grant to collect himself. His phone rang and when he pulled it out, he saw Harold Maguire's name.

"Hello?"

"Joe? What's going on?"

"I'm at the Facility Command Center."

"Joe, I need to talk to you. It's Aiden. I think she's going to be at the demonstration at Chelsea today."

"What?"

"I tried to stop her, but I couldn't."

"Harold, I'm doing everything that I possibly can to make sure this doesn't get out of hand. I'm keeping the Servicemen on a tight leash. But you need to tell her to watch herself. No one here really knows what this thing is going to look like until it plays out."

"What can we do? I've been calling her all night and day. She won't pick up the phone. You need to make sure that she stays out of the Registry at least, please."

Joe Grant looked at himself in the mirror. His skin tone was somewhat pale, and the sweat was building slightly at his temples. Congress was better. "I can do that, Harold. You know you don't have to ask. Just stay at home today and wait for someone from my office to call you. We'll do everything we can to keep her out of trouble."

"Thank you, Joe."

"I'll talk to you later."

*   *   *

Blair crowded around his ProServ comrades, all gearing up for the protests. He fidgeted with his body armor, triple checking everything. He raised the visor that covered his face and unbuckled his helmet to adjust his built-in headset. The grunts were all standing around Humvees and military vans with back doors opened, some inside passing supplies and ammunition to others on riot duty. Jansen saw Blair in the crowd and made his way over to him.

"You ready for this, motherfucker! I can't wait!"

Blair sighed angrily under his breath but the noise around them all was enough so that Jansen couldn't hear. "Have you seen Eckart?"

"He's prepping cadets over there." Jansen pointed across the street outside the Command Center.

"What the hell are cadets doing here today?"

"ProServ was short for bodies; they didn't want to pull priority guards at the security checkpoints. Can't be a dipshit forever, right?"

Blair made for the crowd of nervous cadets, all loading their weapons as Eckart gave instructions. He pulled Eckart over to speak with him.

"Have you heard the orders from Chancellor Grant?"

"It's bullshit, I know. What are you packing today? I'll make sure you get the real thing."

"What do you mean? I'm not disobeying direct orders from the Chancellor…"

"Look, it might get hairy today. I have tactical command of the ProServ contingent here and I'm not sending my men out there with anything less than live rounds. The Chancellor has a problem, he can come down here and do this himself. Remember what I told you?"

Blair got nervous and was afraid to speak.

"Listen, Blair. We have reason to believe that there are terrorist cells infiltrating the demonstrations today. We're going to have our first strikers carry the non-lethal weapons, but I don't want you with them. I want you to have live ammunition because I've got a feeling that this whole thing could go sideways fast if we don't bring it to them as soon as they start the protests. Come with me." Eckart moved Blair through the crowd of Servicemen and the cadets to one of the supply trucks and began to rummage through the back, pulling out shotgun shells by the handful. "Here, take these."

Blair reached out and grabbed the shells after sliding the 12 gauge onto his back by pulling on the strap around his torso. "We haven't heard anything about infiltration. What makes you think that there'll be anything like that?" He stuffed the shotgun shells into his bulky pants side pockets.

"Trust me. You can grab a belt for those in one of the trucks back there. You know most of the guys are swapping the rubber stuff out, anyway. I used to wonder if you could make the tough calls, but I know now that you can. Stay calm and be strong." Eckart put his hands on his shoulders, staring him in the eyes. "Everyone is going to be losing their heads today. I know you've never been through something like this but it's not my first time. This is nothing compared to Tehran. You want to look evil in the face, try staring down hordes of these Jawas. If they come at you and it's you or them, I know you'll make the right choice."

"This doesn't add up, Eckart."

"That's how fast it can turn. That's how fast a protest becomes an insurrection and protesters become insurgents. Today it's our job to stop that dead in its tracks."

Blair awkwardly held his helmet under his arm as he fished for his cigarettes and pulled one from his pack. He lit it with his new Zippo and took a long drag. "What if we make the wrong move today? What if they're peaceful and we unload on them and some Party member's kid gets killed? We'll lose our fucking jobs."

"That won't happen. Who else have you talked to about this?"

"Just you. I wouldn't say this to anyone else."

"Keep it that way. You're sophisticated. Most of these guys aren't. You're just going to make them either too nervous or angry to do the job well and we can't have that. Not now."

"Alright."

"You're thinking too much. All you can do is keep your wits. You lose those, you lose everything."

Humvees started rolling down the street, ProServ sentries manning machine gun turrets on each. They lumbered toward the Command Center, weaving through the crowds of Servicemen.

"That's the Colonel," said Eckart. "Look alive."

The Humvees stopped and the Colonel emerged from the backseat, an aide following him out of the vehicle. The Colonel was dressed in his formal uniform and peaked cap, his dress all gray with red trim and the Party insignia showing prominently on the crown of his cap surrounded by striking bolts and arrows along the band. He wore a thick, warm overcoat which he felt unnecessary enough to let slide off of his shoulders as he outstretched his arms. The aide following him caught it. The Colonel turned and murmured something to his aide, who pointed in Eckart's direction. He cut his way through the crowd, Servicemen saluting him as he passed them by.

"Lieutenant Eckart, how are things looking here?"

Eckart saluted before he spoke. "Things are shaping up well, Colonel Crenna. We'll be mobilizing throughout the area soon, and we'll have every access point leading up to the Facility covered."

"I trust that everything will be as Chancellor Grant has ordered?"

"Of course, Colonel; I've provided some of our rear forces with live rounds, but they won't be called in unless the demonstrations turn."

"See to it that this does not turn, Lieutenant Eckart. The Chancellor has been good to Protection Services and he has been entrusted to run this Facility as he sees fit. I have been sent to see to it that the Chancellor's wishes are indulged."

"Colonel, we are doing everything we can possibly do to provide for the safety of the Facility. We don't know what we're expecting, and I have a responsibility to the men serving here today."

"Barring an act of terrorism, I expect you to do as Chancellor Grant has instructed, Eckart. Restrain yourself and the men under your command or you will answer to me. I'm not here to debate you, is that understood?"

"Yes, Colonel," said Eckart. Blair stood silent as he watched the life drain slightly from Eckart's face. "We will do our best."

* * *

The light was fading from the sky and early evening had set in when it began. A distant rumbling grew louder and Blair could see the wall of bodies, chanting and carrying signs and marching in unison. Blair clutched his gun and eyed the throngs of people making their way up to the line of ProServ troops. The whirring of a helicopter came down fast above the marching protesters and hovered close to them. Thousands, maybe tens of thousands of people were filling the street leading up to the Chelsea Facility. There are more of them than us, Blair thought nervously. Human waves were crashing down. If they wanted this place, they could take it.

The chants grew louder and were audible now for Blair, the protesters lead by booming megaphones as they closed in on Blair's position and the contingent of troops holding the line.

"When democracy is under attack, what do we do?"

"Stand up! Fight back!"

"What do we want?"

"Free Chelsea!"

"When do we want it?"

"NOW!"

This was the point they would not pass, Blair thought. Maybe Eckart was right—look at all of them. They're ready for a fight and they don't care about the consequences. The demonstration was feet away from them and the helicopter had backed out over where the Mystic and Chelsea Rivers met, just before the Facility. Eckart came over a megaphone sitting on top of a Humvee, next to an unmanned machine gun turret. They were all set up at the intersection of Brooks and Condor Streets, the demarcation line. ProServ on one side and the shouters on the other.

"This is an illegal assembly! You have five minutes to disperse! You can find exit points on the following roads: Brooks Street, Putnam Street, and Glendon Street! If you do not leave now, you will be considered in violation of dissent laws!"

The same message boomed from the helicopter as it hovered over the demonstrators. Blair could make out a sniper hanging out from the side of the helicopter, training his gun on the crowd. Then he heard screaming over the chanting throngs.

"Do it now!"

A shout from the crowd echoed out and two protesters emerged, one carrying a dummy dressed like a Serviceman. It was thrown at the feet of ProServ soldiers forming the first line of protection, banging their batons on their clear shields. The second protester lit the dummy on fire, creating an effigy a few feet away from the defense line. Two riot officers emerged from behind the line, let through by a gap that closed behind them. They managed to grab one of the protesters who had stepped forward and began to beat the young man with their batons.

"You like that, faggot?" one screamed as he beat the boy. Other members of the protest stepped forward to try and pull the young man back, but the first line of ProServ riot soldiers began to push forward, beating their shields with batons to make noises like thunder claps as they moved into the crowd. Blair watched as the protesters kicked and punched the shields. One protester bashed a brick over the head of one of the riot officers. He went down fast and was swallowed in the crowd.

"Canisters! Canisters now!" shouted Eckart, and soon tear gas was raining down on the street. The protesters erupted into coughing fits and a general feeling of panic descended on the place. Blair wondered to himself why the Servicemen pulling riot duty today weren't equipped with gas masks as a canister shot into the crowd was hurled back to the ProServ squadrons. It was kicked back to the front line, to where Blair had made his way. He picked it up with his gloved hand and tossed it back at the crowd and instantly developed a running feeling in his throat and his nose. His eyes started watering and he felt compelled to hack up phlegm oozing down his throat, lifting his visor to spit. A rock hit Blair in the side of the head. He threw his visor back down, cocked his shotgun, and fired a shot into the air.

"MOVE BACK!" he yelled at the top of his lungs. The protesters had the upper hand; they were managing to hold their ground despite the line of Servicemen attempting to move them. The chants were louder and stronger. Blair's headset buzzed in burst transmissions from the Command Center. ALL PERSONNEL HOLD THEIR POSITIONS – PREVENT ADVANCES AT ALL COSTS – NON-LETHAL FORCE IS AUTHORIZED. Suddenly a contingent of protesters closed in on Blair and another rock hit him.

"Fuck you, fascist!"

"Who said that? Who said it!" Blair yelled back at the crowd. His eyes were running and he felt compromised, angry enough to threaten the ones closest to him with the butt of his shotgun. He continued to whack a man with his shotgun until the man started moving in the right direction and suddenly some of his fellow officers were at his side, beating the angry crowd back. Then the ground shook and the sound of a boom and shattering glass erupted around them.

An explosion about a hundred feet deep into the demonstration flared up and the plume of fire and black smoke was enough to send everyone back several steps. Fear ripped through the crowd as screams and cries echoed in unison through the streets near the Facility.

"Terrorists!" yelled Eckart through his megaphone. *"OPEN FIRE!"*

Blair fell back and scrambled for cover as bullets ripped through the first line of demonstrators. He could only look on in shock as young men and women fell to their knees with bullet holes in their chests, surrounded by a fine red mist in the air. The protesters dispersed, tearing through backyards and down side streets. The orders came again in his headset, loud enough to make his ears buzz. LETHAL FORCE IS AUTHORIZED – AN ACT OF TERRORISM IS IN PROGRESS – LETHAL FORCE IS AUTHORIZED.

Blair scuttled across the street to another ProServ grunt taking improvised cover, dodging gunfire from what felt like every direction.

"What the fuck happened!?"

"They're bombing us!"

Eckart came over the megaphone again, his voice distorted in terrible static. *"Choke them off! Kettle positions! Eagle Hill is under lockdown. Move now!"*

Blair barely dodged a bullet and fired back in the direction it came from. He sprinted into the streets obscured by white billowing smoke and heard the massive booming of a rifle. He looked up and saw the helicopter hovering, the sniper taking potshots at the fleeing crowd. What the hell was happening? Blair crouched and scuttled forward after another shot whizzed by him. He squeezed the trigger and fired in its direction a few times before tripping over a protester. Blair was face to face with a boy erupting in coughing fits, blood bubbles in his mouth before he turned to Blair and choked on his last breath. Blair started to fling his gear off to sprint faster towards the retreating crowd, chasing one of them who had separated from his group by heading towards a backyard. Blair managed to catch up to him trying to hop a fence, ripping him down by the back of his jeans and throwing him to the sidewalk hard. He dove on top of him with an elbow to his neck and the boy cried out in pain. Blair screamed at him.

"Who did this? Who did this! Tell me now!"

The boy's mouth was gaping, and there were tears in his eyes. Blair couldn't tell if it was the boys' fear or the canisters flying at the retreating crowd. He flipped the young man over onto his stomach and forced his arms behind his back before managing to zip tie his wrists. The boy was incoherent and muttering nonsense as the tear gas smoke grew thick around them.

"Where is she? I have to find her! Where is she? Tell me where she is!"

"Where's who?"

The boy was muffled as Blair shoved his face into the pavement. "Aiden! Maguire!"

Gunfire was still erupting while Blair kept his knee planted on the young man. He looked off into what he could make out in the distance and saw a girl land on her knees and hit the street face first after catching a bullet in her back.

"If you move, you're dead!" said Blair. "Tell me what happened!"

"I don't know!"

Blair heaved the boy up and started rushing him back along with other officers who had managed to detain protesters. The boy dropped out of Blair's grip and to his knees in front of a body, a dead girl strewn out in the middle of the street. Her body was contorted horribly. Blair couldn't make out her features beyond the long hair. Blood was collecting underneath the body and gaping wounds in the chest stained the clothes a dark red. The boy started screaming. Blair went in to pick up the young dissenter and lost the anger he had felt at the crowd. As he picked the boy up, he could make out the girl's features. The eyes were distant and dreamy, unafraid of the terror that had gripped the demonstrations. Blair managed to notice the blue rose in her lapel before dragging the boy off to be charged with dissent crimes.

CHAPTER VIII

Harold Maguire rushed out of his house when what he was watching was interrupted by the Truth. Footage of an explosion ripping through the center of the protest played out, the news ticker below the images reading TERROR AT CHELSEA – MANY DEAD AT DISSENTERS MARCH. The view was up high and hovering over the scene and started playing on a loop as the newscaster started speculating on the origin of the blast. Harold was in his car speeding to the Facility when he got the call from Joe Grant.

"Joe? Why haven't you picked up? Tell me what's going on!"

"Harold…nobody here knew this would happen. We're doing the best we can."

"Where's Aiden? How is she?"

"I'm going to meet you at Mass General, Harold. She's here now. I got you a priority escort; they'll get you through the checkpoints. ProServ is locating your position. I'll see you here soon."

The phone beeped as Grant ended the call and Harold's pulse pounded as he tried to call back but got only Grant's voicemail. The second time he tried to call, he saw in his rear view mirror two ProServ patrol cars appear, one hot on his tail and another passing him in the other lane in order to pull ahead and lead Maguire to the hospital where he would meet Joe.

Everything was a blur and Harold was in his head as the convoy sped through traffic. Those thoughts were the worst thoughts, the unknown and the guessing in an echo chamber that amplified and perpetuated and gnawed at the inside of your skull and anything that you had in your head that was rational was gone. It was hot and it was cold, and Harold felt it in the sweat coming off of him. He nearly lost control of his car on a sharp turn heading toward a checkpoint, jamming on the brakes with both feet and turning hard. The jolt brought him back and for a bit Harold felt relieved that the adrenaline boost would keep him from passing out before he got to the hospital. He got no sleep the night before.

The flow of traffic picked up significantly when they made it onto the highway, burning oil fast before reaching Massachusetts General Hospital. Maguire's escorts bolted from their cars and rushed Harold into the place, past the frantic chaos of the emergency ward. Someone being rushed away had bled on the floor, and a small puddle had formed in the lobby with drops trailing off into another hospital wing. MGH was starting to fill up with some of the luckier victims. Lucky in that they had the right connections and weren't left to bleed out and die in the streets outside Chelsea, Harold thought. Surely that had to be the fate of some. But not Aiden, Harold thought. Christ help me not her.

"This way, Mr. Maguire," somebody said.

The trauma cases faded away, replaced with the odd nurse and patient making their way through lily white halls with color-coded lines running through the floors. The doctors and staff looked haggard and overworked. Harold saw a group of men and women in scrubs soaked in blood, shaking their heads as they left a room for the hallway. They all followed one of the lines until it took them to an elevator bank, the sentries shepherding Harold into an open one before it descended into the bowels of the place. After the doors shut Harold's legs were like rubber and he had to slouch against the side and grab onto the handrail inside. He knew.

The doors opened and he thought he saw Joe Grant at the end of the hallway shove one of his aides before they ran off. Harold hoisted himself up, using all of his strength to reach the end of the hall to meet Joe. As he got closer, Harold read the sign above the door Grant was near and clutched at the wall, gagging bile onto the floor. He collapsed before he reached Grant, who rushed toward him as the ProServ officers tried to prop Harold up.

"Harold," said Grant with a shaking voice. "I'm sorry. The bomb went off and no one knows who started shooting first."

"No," said Harold as the distance grew in his face. "No, this isn't…"

"Let me walk you in. There's someone inside you need to speak with."

Harold shoved Grant off of him when he tried to help him up. Instead he steadied himself against the wall and shuffled into the room Grant had been standing outside of.

"All of you," said Grant with a steelier tone to the officers standing dumb around him. "I want you on watch outside this room. No one gets in, is that understood?"

Grant found Harold leaning over Aiden's body. His heart sank as he thought of her as a child, her mother bringing her into the office like a little mascot and picking her up and playing with her and bouncing her on his knee.

"I don't know what to say, Harold. I failed you."

The coroner lurking in the corner of the room stepped forward, bespectacled and clinical with a dour look on his face.

"Mr. Maguire, can you verify for us that this is your daughter? Aiden Maguire?"

Harold buried his head into his daughter's stomach and bellowed loudly. The coroner looked toward Joe Grant, who nodded and bowed his head. The coroner left the room, Grant opening the door for him and closing it gingerly behind him. He walked over to Harold and put his hand on his shoulder.

"Harold…" Joe Grant paused. "Nobody has to know she was

there. We can take care of this, Harold."

"Fuck you! Nobody has to know? I want them to know!"

"Harold, please…"

"I want them to know!"

"You're grieving now and I understand you're angry, but if we don't protect you then it's going to get very bad for you. We have to do everything to control the situation."

"Who did this?" Harold quivered. "Who killed my girl? I want a name."

"This isn't anyone's fault. They just panicked. ProServ thought they were under attack and they opened fire when the bomb went off."

"I want the one who killed her. Someone has to pay for this!"

"There's going to be an internal investigation of the incident, they're going to discipline-"

"Discipline? Discipline…"

"Yeah, Harold, they're going t-"

"Stop talking, Joe. I don't want to hear it anymore. Why don't you leave us? Just get out."

"Hey, where am I right now?" Grant gestured his hands outward. "You don't think maybe I stuck my neck out here? Always and again, no matter what! I mean how am I going to do this? I've got who knows how many dead kids back there, I've got injured ProServ officers, I've got security threats, and where am I?"

"You want a damn Medal of Freedom for not being a reptile for ten consecutive seconds? You ruined me, you bastard. It's done. My life is over! You took my wife and now my kid!" Harold bellowed. "You took my only child from me, you gutless fucking fascist!" He lowered his head and sobbed into Aiden's remains.

Joe went for the door but turned back before he could get to it. "You know, you don't think this hurts me, too? Harold? You don't think I've got a hole in my fucking heart being in here with you? Like this?"

Tears welled up in his eyes and he held his hands on his waist. "We used to be like family, all of us. What the fuck happened?"

Harold laid Aiden back down and stroked her long, tangled hair. Her eyes were closed. Her face was calm. He stared at her for some time. Grant was a shadow on the wall.

"She doesn't have to fight anymore. Maybe now she can just exist somewhere else, wherever it goes on…or maybe she's nowhere. Maybe her spark just went out and the last time I saw her she hated me because I'm a coward."

"Harold, you're not a coward."

"She knew that I loved her, right?"

"She knew. Harold, there was no way she couldn't know."

"She was too much like us. She stood up against all this and demanded victory or death, and I couldn't stop her." Harold looked deep into his daughter's face. "And now I don't know if she died hating me. She's on a slab and she puts me to shame."

Grant drooped into himself, standing stupid and observant. Harold pulled two of her bobby pins from her hair, placing them in his pocket. He noticed the blue flower in her coat lapel, blooming brighter than he had remembered when his daughter fiddled with it just a few days ago. He plucked it from her coat and held it close, seeing no signs of withering or death on the petals. He placed the flower gingerly in his coat pocket and stroked Aiden's cold face. He picked her up and held her body close to his, supporting her neck and keeping her head close to his own. What a thing of beauty, he thought.

*   *   *

Harold was escorted home by the ProServ patrols. The dusk deepened as he made his way home and night caught him at his front doorstep, the sky all dark and swirling and obscured by clouds. He shuffled through his doorway and slunk off to his chair at the corner of the room, where he hung his head in his hands to sob. The television was still on when he sat down and the Truth had several commentators on at once, four split screens with an anchor and three talking heads bobbing back and forth and up and down all saying virtually the same thing at once.

"This is how bankrupt their ideology has become! Trying to bomb Chelsea after the new management wants to address some of the claims of living conditions – this is insane!"

"What we need to start talking about finally is infiltration – how deep have the terrorists dug into dissent movements across the country? The American people deserve to know!"

"You still think there's a difference between these protesters and the terrorists? You're out of your mind if you don't think this is a blatant attack on the Restoration and the beginning of open rebellion in the streets!"

"This is certainly a spirited discussion. Some may begin to ask if the events today warrant tougher penalties for dissenters and a zero-tolerance policy for protests. Let's take a look at that bombing footage again…"

Harold turned his television off and thumbed through his records until he found *The Division Bell* by Pink Floyd, slipping it out of the sleeve and placing it on the turntable, moving the needle midway through the grooves to get to the fourth song of the track list. He turned the volume up loud enough so that it could be heard throughout the house and made his way upstairs into Aiden's room. He hadn't entered the place since she had vanished on Christmas. There was an envelope with Dad scrawled across the front on the pillows above her sheets on the bed.

Dad,

None of this is easy for me. If something happens tomorrow – if I'm detained or worse – know that I understand why you're doing what you're doing, I just don't agree with it. You're better than Joe Grant and all of his bullshit. So was Mom. I'll never understand why you two didn't keep fighting for what you thought was right. Your ideas, your beliefs shaped mine. You made me want to be involved, you taught me so much… and then you just gave up. You compromised, and all of a sudden the world turned for the worse, and you watched it happen, and you didn't do anything.

I'm not going to give in like that. I can't and I won't. I'm too young to see the world as a lost cause, even if you do. I know life hasn't been fair to you or me, but a lot of people have the right to say that these days. What about them? I know you want to make things better, but you never even try anymore, and it breaks my heart. I look to you for advice and for inspiration and all I see in you now is hopelessness. But it doesn't mean I don't love you.

I remember when I was really young, no more than four or five. You were trying to discipline me or something and I was a brat and told you I hated you and I didn't want to be your daughter anymore. I remembered how shattered you looked when you came into my room. You did something that was extraordinary – you didn't get mad or yell at me, you leveled with me and told me how bad you had it when you were a kid and that you hated your father. You told me that you felt lucky that he wasn't alive and that I would never know him – and then you choked up and begged me not to hate you and I gave you a big hug and from then on I felt more like an adult than a child. I loved you then and I love you now. I always will no matter what.

I love you enough to challenge you when I think you're wrong. I love you enough to urge you to be more involved and to not lose hope. Maybe you're right about some things, too. Maybe you can make a difference in Chelsea and make their lives better – and I hope that you do. But prolonging their misery isn't enough. They should be free and so should we. There's a lot that needs changing and it will never happen if everyone thinks like you. Don't let things get you so down that you don't want to fight back! No matter the odds or how impossible it seems or even if it means you lose something in the fight. You taught me all that. But if you won't act on it, then I will.

> With Love,
>
> Aiden

Harold clutched the letter close to his face and fell onto Aiden's bed. This is worse, Harold thought. She didn't hate me. She pitied me. He shifted and slunk down on the ground next to Aiden's bedframe and leaned against the mattress, still clutching his daughter's letter. The tears flowed freely, and there was a deep dull ache in his chest. There is nothing now, Harold thought. There's no rest, no feeling but agony. This is how my story ends, middle-aged and alone in the world with a chasm in my chest because all the good things were torn away for the most despicable reasons. My world collapses in on itself spectacularly before it ends, like a star in supernova.

"Now you know why I'm hopeless, sweetheart." He said the words aloud looking around his daughter's room. Something in Harold, innate and elusive, knew that this was coming. He knew deep down that Aiden was on a collision course with America in Restoration, the Nats, Robert Wright, and all his corporate henchmen. They would never give in to one another, so the result was simple: two unstoppable forces, one fierce and miniscule and another brutal and leviathan. They collide, and the larger one prevails, runs the smaller one right over and obliterates it instantly without thought. Like the elephant swatting a fly on its rear with its tail. To oppose this beast is useless, he thought. It will beat you and you'll lose. But then again…didn't he keep out of such matters and lose regardless? Does it get any worse than right now? Not for me, he thought. Not for me.

Harold managed to get himself up off the floor. He folded the letter up and looked around her room for her trinket box, finding it on her drawer chest at the far end. Harold creaked open the metal box, observing the colors and the swirling designs that gave the impression of the waves churning in an ocean. The letter and the bobby pins were placed in the box, but when Harold pulled out the blue flower, he simply observed it as he held the bit of stem still attached to the vibrant petals bunched tightly into a thick bulb. The flower went back into his pocket, closest to his heart as it could get, and it would stay there until it disintegrated completely.

Harold closed the trinket box and looked in the dresser mirror, his eyes cloudy, his cheeks puffy and moist and his slack jaw moving slowly from side to side. His head hung low and he looked up to see himself, slow to rise to his own image. Gripping the dresser with both hands he was struck with the thought of Aiden's funeral and how he would plan the event.

*   *   *

Lieutenant Eckart stood in Lo Presti Park looking at the Boston skyline. The ProServ patrols had been doubled in East Boston and he heard the Humvees moving down the street, still on the lookout for stragglers who had made it out of the protests. No one was on the streets now. His left hand dug into his pocket, he marveled at the lit-up skyscrapers and the massive cranes guiding steel girders, protruding up into the night air. The waters churned between the park and downtown, waves chopping in natural rhythm. The city lights and the stars reflected off the harbor. Eckart turned as he heard noise coming from behind him and saw his contact, a well-dressed man with slick, undercut hair and a pale angular face. Eckart met his gaze, the clear-blue eyes of the Leader's advisor staring back at him.

"Hell of a day, Lieutenant." The man had his hands dug into his pants pocket.

"Exactly as planned."

"You performed admirably. The bombing act was inspired. The Leader is very pleased with how events are unfolding."

"I appreciate his vision. I've watched too many come before him and lack the heart to see things through to their logical conclusion."

"That's why he considers you such a treasured asset. We stay on this course and the Restoration is guaranteed."

"What about loose ends?

"All taken care of – as always. Power struggles are unpredictable, but the purges in Washington are moving faster and have been more effective than we could have ever anticipated. Couple that with nationwide attacks on all the major protests, and the next wave we have in store…"

"I'm still concerned. Our pick isn't leading the internment program here. It's that snowflake Grant – he's managed enough pull in Arbitrage to treat this place as his golden parachute. He could blow this entire operation. Meanwhile I'm facing disciplinary charges for doing my fucking job."

"No need to fear. I'll see to it that you'll be fine. Expect little more than a slap on the wrist. Your position in Protection Services is entrenched as long as you keep this up." The man walked up to Eckart and patted him on the back. "You've made us very proud today. We're this close to living in exactly the country we deserve."

Eckart looked at the man with steely satisfaction. "Perhaps it's time then to explore moving to the next phase. As long as you still think it'll work."

The man smiled. "It's been working since Orient Heights, hasn't it?"

CHAPTER IX

"The tragic events at facilities nationwide – Chelsea in particular – are regrettable," said Joe Grant, his shoulders back and upright and his eyes trained on the television camera in front him. "I wish that it hadn't gotten to the point that it did. But at the same time, we can't lose sight of our mission. Look, ever since I can remember I loved politics. I'm a political person. My time in Congress representing the people of Massachusetts is something that I'm going to treasure forever. But you can't govern or manage based on politics. You've got to deal with the reality; and the reality is that these demonstrations were the cover for something far more sinister. We were lucky to have the caliber of Servicemen that we had there. Otherwise, I fear that there would have been more bloodshed."

Joe was comfortable sitting in the Command Center's remote TV studio, having digested the Party Talking Points before the interview. He amended some and glossed over others, giving them his own personal touch. He still had some measure of control. The Truth interviewer began to buzz in his earpiece.

"No one could have foreseen the events of December 26th. How have you been coping with these events so shortly after your taking the helm?"

"It certainly isn't easy, I can tell you that. My heart goes out to the people who lost somebody that day, who had members of their family or friends duped into showing up to what became another act of terrorism."

"Now we're hearing reports coming out of Boston and cities around the country that experienced similar attacks that this may not be Ikhwaan-related, that

this could have been perpetrated by terrorists born and raised in America. These reports suggest that these could be a whole new breed of terrorist – dissent terrorists. Can you comment on that?"

"I am privy to some information concerning the origins of this attack and I can confirm for those watching this broadcast that this attack was not perpetrated by Ikhwaan and that a domestic group is responsible. But whoever is to blame, Protection Services has been tasked with capturing those responsible. They're sweating leads now and some of those who are responsible for the bombing outside Chelsea have been captured while some may still be at large. Rest assured that they will feel the full weight of justice. It's only a matter of time now before all responsible have been caught – that much I can promise you."

"I think we can all agree with that. That was former Congressman from Massachusetts' 9th District and current Chancellor for Internment Services in that very same district, Joe Grant. Chancellor, thank you for your time."

"Thank you for having me."

"In other news to ring in the new year, a truck bomb in Caracas has claimed the lives of three Security Solutions executives and scores of ground forces in that beleaguered capital this morning. We'll have the details after this commercial break."

Grant watched the camera and when the red light went off, he pulled his ear bud out and took some of the taping equipment out from under his suit jacket. He got up and left the clutter on his chair when McGonagall appeared behind him.

"Why didn't you take the cue?"

"What?"

"The talking points the Party sent to us. You didn't say anything about that People's Liberation whatever group, why not?"

"Who gives a shit?"

"It's good to know about. I mean, in the future. The Party's all gung-ho about driving home the 'new threat from within' all of a sudden."

"What's the difference?" Grant checked his phone for the time.

"When's the funeral?"

"10 in the morning today. You still trying to bring Maguire on board?"

"Yes."

"Why are you bothering with him anyway? We could find a hundred people more qualified than he is to do what you're bringing him on for."

Grant started to adjust his tie, loosening it, and unbuttoning his collar. "I could say the same thing about you. Not your concern, Ed. I want Harold Maguire working for me at Chelsea. Is that understood? Does that satisfy your curiosity to the point where you can finally feel at ease?"

"Whatever you say, Chancellor. We should get going. If we leave in the next five minutes, we'll be on time."

"Should I change my tie? Do I have time to pick out another suit?"

"You'll be fine, it's appropriate looking. You don't need to worry about it."

Grant fussed with his hair using both hands. "I'm gonna go change my tie."

*   *   *

Harold Maguire made his way up the gently rolling hill, toward the site of Aiden's grave. He had chosen to bury his daughter next to his wife's headstone, under the weeping willow at the top of the hill in the cemetery closest to his own home. Each step felt like his legs had turned to lead. The guests followed his slow, stoic strides up to the gravesite. The aching in Harold's chest was constant. The knife had been broken off in his torso, always churning. His hands were dug in his pockets as deep as they could go, and his trench coat was spotted with a light rain that started and stopped and started again. Harold reached the top and looked off into the distance at the dense and growing Boston skyline. A small assortment of guests slowly made their way up to the site and stood in silence around the casket.

"Good morning, all," said the man from the funeral home whose name Harold had forgotten. The man had a light demeanor, which made Harold angry, but he did a good job of hiding that feeling. The funeral director smiled through his words as he continued on.

"We are here today to lay Aiden Maguire to rest, next to her mother who loved her so dearly. Aiden was a girl who grew to see young adulthood, always surrounded by friends and her family who have gathered here today to celebrate her memory. This is not to say she did not see her share of tragedy and hard times. At a young age she lost her mother to a senseless act of violent terrorism in the bombing at Orient Heights…"

The funeral home fellow was making big gestures with his arms and hands. He spoke to every person in the crowd individually, which seemed to make Joe Grant uncomfortable. Joe made his way over to Harold and the two stood in silence next to each other. Harold counted the seconds as they passed, hoping for an end to the entire affair. The man from the funeral home finished his remarks and Aiden's casket was lowered. Flowers were distributed to the attendants and each was able to toss theirs onto the coffin in the ground. Each rose distributed was a brilliant shade of blue, at Harold's request.

"How are you holding up?" said Grant as he placed his hand on Harold's shoulder.

"How do you think I'm doing?"

"The official was good. He did a great job honoring Aiden."

"He used to be a priest. I guess he thought this was more lucrative. He was strange; I don't know why he was so cheery."

"I think that's for the benefit of other people. Helps them move on, maybe."

"Maybe."

"Will you take a walk with me?"

The two moved slightly away from the ceremony grounds to the other side of the top of the hill under another tree overlooking Boston.

"I understand why you wouldn't want to talk to me as of late, but we need to do some things if you're serious about coming to work with me. It's going to change your life: you'll have a great job that you can start turning into a career and you'll get to know some important people. You could move into the city."

"Do you think I give a fuck about that right now? She's dead, Joe. I don't have anything anymore."

"Jesus Christ, Harold, you have my friendship and my trust."

Harold raised his hands in front of him at Joe, with tears welling up in his eyes. "I can't do this right now."

"It's a great opportunity and I want to make sure that you're going to go through with it. I'm trying to watch your back, Harold. Believe me when I say it…"

"What did I just say?"

"Just take the oath and join the Party at least. I can have you sworn in today. My car's at the bottom of the hill."

"I need time to myself right now."

Nigel emerged from the sparse crowd. Joe saw him and became fidgety.

"Well, just call me soon. You know how to get in touch with me."

Joe gave Nigel a bad look as he walked briskly away from Harold.

"Harold," said Nigel. "I'm sorry."

Harold nodded.

"Was that Joe Grant? Why'd he leave in such a nark?"

"That's Joe. I can't imagine he'd want to be seen with someone who was just cleared of dissent charges."

"Thank you for helping me keep my name out of the Registry."

"I don't want you confusing things. You were dating my daughter, and now she's in the ground. You're a good kid. I wanted to make sure that you didn't ruin the rest of your life, but that's where this ends. We don't need any further contact and you're not under any obligation to play son-in-law."

"So that's that, then?"

"Yeah, Nigel. That's that."

Nigel looked around and saw that the guests had cleared out.

Nigel spoke in a low whisper. "We can get back at the people who killed Aiden."

"What? What are you talking about?"

"The movement isn't losing strength, it's growing. The Nats can't hide what's really going on. But the time for protesting is over: the only way we're going to have an impact now is if we actually fight. I want to introduce you to some people-"

"You have no idea what you're getting yourself into."

"Just hear me out."

"Listen and understand: the moment you seriously consider what you're suggesting is the moment you decide you don't want to live anymore. Do you get me? Are you ready for that? You're a damn child."

"I'm ready to die. It's time to act. We need to do something!"

"Shut up! I don't want to hear it. You want to keep playing games you go ahead, just leave me out of it!"

"Who do you think is responsible for the rioting inside Chelsea? The gunfights? I have a contact who knows some of the people who got weapons in. A lot of the people who were at the Chelsea protest want to get involved. I'm serious, Harold. I want vengeance, that's what I'm living for now. We need to do something radical, something people can't ignore."

"I'm not going to debate this with you."

"So that's it, then? Your daughter gets murdered by these people and you're going to roll over and keep being a fucking coward?"

Harold swung hard at Nigel and connected with the side of his face, knocking him down. He eyed Nigel on the ground with a grimace.

"I'm done with you, Nigel. You stay away from me from now on. I forget everything you just said to me. We're finished. Is that clear?"

Nigel eyed Harold. He held his jaw and laid on the ground. "We need you, Harold."

Harold walked down the gentle sloping hill leaving Nigel at the top, on the ground and staring at Aiden's grave. He held his hand gingerly as it started to throb. Nigel had some nerve – at her damn funeral no less. He was just a kid; he didn't know what he was doing. Harold regretted having hit the boy. He didn't deserve it. Still, if Nigel kept up all this nonsense about revenge and rebellion, he'd be Chelsea-bound. He needed to get it out of his system. Harold climbed into his ride, his hand still hurting. He started the car with a boom and a fit and Harold drove his old sedan out of the cemetery, heading home in the off-and-on rain.

CHAPTER X

The barracks hearing room was clinical and modern, with a row of ProServ executives, field personnel, and higher-ups in the Party all sitting in front of Blair as he stared back at them. He was staring at the walls, consumed by the off-whiteness of the entire room. Taupe, maybe. Not quite an eggshell. One executive spoke into the microphone at his table.

"Officer Blair, how would you describe the mood of your fellow Servicemen the day of the bombing at Chelsea?"

Blair leaned forward into a microphone of his own. "Tense, for sure. Everyone was on edge. Trying to stay vigilant and alert."

"When the protesting started, what did the people who showed up actually look like?"

"What do you mean, sir?"

" You all had a certain idea of what the day's events would have in store, but did it match what it was that you all were told? Was this largely a group of civilians? Respectable looking people?" The executive adjusted his eyeglasses. "In sum, did this look like thousands of people gathered for anything more than a peaceful protest?"

"Sir, I watched them inflame fellow Servicemen on the front lines. An effigy was burned at a distance from other officers that could have gotten out of control. We had rocks thrown at us. Protesters were pushing the line we had set up to ensure that Chelsea would not be compromised, as well as to ensure the safety of protesters. All of that happened before the bomb went off. It was only then that we responded with live rounds."

"I understand entirely. I'd like to know more about the demeanor of your commanding officer, Lieutenant Frederick Eckart. How would you describe him to us?"

"I would call him a very dedicated officer and a patriot."

"Dedicated?"

"Yes."

"Would it be fair to say that dedication could be misconstrued as overzealousness?"

"What do you mean?"

"Were you or were you not given live ammunition as opposed to less lethal weaponry to deal with the protests that day?"

"I was given live ammunition, yes. But we ended up needing it."

Another executive leaned forward to her microphone after taking a sip of water. "How would you have known that beforehand?"

"Lieutenant Eckart has seen a lot of combat scenarios in his life, and he was planning for every contingency. I held back from firing until aft-"

"Combat scenarios? Officer Blair, a slew of young people – many of whom with familial connections to highly respected and indispensable members of the National Party – were shot at in the streets. Many were wounded and killed. The pattern repeated itself many times over across the country."

"Officer Blair," said a ProServ captain, looking sharp in his full dress uniform. "We have to be perfectly blunt with you. We are still contending with exactly who was responsible for the spate of bombings that were coordinated to strike at these demonstrations. We don't know if it's Ikhwaan, Antifa, Black Lives Matter, or another terrorist group altogether. Most of the casualties, if not all of them, seem to be civilians with no connection whatsoever to any organization that we know of. That represents an unacceptable failure on our part."

"Captain, with all respect, I don't know how we can come to that conclusion." Blair sat up straight. "If anything, Lieutenant Eckart was the only person who accurately saw this coming."

"That's an excellent point." Colonel Crenna said the words with a displeased air about him. He leaned back in his chair.

The captain continued. "When all is said and done, Lieutenant Eckart had tactical control over the Protection Services response to the Dissenter's March at the Facility. That supersedes the command of Colonel Crenna. Thousands of people were killed nationwide during these demonstrations. Eckart is responsible for the ones who died here."

"The situation may be different if Eckart's conduct on the 26th were a singular occurrence," said Colonel Crenna, leaning forward towards his microphone. "We've long suspected Lieutenant Eckart's behavior is an indicator of something more troubling. Perhaps you could shed light on that?"

Blair sat for a period of time, staring at all of them. He swallowed hard.

"Officer Blair," said the Colonel. "We do not intend to hold you responsible for the misconduct of another Serviceman, or those under Eckart's command. It's not how things are done here. What you tell us is going to be in the strictest of confidence. Now I want to ask you again… has Lieutenant Eckart done anything up to the point of the events of the protests that would make you feel as though he were unable to discharge his current duties effectively and properly? Anything at all?"

Blair thought carefully about the words he was going to use.

*　　*　　*

Blair stood outside of the barracks hearing room, waiting for Eckart to emerge from his disciplinary hearing. He felt sick to his stomach. When Eckart emerged from the hearing room, Blair stood up at attention to address him and fought the spinning in his head.

"How did everything go?"

"I've been officially reprimanded and demoted."

"How can they blame you for what happened? Nobody could have seen that coming."

"I was expected to fall on my sword. There's nothing that can be done about it now. It wasn't as bad as it could have been."

"They can't hold you responsible for this. It shouldn't matter who was protesting." Blair paused to collect himself. "Now I know where you're coming from. How are we expected to do the job if they intervene whenever someone somewhere applies some pressure? Management doesn't know what it's like out there!"

The door to the hearing room opened and Colonel Crenna emerged, surrounded by an entourage of ProServ brass and executives on their way out. Eckart and Blair looked on as the Colonel made his way towards them.

"Sergeant Eckart," said the Colonel as he nodded in his direction. He turned to face Blair. "I'd like a word with you, son. Come with me."

Blair and the Colonel walked off, away from the brooding Eckart and down the long corridor of the ProServ barracks. The Colonel put his hand on Blair's shoulder and spoke in an easy manner.

"David, isn't it?"

"That's right, Colonel."

"David, how long have you been serving?"

"Not long now, Colonel."

"How does Corporal Blair sound to you?"

"I don't know if I deserve that sir…"

"You most certainly do…you did a very courageous thing just now. Between how you handled yourself during the demonstrations and the Malone Park raid, you deserve a title more fitting. You're of good stock to boot, and I'm glad you understand the seriousness of our current situation. How important it is for us to have a backlog of recorded patterns of behavior – should it be necessary."

"Thank you, Colonel. I appreciate it."

"I know Eckart is close to your brother, Stephen?"

"Yes, that's right."

"They served together for a period of time. I understand you had something of a leg up on many of the recruits in your training class as a result of your relation."

"My brother showed me a lot of what he knows. He came up with Eckart in the Army, all the way to their berets. I'm nowhere close to that, though…"

"Enough modesty. You've got talents. I'd like to move some things around on your behalf, I think we can start elevating you to more serious work in SubCrimes. Consider your time shadowing your brother's friend coming to a soft close. You'll stay with him for the next few days or so, but your new role will have you working with others."

"Do you think that's a good idea…I mean, after the hearings? Wouldn't it be smarter to keep close to him? It would arouse less suspicion."

"Eckart has led you this far. You had an impression of him taking you further, I'm sure. But I want you to trust me when I tell you, Corporal: it will serve you better to go your own way." Colonel Crenna put his hands on Blair's shoulders, bringing him in close. "Eckart's demotion will be quiet, and the Truth is helping us a great deal in navigating the course ahead. But he's standing on quicksand and he's going to bring you down with him. The true believers aren't the juggernauts they'd have you think they are. We still need to have a country left to fight for when this is all said and done. Do you understand?"

"I understand, Colonel."

"Very good, Corporal Blair. Has a nice ring to it, doesn't it?" The Colonel was smiling through his words. "I'm sure you'll make us proud. Just like your brother did."

"Thank you, sir."

Colonel Crenna waved to his aide, who made his way over to the two of them.

"See to it that David Blair's promotion goes through."

"Thank you again, Colonel." Blair saluted Colonel Crenna and made his way back to where Eckart was standing, still meandering outside the hearing room alone.

"What did the Colonel want?" said Eckart.

"I've been promoted to corporal."

"You didn't tell him about al-Haqq, did you?"

"Of course not. You told me not to mention it to anyone."

"Crenna's a politician. He's too concerned with climbing the ladder and ingratiating himself with the Party elites. He's gunning for a plum job at Arbitrage as an executive and somehow he's gotten the idea that putting me on the chopping block is going to get him there."

"Beyond that, I have to ask you something. Why didn't we move on the breach at Chelsea faster? Maybe the unfits exploited the gap to attack the protest and if that's the case then we could have stopped it from happening."

"There was nothing we could have done to stop that." Eckart gritted his teeth and Blair could see his ire rising. Eckart exhaled deeply and calmed himself. "Listen, Blair: there's a power struggle in the National Party. The Leader is purging high-ranking Party members now because they're undermining the Restoration. We have to be very careful. I'm not quite sure who to trust right now."

"Then let's work on it ourselves. Maybe the Council President could point us in the right direction. Or do you think he was in on it?"

"Raikenov is a gangster, he's not a revolutionary. He's not interested in anything beyond the leadership in Chelsea. He wants a nice life on the other side of the Wall, that's all he's interested in. He's not going to involve himself or his people in anything that could jeopardize that. All he wants to do is keep us happy and his own people placated. Everything that happens inside Chelsea flows from that simple fact."

"If the unfits knew how he lived, he'd be finished."

"You're probably right – but they'd have to get to him first. He's got his own detail of hardened thugs to protect him. He's fortified himself within a section of Chelsea they're calling the Forbidden City – only for guests of the Council. I'll arrange for a meeting."

"I can start working over some of the informants we made from the protests."

"Excellent. You do that."

Blair made a move to turn and walk away but Eckart grabbed his arm.

"By the way…congratulations, Blair. At this rate I'll be the one saluting you."

"Stop."

"I mean it. You're good at this. You're proving yourself faster than I ever thought you could. You should be proud of yourself."

"I don't know," said Blair as he turned to face Eckart. "I barely got any sleep last night. None of this is as black and white as I wish it were."

"Nothing ever is, on the surface. You need to remember that everything we do is for a greater good. It's not easy, but we do what we have to do."

Blair looked down and recited the ProServ motto. "We do what it takes."

"That's right. It's late, Blair. Why not call it a night? We'll begin with all of this tomorrow."

Blair nodded. He walked off feeling not much better about things.

* * *

Harold Maguire sat in his living room chair cradling the handgun he usually kept buried underneath the clothes in his dresser drawer. He got it through an old friend years ago, keeping it unregistered and never feeling the need to carry it outside of the house. His eyes welled and the TV was on with the volume turned up loud, Grant's interview with the Truth bellowing out of the set. All he could do was stare at the gun. He could think of no music he wanted to hear now, and he wondered what would happen to his record collection afterwards. It was just him and the gun and the blue flower in the breast pocket of his shirt. Harold cocked the gun and put the barrel in his mouth.

He agonized with his finger on the trigger. Harold pulled the gun out of his mouth and stomped on the ground. He pulled his hair and bit his lip hard enough to bleed. His hands were over his face while he still held the gun with his finger off the trigger, the metal cold on his skin. He reached down for his bottle of whiskey, took three long chugs, and gasped at the burn that hit his throat and radiated up into his mouth. Harold breathed in deep and sniffed to clear his nose. He swallowed hard and tried to put the gun in his mouth again after a few more deep breaths. His finger hovered over the trigger in an uneasy way as he tightened his lips around the barrel. He jumped out of his seat when he heard a shattering noise and saw something come through the window. Harold leapt up with the gun and made for the front door, whipping it open wildly and screaming at the top of his lungs.

"I'll fucking kill you! You hear me you little shits! You're dead!"

Harold thought he heard the patter of feet growing fainter into the dark of the night. The gun went into his waistband behind his back and Harold stood looking out at his neighborhood. Half of the houses weren't even lit up and many of the streetlights were out. He could make out the signs that read FORECLOSED on many of the lawns around his own house. No one emerged from their homes or their apartment balconies to see what had happened. He made his way back indoors, his adrenaline still up.

The little snots left in this neighborhood. He felt fear like lightening run up his spine. It might not be neighborhood kids at all. It may be the Wright Brigades, the youth contingent of the Leader's movement. Junior honorary members of the National Party that served as a feeder organization for employment with the Party or at one of the military companies. They informed on their classmates at school and on friends and acquaintances in their neighborhood who had slipped under the radar of the usual authorities. Maybe they were targeting me now, Harold thought.

Shattered glass was strewn out across the living room floor and on his couch below the window. Half of it was still intact and the other half lay across the room in small breakaway bits. Harold made his way into the kitchen to find a broom when he accidently kicked something across the floor and into his kitchen. It was a good-sized rock with paper rubber banded around it. Harold took the band off and read the piece of paper in his hands.

Find justice for Aiden. Meet at Trocoa Mill
tonight, 10pm. Leave your phone at home – they use it
to track you. Join the movement. Vengeance is yours.
        -PRF

The work of the *People's Revolutionary Front* had been all over the Truth as of late, a slew of high-profile bombings and gunrunning into internment centers to train unfits how to use them. They were fanatical terrorists, a pitiful gaggle of rebels bent on the upheaval of civilized society. Or they were sowing the seeds of a revolt against the Nats, the first serious domestic group fighting the Party regime if you were delusional enough to think that way. They seemed suddenly to be everywhere.

Harold wobbled on his feet before remembering that he had

drank enough to put himself to sleep before eight o'clock. He steadied himself against the counter, trying to think reasonably about what had just happened. How did he even know this was really the PRF in the first place? Maybe this was all a convoluted sting operation or the Brigades making him miserable. After Aiden died, Harold felt like she left him sitting in a dead-end neighborhood with a big red flag over his head that might as well say put me in the Dissent Registry or declare me an unfit. How long before they started looking at me less like a victim and more like a loose end, he thought. It probably was ProServ: they'd have a unit waiting at that crumbling, burnt out mill building on the marsh. Waiting in the weeds to either shoot him or haul him off to the Chelsea Ghetto. Who has the mind for this kind of theatrics anyway? Rocks through the window with typed notes wrapped around. One thing struck Harold as he stood unsteady over his counter; the thought was so potent it fell out of his mouth.

"I need a drink."

The words sounded slurred and sloppy, but he paid no mind. He grabbed the note and crumpled it up as he belched and felt some of the contents of his stomach at the back of his throat. He stumbled into his living room where he grabbed his jacket and made his way to the front door. Glass was still strewn out across the room and the gap in his window was large enough that someone wouldn't have a tough time trying to get in. The bastards can have all this if they want, Harold thought stupidly. He closed the door behind himself and made sure he locked it as he left his house. Another brilliant idea struck him as he pulled out his phone to text a contact TOMMY. He sent him three snowflake emojis followed by a question mark. Harold put his phone away and rubbed his hands to warm himself a bit. He used the time to struggle to put his coat on. In less than a minute he got a response. Thumbs up emoji, followed by MEET ME AT RIORDAN.

He stumbled off of his front steps and toward the Riordan

Café, the only place walking distance from his house. Who are they kidding, Harold thought. They'd have done better naming it the Infinite Shithole. Walking felt more like stumbling, and Harold had to stop twice to collect himself before he turned the corner. It was a cool night and the clouds had parted, but still warmer than what January should have to offer. The Riordan wasn't far off now; Harold could see the glow of the cheap neon sign.

When Harold reached the bar, he ducked to the side of the one story building to vomit by the warped and rusted chain link fence where they kept a few plastic barrels with odd holes chewed into them from the vicious rats in the neighborhood. After he was finished he spit three or four times before wincing as he swallowed. He felt like he had gotten something off his chest. Like hitting the reset button. He groaned as he leaned back up and felt less embarrassed when he realized that no one was near enough to see what had happened – the only car parked on the street was an empty-looking van. Above the Riordan entrance was a sign advertising two-dollar drafts.

The bartender nodded at Harold as he came in. There was a slew of people all gathered around the band playing. The guitar riffs and the vocalist pierced his head in unimaginable ways. The floors were warped, made from cheap old wood, and stale beer stunk up the place something awful. Harold took a seat and flagged the barkeep down.

"What'll you have?"

"Two-dollar draft," said Harold as he held up two fingers.

On the TV hanging overhead at the end of the bar, one of the Leader's fanatical shitheads addressed the press corps about the Dissenter's March attacks and how the victims would be alternately brought to justice and honored for their sacrifice. It was totally whitewashed at this point: the facts and the logic just seemed to melt away entirely. They coated reality in so much deranged misinformation that Harold couldn't even compute it all. He looked away from the set to watch the man pour and suddenly heard his name come from behind him. He turned around and saw Tom.

"Hey, Tommy. How are you?"

"Pretty good, man. Haven't heard from you in a long time now."

The cheap draft beer appeared in front of Harold, who took a swig. "My daughter died."

"Damn, I'm sorry."

"I'm all fucked up."

"You need to get lifted?"

"How much do you got?"

"I'm holding for the band."

"Could you give me an eight ball?"

"Come with me."

Tommy ushered Harold to the men's room, where he emptied a baggy of white powder on the countertop surface by the sink. He chopped it and put it neatly in a few straight lines with a razor blade. Harold felt the itch as soon as he saw the stuff emptied into a mess of a small mountain next to the sink. He found a dollar bill and started rolling it tightly.

"Just like old times, Harold. You'll be feeling better in no time. This is good shit."

"I heard the Nats are spraying all the coca fields in the Western Hemisphere with some poison. Like a biological agent."

"Yeah, I heard that too." Tommy leaned over the countertop and took the first line. "This has been test run, we're good. Barely stepped on. Have at it."

Harold could hear the band outside had stopped, and the jukebox started playing *Lazarus* by David Bowie. He took the dollar bill to his nostril and inhaled half a line, clearing his throat before going back to finish the other half. He blocked one nostril and alternated as he felt the drip in the back of his throat.

"God dammit," he said before going back for another. "I don't want to be running back in and out of here. I'll just do it now."

"Be careful. This is a lot."

Harold kept going. "So what? It's time start having a good time for once." He splashed some water on his face, sniffing one long last time before going for the paper towels. He put a few $20 bills in Tommy's hand. "Thanks for the hookup."

"I hope you do OK, man."

"So do I." Harold smiled and grit his teeth. "It's time for another beer."

Harold walked out of the bathroom and back into the bar as the jukebox shifted to *Stand Back* by Stevie Nicks. The place was thinning out. As Harold leaned in for another draft, he sensed someone hovering close to him. He turned and came eye to eye with Nigel Whitmore.

"What the fuck are you doing here, Nigel? I'm trying to have a good time."

"I feel sorry for you if there's any hope of that."

"Fuck you, you little limey pissant!"

"You'd rather circle a drain than do something about what happened!"

Harold put his finger in Nigel's face. "Why don't you go back to my house and fix my window. You did that, didn't you?"

"Can we just talk outside? Take a walk with me."

"I'm not going anywhere with you."

"I'm not going anywhere, then."

"Yes you are. Get out. Go away. Fuck off and never return."

"How was your bathroom break?"

Harold kept wiggling his lower jaw. He shoved Nigel away from the bar. "You want to keep pushing it, you fucker?"

The bartender showed up a few feet from Harold and Nigel. "You two need to take this outside."

"Are you serious?" said Harold. "This little shit comes in here and fucks with me now I'm out?"

"Yeah," said the bartender. "Time to go."

Harold stood in front of the bartender and chugged the rest of his beer. "You suck."

"This is going to get bad for you the rate this is going."

"What's my name?"

"What?"

"What's my name?"

"I don't know your name, pal."

Harold shoved the bartender from over the counter and threw his empty glass at the shelves of liquor behind the bar, shattering many of the bottles. "Fuck you!"

"I'm calling the cops!"

Nigel grabbed Harold and the two ran out of the Riordan, running clean down the street in a sprint. The two slowed down a few blocks away and started panting.

"That was really stupid, Harold."

"What is it with you? You need a father figure that badly? I'm not up for it."

"Clearly."

The two stopped under a broken streetlamp and Harold looked around somewhat puzzled. In just a few blocks he seemed to be standing in a nearly abandoned neighborhood again. A screech roared up next to him. The dark van door slid open, and two men in ski masks jumped out to pull Harold into the vehicle. He was on his back struggling against Nigel and the two men as he heard the van door slide shut.

"Harold! Stay still and you won't get hurt!" Nigel screamed as the van lurched and pulled away. Unfamiliar voices were yelling all around.

"Get him tied!"

"He's got a gun here-"

"Keep him quiet!"

A piece of tape went over Harold's mouth, strong enough so that moving his jaw and trying to scream proved useless. Harold flailed around, trying to free himself as his hands and feet were bound. One of the thugs in a ski mask searched until they found his phone, pulling it out of his front pocket. A black bag went over Harold's head and the van took another sharp turn before picking up speed.

CHAPTER XI

The bag came off of Harold's head and the light shining on his face overpowered him. The tape was ripped from his mouth and he squinted and turned his head away, scared and unable to speak. Gasping, he tried to see the faces around him, all intense eyes. As he adjusted to the brightness of the light, the gang slowly fell into focus.

"Harold Maguire – you are being detained by the People's Revolutionary Front. The PRF demands the unconditional release of every human being deemed unfit for trial. We demand an end to overseas occupations, as well as the impeachment and trial of Robert Wright for crimes against the human family. We demand self-determination for all peoples oppressed by American imperialism and the abolition of the military-industrial comple-"

"Alright," said Harold. The voice was young and Harold felt more at ease when he realized that the band of revolutionaries were as old as Nigel and probably as naïve. "You've got your work cut out for you if you think you're going to get all that by giving me the black bag routine. Where are we?"

"Trocoa Mill." Harold recognized Nigel's voice and squinted. Nigel was the only one without a ski mask over his head. "I'm sorry we had to nab you like this, but we didn't think you were going to make the meet on time." A small rat came scurrying out of a corner and up to Nigel's foot. He shoved it off with the tip of his shoe, nudging it in the opposite direction.

"Turn that thing off, will you?"

Nigel turned the light upright, illuminating the mill. Harold could make out large windows at the far end of the floor space, half of them grimy and busted out. Bits of wood and broken window lay all over the floor, caked in filth. There were five or six people standing around, all of them fixed on Harold Maguire. The flimsy metal chair squeaked when Harold shifted. Apparently, they had untied his feet before they sat him down.

"Which one of you plans to pay for my window?"

Harold heard the sound of a gun being cocked. A woman stepped forward holding Harold's pistol. "You're not running the meeting, Harold."

"Who are you?"

"My name is Leona." She held the gun with both hands, pointing it at Harold's chest. "We know what they did to your daughter, and we know you're close with Joe Grant. Grant thinks you can be bought off. Your wife and your daughter become parts of a life you leave behind, and their deaths become the price you pay for admission to the ruling class. But we know you don't think that way."

"You know an awful lot about me for someone I've never seen before in my life," said Harold.

"Aiden told me all about you." Nigel crossed his arms. "We were in love."

"You have no idea what that word means," spat Harold.

Leona uncocked the gun and pointed it at the ground. "We're not going to dispute how much you cared for your family or how much Aiden meant to any of us. We're here now because we know that nothing is going to change unless people who are tired of all this start taking real action. We need to fire another shot the whole world can hear. We need people in the streets, ready to fight and die for the cause."

"What are you going to do?" said Harold. "Start lobbing

Molotov cocktails at the ProServ patrols? You're children. You don't have a chance."

"We know enough to sneak some of our people out of Chelsea already," said Leona. "We know how to get weapons in, and we know how to organize well enough so that ProServ can't get to all of them in one bust at Malone Park. We make phony IDs real enough to go undetected. It's how we move around."

"And we know how to scramble your phone so that when you bring it with you like some asshole they can't pick up on the signal and realize you're here." One of the voices spoke from the shadows.

"Fenster," said Leona as she raised her hand, signaling his silence. She turned back to Harold. "But he's right. So, for kids I'd say we're doing just fine – and remember that we're just one cell. There are a lot more of us."

"And if you don't like what you're about to hear we could kill you right now, Harold." Fenster stepped forward. "We could put an end to your whole slow-motion suicide act and leave you here with your throat sli-"

"Cancel that shit, Fenster! We're here now." Fenster went silent, and Leona turned back to Harold. "We're not asking you to do much for now. Only to trust us. We are not the enemy, Harold."

Leona made her way over to Harold, getting on one knee to be at eye level with him. She took the ski mask off of her head and revealed her face. Her eyes were hard and trained on Harold's. The only blemish on her dark skin was a small scar on her left cheekbone that had the appearance of a tear streaking down her face.

"You think the Nats would let me into the Services? You think I'm here to bring you in?" Leona motioned to one of the group to come forward. "I'm gonna show you something." Leona was given a tablet and she began cycling through images of two men, showing Harold a story in photos.

"We tailed a Party member from DC, one of Wright's top people. He got to Chelsea a few hours before the protests. After the bombing, he showed up at the Facility HQ and then he had his driver drop him off at a park in East Boston. He met with a man named Frederick Eckart, a ProServ officer in charge of riot control that day."

"What is this?"

"Just listen."

Leona started playing a video of the conversation between Eckart and Wright's advisor. The sound was grainy and sometimes dropped out, but mostly audible. Harold sat for some time, a middle-aged man with a coked-out stare and a heart beating too fast for good health.

> *"Perhaps it's time then to explore moving*
> *to the next phase. As long as you still think*
> *it'll work."*
>
> *"It's been working since Orient Heights,*
> *hasn't it?"*

"What? Orient Heights? What did they do?"

"They were responsible. They didn't just take your kid from you, Harold."

"No, they caught the ones who did it. Ikhwaan, the Muslim group. They did it. No, I can't…"

"They've been doing it for years. They started to spread fear and build support for Robert Wright and the Nats, and now they want to justify something worse than internment. They want to start killing off the unfits…systematically."

Harold squirmed in his chair, the ties chafing at him. Looking around, he saw pity on the faces of the people standing around. All but Fenster. Part of Harold felt affirmed in the worst way. He was more afraid now than he had ever been in his life. In just a few minutes he went from feeling like he was circling the drain to being totally adrift.

"That person we've been tailing is Richard Cantwell – he's one of the Leader's bag men. Party members get out of line and Cantwell makes sure they get hit by a car while they're jogging or have a heart attack at a show trial. Eckart works in SubCrimes, and he's Cantwell's operator in Boston. He orchestrated the Malone Park murders not long ago. Someone we helped a few months back wasn't as careful as he should have been and this guy zeroed in on him...declared him an unfit on the spot and executed him while Malden PD had him in custody. We don't know much more about Eckart. We don't have many opportunities to get close to them, either...then we thought of you."

"You want me to be your inside man at Chelsea."

"You might not think it, but we care about you, and about the safety of our people. We take precautions. We don't encourage unnecessary risks. But when you're at Chelsea, you'll have a seat at the table. You'll have information we need and you'll be able to get it to us."

"You're in over your heads."

"Don't you want justice for your daughter?"

"Getting justice for her is one thing. Going around killing people for a doomed cause is something else. If any of you have any sense left, you'll walk away from this."

"Nobody here is gonna walk away," said Leona. "No one but you, Harold – and you know what I'm talking about. We know how close you came to taking the easy way out."

Harold locked eyes with Leona. "If you came that close you'd know there's nothing easy about it. How long have you been watching me?"

"Long enough. This is your chance to put things right. Just give Joe Grant a call and tell him you want in. Once we're ready, we'll contact you again." Leona made to put her hand on Harold's shoulder. "Take a deep breathe. All those things you used to believe in, they're still inside you and now you finally have a way to do something. You can help people. You could save so many lives Harold. You have no idea how important you are. Just take this leap – that's all we're asking. If you change your mind, we'll walk away from you and make like all this never happened."

"Walk away? You tell me about all the Party members and ProServ thugs you're targeting and you're going to tell me with a straight face that if I take a job at Chelsea and have a change of heart, you're just going to let me walk away? If I don't do what you're asking me to do, you'll kill me. Or better yet, you'll follow me around for a while and convince yourselves that you're gonna kill me."

"You can call us a lot of things, Harold. Don't call us soft. Or naïve." Leona raised her sleeve up on her shirt to reveal her left shoulder. The scar morphed as she flexed her bicep. "That's where they put the implant when they started putting people in the Lawrence Ghetto. It's a biometric chip to keep people from escaping. Like they use for dogs." She rolled her sleeve back down. "Then they sent me to Chelsea. Eventually, we figured out how to offset the signal. I had to cut mine out with a piece of scrap metal. After I got out and got hooked up with the Front, I went back in to get food and medical supplies to our people. I looked people in their eyes and promised them that they'd be safe when they went with me. I mean it when I say it. If I say we will let you walk, it means we will let you walk." Leona lowered her sleeve. "You know where we stand and what we're about. If you take the job, we'll know about it and we'll be in touch soon."

"Leona, I didn't–"

Leona put her hand on Harold's cheek. "Make the right choice, Harold." She leaned into his ear, where no others in the room could hear her words. "We meet at the dark end of the street."

"What?" said Harold.

"When you hear it, you'll know you're talking to one of us." She turned back to the ones standing behind the bright light. "Let's move him out."

The group came toward Harold, and the one named Fenster

had a toothy smirk on his face as he opened the bag to put back on Harold's head.

*   *   *

The van idled outside of some abandoned houses that Harold was told were near his neighborhood. He heard the van doors open up and then his sight returned as the bag came off his head. Nigel neatly cut Harold from his ties. Harold rubbed his wrists.

"Where's my gun?" said Harold.

Leona took the pistol and held it up. "We'll hang on to this for you. Maybe you'll get it back when we know we can trust you. You're about five blocks away from your house if you head down the street."

"Wait, Leona?"

"Yeah?"

"Can I ask you something?"

"What?"

"What's it like on the inside?"

Leona paused for a long moment. "We'll be seeing you, Harold."

Harold was forced out of the van and onto the street. He heard the van doors close and the sound of the accelerator. The van disappeared into the night. Harold was left standing in the street stupid, hoping that no one was hiding out watching him. His phone had been given back to him. As he turned a corner, he stared at the screen before he put it back in his coat. The streetlights zapped off and the few lit houses lost power, leaving only the dark of the night ahead of him as he made his way back home. The streets were lined with litter and cracked sidewalks and bent metal fences rusted over and all of it shrouded in black. It was strange, Harold thought. There was no fear anymore. The aching and the longing for a quick death had vanished – or were at least less intense than they had been not an hour ago. Maybe it was still the coke.

Or maybe it was the names and the faces and the recording. It was the first time Harold had been handed a gift-wrapped excuse to feel everything he believed in for decades of his life. His worldview was vindicated. The world's turn wasn't just some expanding overcast or a monstrous cancer consuming all the things in its path. It wasn't an ideology, morphing and changing until domination over the land and the seas and the skies, over cyberspace and outer space and all points outside and in between seemed like a logical conclusion for any patriotic American. There were lines now, where conjecture and conspiracy ended and human beings who killed his family began. It's not overwhelming and unconquerable anymore. It's sitting at the tips of my fingers and at the edge of my reach, Harold thought. He just needed the nudge to grab it.

Harold found himself climbing the front stairs of his house. The temperature inside had dropped, and Harold fetched duct tape and plastic bags. He did a decent job of covering the half-broken window so he couldn't feel the wind blowing into his house anymore. After he was finished, he searched his record collection before he found *Stealing Fire* by Bruce Cockburn. Before he pulled it out, he took a deep breath and sighed. He pulled out his phone and dialed.

"Hello?"

"Hey Joe, it's me. It's Harold."

"Harold – hey, how's it going?"

"I'm not waking you, am I?"

"No, no. I was just going over something. How are you doing, Harold?"

"Good. I've been doing a lot of thinking. I just needed some time to myself, you know?"

"Sure, Harold. I understand."

"I'm calling to tell you that I'm still up for taking the job if you'll still have me."

"That's great news, Harold. Are you free tomorrow?"

"Yes. Yes, I'm free tomorrow."

"I can meet you at your house tomorrow at 10 in the morning. I'm gonna have you sworn in as a Party member and we'll go over a few things. You have the whole day freed up?"

"I can make that happen, sure."

"Excellent…you're making the right decision, Harold. I'll give you a call tomorrow when we're on the way."

"Very good, thanks Joe."

Harold took the record out of its sleeve and blew on it before playing the second to last track on the album. The song filled the room as he sat down in his chair, rummaging through his shirt breast pocket to find something Leona had given him. *Here comes the helicopter, second time today / Everybody scatters, and hopes it goes away.* Harold plugged a small penny-sized port with a foldable USB jack into his phone. His screen displayed one of the PRF surveillance photos, a still of Cantwell and Eckart talking on the edge of Boston Harbor. He stared intently at the image and studied the faces of the two men, particularly the ProServ veteran. The image had become etched in Harold's mind. *How many kids they've murdered, only God can say / If I had a rocket launcher…I'd make somebody pay.*

CHAPTER XII

The roar of rotors kept Corporal Blair on edge as he looked out the helicopter's window. They descended on a fortified sliver of squat red brick buildings by the section of the Wall that ran alongside Route 1. *The Forbidden City.* He and Eckart had a squad of ProServ commandos with them, all either readying or cradling their weaponry. Blair gripped a handle above his window and looked at the scene below as the ground and the unfits standing around came closer to him. The only thing between me and a hard landing was a seatbelt and maybe a few hundred feet, Blair thought. His musings ended as the helicopter pilot came on over the speaker system, his voice broken up and with a constant hum of static obscuring his words.

"Listen up guys. We're coming in now. When we let you out, we're dusting off past the Wall. We'll be back in a few minutes of your signal — backup is on standby. Call it if you need it."

"We'll be fine," yelled Eckart over the whir of the blades and looking back at the chopper pilot. "Raikenov isn't stupid!"

The helicopter steadied and sank into an old basketball court, pushing down the brown weeds that sprung from the many cracks running through the court and blowing refuse around. The blades slowed, but the whole thing seemed just as loud to Blair.

"You ready?" said Eckart.

"Let's go."

They both climbed out of the helicopter and set foot in the

Forbidden City. Raikenov's people stood around staring at the bird. They all wore armbands on their right arm with an acronym *AF* drawn on, *Auxiliary Force*. The commando detail accompanying Eckart and Blair were armed with submachine guns and had them on hair triggers; they had moved out of the chopper to cover the two senior Servicemen. Blair looked around at the red brick buildings ahead of him, all long and dumpy looking with cheap siding and busted air conditioners jutting out from them. He made out a nearby sign that should have read SERIVANO APARTMENTS but some of the letters had fallen off. Dhananjay walked towards Eckart and Blair, his hands buried in his heavy overcoat pockets. Blair kept his right hand over his hip holster. The helicopter touched off and the whirring grew distant before it was gone.

Blair eyed the terrain and thought of how quickly ProServ could wipe out the Council and all of Raikenov's muscle with just the ten ProServ grunts and enough bullets. From what little Blair could glean from Eckart, Raikenov and the Council handpicked many of the Chelsea Auxiliary Force now numbering nearly 3,000 strong. For all their graft and thuggery, Raikenov seemed to be able to keep a grip on them. The few that couldn't be bought off or cajoled into behaving could be dispatched with ease by the real authorities, Blair thought. Ten men with assault rifles and machine guns could beat hundreds or even thousands of fools with sticks and stones any day. At least that was the extent of the hardware they were supposed to be walking around with.

"Not a bad headquarters for the Council," said Dhananjay as he met Eckart and Blair at the center of the court. "It's the old Chelsea Housing Authority."

"Where's the man we're here to see?" said Eckart.

"I'll lead you to him. Follow me...Sergeant."

Eckart scowled at Blair before Dhananjay led the two into the main building of the old Housing Authority. A few ProServ shooters followed. Eckart clicked the communications bud in his ear and ordered the rest who were positioned near the court. "Keep the landing zone secure. We'll signal you when to get the bird back."

"Pretty quiet in here since you guys raided the al-Haqq brothers' place," said Dhananjay as he guided Eckart and Blair into the main building. The halls smelled of mold and stale air and the white floor, walls, and ceiling were tinged in yellow water stains. "You're lucky to have me in your lives, you know that? If it weren't for me, you'd have no hero stories to tell. The riots would still be going on. It could've been a revolution."

"How did you know al-Haqq?" said Blair.

"He was in the Auxiliary Force. Served for a month or so – but he wasn't down. Didn't have the stomach for it. Truth be told, he was probably a mole for the rebels. We asked him to round up a few girls for a big night at the Joy Division, you know Raikenov's place? He just wasn't having it. He quit. That was the last anybody saw of him. But we keep our own informant lists on where these guys live, who they visit. Everybody's watching everybody these days."

Eckart motioned for the commando escort to stand watch as Dhananjay pushed a large set of doors open to a converted office complete with staffers for Grigori Demetrivitch Raikenov, who sat at a good sturdy table and held a porcelain coffee cup.

Raikenov was an older man of below average height, lean for his age but healthy still. He blew on his coffee for a few moments before taking a measured sip. The Auxiliaries stood around, some smoking cigars and cigarettes, telling stories, and others drinking. There was no air of this kind of ease around Raikenov, whose face had taken on what seemed to be a permanent state of hard thought. He was white but his eyes were vaguely Asiatic, the push and pull of Western and Eastern Civilization showed through his face. His hair thinned slightly at the top of his head, now all salt and pepper. Mostly salt. He motioned to Dhananjay and the two ProServ officers, who sat down – except for Dhananjay, who moved deliberately to the other side of the table and stood.

"Gentlemen," Raikenov said calmly with a well-managed accent. Blair was surprised. He imagined the man sounding exaggerated and unreasonable, like a caricature of a Russian gangster. This man sounds like he's lived in America as long as he's lived in Russia, Blair thought. Maybe longer.

"Welcome to my office. Would you care for something before we discuss our business? We have beverages and crackers, vegetables."

"Tell Babu to go fuck off," said Eckart. "We're not talking business as long as he's hanging over your shoulder."

"I'm trying to help you," said Dhananjay.

Raikenov had an amused look on his face. "Danny, don't fuss. I'll speak with you soon."

"You're the fucking cracker." Dan looked more deflated than angry as he cast a look at Eckart and trudged off.

"We wanted to talk to you about a security problem," said Eckart. "Unfits are getting out and contraband is getting in. What do you know about it?"

Raikenov raised his hands up after putting his coffee on the table and put them down just as fast. "Naturally, there is always some underground activity inside internment facilities, prisons, what have you. We do the best we can with the resources provided…and as resourceful as we are, we cannot be expected to stop it all. Could we?"

Blair reached for a cigarette. "You ever hear 'the buck stops here?' Might be something useful to remember as long as you're Council President. You might not have a hand in it but how are we supposed to know that? You're in charge here." Blair spoke with the unlit cigarette hanging from his mouth. "You've got a leaky ship and you don't even know you're going under."

"I do not appreciate accusations. I handle business here inside Chelsea. Why would I do something that hurts business?"

"Business?" said Blair as he lit his cigarette and chuckled. "What business? Drugs? Intimidation? Extortion? Sex trafficking? If you call that business, you're some kind of businessman."

"I do not believe we have had the pleasure of meeting yet, young protégé of Eckart." Raikenov took another sip from his cup. "You sound highly appreciative of your obligations. I commend you. It takes a man of great integrity to never give in to the many temptations to abuse their power and violate the Serviceman's moral code. They might end up unfits themselves if they did…"

"David." Eckart spoke as the smoke from Blair's cigarette drifted into Raikenov's face as he exhaled. "We're here to solve a problem. That's all."

Blair contorted uncomfortably, Raikenov staring at him without breaking eye contact. His mouth barely moved as he spoke. "Right."

"Have either of you considered the possibility of a leaky ship on your end? Perhaps there are those in ProServ less scrupulous than yourselves…"

"That's not possible," said Eckart. "Why suggest it? Have you heard anything specific?"

"Nothing that I could guarantee. But I will tell you it would be wise to instruct Servicemen who may pass through certain establishments to remain buttoned up. I spend more time looking the other way than doing almost anything else. The Council is filled with those who would do much to see themselves in my leadership role. Every Council meeting entertains a host of issues that keep cropping up – 'not enough food, no running water, no medicine.' And the drug use…by our calculation we have 30-50 overdoses a day. More if we didn't stem the flow and work so closely with you all." Raikenov put his cup down and gestured with his hands calmly. "In all fairness, most who live in Chelsea do not live with my level of comfort. Perhaps contraband would cease to be an issue if people's conditions were materially improved."

"What about an exchange?" said Eckart. "You do something for us, and we'll do likewise."

"What were you thinking?"

"Simple deal: we make sure you keep your position if you find the breach and who's running it. The real breach – how anyone could get out or how the weapons and unauthorized food stuffs could get in. I don't really give a shit if the unfits are overdosing. What we need from you is to double down. Put the Auxiliaries on this full time. Make any rebels or troublemakers in here scream. Put the squeeze on them and at some point, you'll come across the security gap. We'll do likewise on the other side of the Wall."

Raikenov sat with a smirk on his face, taking a long sip of his coffee. "Alright. But I need leeway. I will find the gap, but it will mean that things will be ugly for a time. It may be best to keep the Truth cameras out of here."

"No one is going to interfere," said Eckart. "Nobody gives a shit about unfits after what happened just outside here anyway. No one's crying over a few dead jawas or illegals." Eckart stood up from his seat and adjusted his belt. "We'll be in touch."

"Very well, Eckart." Raikenov placed his cup on the table and looked squarely at Blair. "I don't believe I ever learned your name."

"You can refer to me as Corporal Blair." He stood up and eyed Raikenov.

Raikenov moved to his feet to match Blair's posture. The flick of something could be heard, as if something had just clicked loudly into place. Raikenov moved his hand and showed a switchblade. Blair thought about drawing his weapon and putting a hole in Raikenov's forehead. Blair felt jittery and he was in his head, praying that the Russian couldn't see him shake.

"How many lives have you taken, Corporal? How many people have you killed?" Blair eyed Raikenov and neither budged for some time. Eckart watched in silence. Raikenov raised the switchblade after a few tense seconds and clicked it so that it sheathed itself before he put it away. "Those who steal from me often lose their fingers. Those who betray my confidence have their throats slit ear to ear. The ones who talk back usually live the rest of their lives without tongues."

Blair stood mortified, swimming in a sea of his own fear. Eckart stared him down.

"It would shock you what people are willing to eat when the pangs of hunger become too much for them," said Raikenov. "I look forward to our next visit. We will have good news for you then, I hope. Enjoy your day."

Blair looked away from the man and noticed a small picture frame sitting at the corner of Raikenov's desk. Blair picked it up and weighed it with his hands, tossing it lightly back and forth twice. "Nice, Grigori. Who are they?"

"My family," said Raikenov with a dry smile.

"You play knife games with them?" said Blair. "You know I could find out exactly where they are before lunch, right?"

"Corporal," said Raikenov. "You have much less leverage than you're imagining. Don't entertain the thought."

"Don't you ever fucking muscle me again." Blair's voice shook slightly.

Eckart grabbed the photo out of Blair's hands and put it back on the desk. "We're leaving now. I'm glad we could come to an agreement." He forcefully turned Blair around and walked him out of the makeshift office. The ProServ commandos outside Raikenov's quarters closed ranks on the two senior officers as Eckart shoved Blair into a wall, spinning him around so that the two were face to face. "What are you, a fucking child?"

"What the hell is going on in there?" said Blair. "Why are we bending for that piece of shit?"

"He's going to be the one who finds the breach. He's good for these kinds of things and you want to piss him off so badly he doesn't come through for us?"

"Do you really know him? Have you read his file? I looked him up in Genisys and he's all but completely redacted. Any background history can't be accessed by ProServ field personnel. So I really got to ask you, how well do you know the King of the fucking Unfits? And weren't you the one who blew away al-Haqq? If we had time with him he might have given us something useful. Maybe not right away, but-"

"Put it to bed," said Eckart. "That was out of line in there. You're acting like you're not in control."

"And you do it 20 times a day!" Blair pushed Eckart away. "So don't give me any of your shit. You act like a psychopath and nobody bats an eye. The first time I give somebody the squeeze and all of a sudden I'm out of control?"

Eckart pointed in Blair's face. "If you weren't Stephen's brother, I'd break you in half."

"Sir," said a commando, "should we signal the bird?"

Eckart stepped back from Blair, still fuming. "Call it in. We're done here." Eckart left the main building. All but one commando followed him. The remaining commando steadied his gun to his chest and stood to face Blair.

"Corporal, we should move out."

Blair shoved off from the wall and walked coolly out the front door with the commando close by, strolling towards the extraction zone with his hand on the holster of his gun. He found Eckart idling on the basketball courts, the faint sound of the helicopter in the distance.

Eckart asked, "What's on your agenda for the rest of the day?"

"I want to call in some informants," said Blair.

"Why don't you look into something else? Get your head away from this for a while. The campus police found a car bomb parked outside MIT. Take a drive down there, check it out. I'll keep you briefed on all of this."

"Why won't you chase this thing all the way?"

"I told you. Think of what's going on in the Party right now, in Washington. I'm trying to protect you."

The sound of the helicopter intensified as it came down on top of them. "I don't need you babysitting me anymore!" Blair climbed into the helicopter and sat back down next to the same window. Across from him was Eckart, climbing into his seat and staring intensely in his direction. The rage was etched on his face, the icy veneer always a moment removed from slipping entirely. Without words, Blair could read him. Eckart was going to do everything he could to get me back under his thumb, Blair thought. The rotors of the helicopter were intense as it lifted them back into the sky.

*   *   *

The doors to Asiyah's squat were being pulverized. The banging wouldn't stop. She took some of the medical kits she could stuff into a backpack before going out of the apartment window onto a fire escape. Soon after she ducked down, the door exploded. One of Raikenov's hulking goons in the Auxiliary Force started turning things over and kicking furniture clean across the room. Yevgeny, Asiyah thought.

"Where are you?" Yevgeny spoke in clipped, Slavic-sounding English. "Stupid bitch! Don't make me look for you!"

Asiyah slid down the fire escape, nearly breaking it as she landed on the sidewalk. She bolted up and started sprinting down the crowded street before someone appeared from around a corner and grabbed her by both arms. An old, black luxury sedan pulled up to the scene and the man shoved Asiyah into the open door. He slid in next to her. On the other side of Asiyah was Grigori Raikenov. The sedan drove off, honking its way through streets teeming with unfits.

"Hello my dear," said Raikenov.

"What do you want from me?" said Asiyah.

"You've been very difficult to track. You never perform surgeries in the same place twice. Smart. Until you worked with the wrong person."

Asiyah struggled as the man grabbed her again, wrestling her into her seat.

"We're not going to hurt you," said Raikenov. He grabbed Asiyah by the chin with force. "It gives me no pleasure."

"Son of a bitch!"

"Asiyah, dear. You haven't even heard what we propose for you." Raikenov took his hand away.

"You tell me I'm dead unless I'm you're fucking whore!"

"Well you've served us well in that department! But we could offer you something better."

"Alright," said Asiyah. The man released her from his grip as she straightened her clothing. "You're not going to kill me?"

"I can't bring myself to it. Having tested the goods myself." Raikenov stroked her cheek as Asiyah recoiled. "You may be better served by life on the outside."

"You're lying…"

"I'm talking about legitimate release. You have special skills. We could use someone like you on the other side of the Wall."

"What do you mean?"

"You're good. You've performed life or death surgery more than once in these conditions. I have much confidence in what you can do outside of this place. Before I was interned, I had many business interests in Boston. My outfit that's still outside could use someone like you."

"You want me to be your mob doctor?"

Raikenov smiled. "No. You *get* to be my mob doctor, as you say." His knife unsheathed itself, and he put it against Asiyah's check. "Or I *get* to slit your throat."

*   *   *

"What do you know about Grigori Raikenov?" said Blair. The low hum of the crowded Cambridge bar rang in his ears.

"Not much," said Carver as he raised a pint glass to take a swig. "He's the man to be in Chelsea. Heard he had ties to the Russian Mob. He's probably into whatever it was they were doing in Boston. Or are doing, whatever's left of them."

"We got into it today, in Chelsea during our meeting. He pulled a fucking knife on me. When I put some pressure on him he just stared right through me."

"What pressure?"

"I picked up a photo of his family and implied I could get to them whenever I wanted to."

"Are you crazy?"

"It was not a banner day at the office."

"Have you checked his file?"

"It's all redacted, I can't read anything on him. It's like he's been scrubbed."

Carver laughed. "You realize you're talking to me, right? I'll look into it." He finished his beer and put it on the table. "But you should know that redactions happen for a reason."

"What do you mean?"

"ProServ doesn't want its grunts knowing anything about Raikenov. Or anyone who might be able to look at his files."

"You think there's something to that?"

"There's always something to that."

"The guy was so dead calm. Like nothing rattled him. He made Eckart squeamish."

"Oh, I would have liked to have seen that."

"You know, they're moving me up in SubCrimes. They want me

to start running informants, helping to put operations together."

"Congratulations." Blair poured some of his beer in Carver's pint glass. They both raised their glasses. "That's a big deal. Cheers."

"Would you ever consider helping out? Like, coordinating with me directly? Off the books."

"You mean you want help cutting through the bullshit, right?"

"I need somebody I can trust to get me intel. Someone I know isn't going to get me killed by asking the wrong questions to the wrong people or giving me bogus info to keep their boss happy."

"I get what you mean." A new beer appeared in front of him as a waitress made her way by. He took a long swig. "I could be interested."

"Well, let's start with Raikenov at least. I want everything there is to know on him."

"Anything in particular you suspect?"

"He's too chummy with Eckart. Something's up."

"You know I've heard stories about the Russians going back to the Soviet Union. Games they used to play. Their security services called them *active measures*. Social media influencing, financing fringe opposition groups, false flag incidents, poison a few intrepid anti-Kremlin activists with a nice shot of dioxin in their morning coffee. All kinds of stunts."

"What's dioxin?"

"It's the main ingredient in Agent Orange." Carver took a sip of his beer.

"None of this makes any sense – Eckart's doing Russia's bidding? That's not possible."

"Maybe Raikenov was a spook and Eckart turned him for his own ends as opposed to Russian interests. A lot of these mob guys used to be involved with the military or the spy game. It's how they made all their connections. When the Soviets fell, all the top Communist Party members took all the state functions and privatized them. All the money went into their back pockets. The difference with the mobsters was the stuff they could get their hands on first was usually AK-47s."

"That sounds oddly familiar. You're talking about arms dealing?"

"Exactly right. Eckart's worked all over the world, and the Special Forces community is surprisingly small. They could have crossed paths."

"Do you want to step outside?" Blair showed Carver his pack of cigarettes.

"Laying low tonight, huh?"

Blair slid out from the booth they were sitting in. "Something like that."

The pair moved through the half-emptied bar and Blair held the door open for Carver. The cold wind sent a chill through him. Carver took the cheap disposable lighter from Blair and made a small circle with his thumb and index finger around the flame, lighting the cigarette Blair gave him with little effort.

"That's a neat trick."

"I never showed you that?"

Blair took the lighter back and covered it as he tried to light up. The wind kicked up and it was no use. "Jesus."

"Give it to me." Carver pulled the lighter trick again.

"Thanks." Blair took a long drag and exhaled. "You really think there's something there between those two?"

"Based on what you're telling me, it sounds like there's a good chance." Carver took the cigarette out of his mouth and blew smoke away from Blair. "Tell me something."

"What's up?"

"Why did you freeze up with Raikenov? What made you stop from at least pounding his head in?"

"He's not just an unfit, the way Eckart talks."

"You didn't freeze up with al-Haqq."

"He had a gun on me. Plus, I wasn't thinking. It was all just action."

"An unfit pulled a knife on you. A good officer would have your back however that played out. What did Eckart do?"

"He just stood there."

"I think you've got your answers, brother."

"He's the head of the Chelsea Council."

"He pulled a knife on you and the dude who's supposed to have your back watched and waited."

"Maybe he's just steadier than I am, more restrained."

Carver laughed. "I know that's not something you expect me to believe. You trying to convince yourself?"

"That sounds about right."

"Let me dig around and see if there's anything. Because now I'm really interested. But I hope you know, this isn't going to be an overnight thing."

"How long do you think?"

"Redacted files? Probably months."

"Christ."

"General Information Systems isn't a joke. But I will get it done, that I promise you."

"Good. I appreciate it." Blair flicked the rest of his cigarette into the road. "I'd prefer not to live my entire life not knowing which way is up."

SPRING

CHAPTER XIII

Harold Maguire stood near the windows in one of the corners of the large function hall, off and away to himself after a few hours of nonstop schmoozing. He looked out over Boston from Arbitrage Tower, finishing his cocktail as some of the city's elite Party members and corporate types laughed and drank and traded gossip and told great tales. Harold fiddled with the cherry stem as he stared out at the city skyscrapers and the sea of construction cranes lit up at night. What a difference a few weeks makes, he thought.

A waiter made the rounds. Harold adjusted the pocket square in his suit and ordered another Manhattan as his old friend Joe Grant approached him.

"Harold! How are you holding up here?"

"Doing fine. Just taking a break from the beautiful people. Great views here. I haven't been in a skyscraper this high in ages. When I was, it was the observation deck."

"Picture windows," said Joe with a laugh. "Get used to them. Play your cards right and you'll be doing all your work out of the Tower. You know, you're a big hit at this get together. You're doing everything right, and I think a lot of people are excited about what we're planning with the Facility. Our strategy could be replicated nationwide if we get this right." A fair woman in her early forties and a slim figure came up behind Grant and placed her hand on his shoulder, enveloping him in an embrace. "Speaking of me getting it right…"

Harold smiled timidly and extended his free hand to shake hers. "How are you, Jackie?"

"Harold, it's wonderful to see you. I trust Joe has been treating you well. You can tell me you know. I'll straighten him out if he's not treating you right!"

Joe laughed. "That's right, she will!"

Harold looked down at his empty glass.

"Harold," said Jackie as she readjusted her tone. "I want you to know how much this means to us. I know that it means the world the Joe that you said yes to working with him. Particularly after everything."

"Thank you, Jackie," said Harold. "I'm learning to go on. There's still work left to be done."

"This is why everybody loves you, Harold!" Jackie gave him a hug. She held him by the back of the head. "You're the strongest man I know. I feel honored that you're in our lives."

They must be half in the wrapper, Harold thought. He's bright pink and she's doing the weepy drunk shit. Jackie relinquished her grip as the waiter came back and handed the Manhattan to Harold, who traded in his empty glass and had a good gulp of his third cocktail. "How's your son doing?"

"Tony's taking a semester off," said Joe. "He went with his friends to Bali for the Spring Term."

"Does that have you guys nervous?" Harold thought of how he had deliberately kept Aiden away from Tony Grant after a certain age. Aiden was growing into such a wonderful child. Tony was a snot from the get-go, a brat who acted like his entitled sneers were divine commandments. He was college-age now and Harold didn't have a hard time believing that the kid was growing well into the role of an Ivy League date-rapist. Now the twerp was living it up in a tropical paradise while his own child was in the ground.

"Let me tell you something…Bali is safer now than it's ever been.

Our organization is doing tremendous things in Indonesia. But that's not to say there isn't room for improvements. We can always do better. But Bali is totally safe. There's better security there, uh, well I probably shouldn't say it's better patrolled than Chelsea, right?" Joe finished his sentence with a put-on laugh. "In all seriousness, Bali is safe. We wouldn't have let Tony go if it were dangerous."

"Glad to hear it," said Harold.

"Are you ready for the introduction?" said Joe.

"Introduction?"

"I'd like to introduce you so you can say a few words."

Harold felt a jolt of nervousness hit him in the stomach. "I haven't spoken to a crowd this big since college."

"You'll be fine," said Jackie to Harold. "Better get used to it now or you'll be hopeless."

"That's right. Come on, come with me." Joe guided Harold through the crowd toward an area where an aide of his was holding a microphone, who handed it over to Joe.

"Excuse me," said Joe. "Excuse me, everybody. If I could have your attention for a few moments." Grant had a natural forcefulness that didn't come off as pushy or rude. The room quieted to a low murmur as the speaker system carried his voice throughout the function room.

"I'd like to thank all of you for attending tonight. I'd like to thank each of you for the hard work you're doing every day, whether it be in the public or the private sector. Many of you know each other in a workplace setting, but I really feel that it's at events like these where we really get to enjoy each other's company with a little less stress attached and we can really get to know one another.

"I'd like to introduce you to someone you'll recognize as a new face tonight. His wife was one of the greatest talents I've ever had the privilege of working with when I was in Congress. There isn't a day that goes by when I don't think of her and wish she were still with us. The man

I'm introducing could be best defined as tough. Resilient. Down-to-Earth. We met in college and he's been a friend of mine ever since. He's been engaged in the many neighborhoods around town in a number of roles working with community groups and solving issues that most concern the people who make up the City of Boston and its surrounding communities. He brings tremendous experience, uh, in that regard…"

Joe was doing what he did best, thought Harold. But why was he bringing this stuff up? He's going to get me killed, Harold thought. Half the groups Harold had anything to do with picketed Joe's office at one point and Harold never had a real job with them anyway. It was all activism. He had drifted away from it all even before the Party came on the scene. Harold couldn't tell if his success was due to misguided nostalgia or self-important pity on Joe Grant's part, but that didn't matter now. What mattered was how the hell he would introduce himself to a group of high-powered fascists glaring at him with feelings ranging from amusement to suspicion.

"…ladies and gentlemen, our new Vice Chancellor for Outreach and Administration: Harold Maguire!"

A round of applause came over the crowd and Harold took the microphone from Grant without putting his drink down. "Thank you, Joe. Joe Grant everybody!" It was enough of a line to keep the applause going a little longer and to allow Harold to think of something to say. "I want to say what a pleasure it's been getting to know all of you here tonight. It's really been an honor and a privilege." Harold paused and looked around the room. They were all staring at him now. "I know that we're all concerned with the situation in the Chelsea Facility, and places just like it all over the country. All too often we can look out on the place and see the smoke rising because of what's happening there."

Some of the faces staring at Harold contorted in discomfort. You don't have anything left, Harold thought. Fuck it. "And you – we – can't afford to ignore it anymore. We can't sweep it under the rug and pretend it's not happening. Otherwise the situation on the ground in there is just going to get worse. I've been having discussions with Joe and with members of his team over the past few days and soon I plan on going into the Facility myself with a security detail to see the situation up close. Everything that I've been learning so far about this place really strikes me: the resources are scarce. The unfits who live on the other side of the Wall don't have basic necessities. They go without enough food, they go without electricity, in fact most unfits in Chelsea are living in a world that looks more like the 19th Century than the 21st Century. Potable drinking water is becoming an issue. I'm sure a lot of you are wondering why that's even our problem."

Chuckles rose from the crowd. It unnerved and excited Harold all at once. They haven't turned on me completely, he thought. "My point is this: when you have unfits who see their living conditions deteriorate to this point, they're not going to be very happy. They're going to look to the groups and the factions there who are offering an outlet for that anger. As you've seen, that means riots in the streets.

"Now, that means we have a real opportunity with Joe Grant as Chancellor. We can reverse this trend, because we have a leader who's tough enough to know when to crack down on trouble groups and who's smart enough to know that we need a holistic approach to dealing with unfits in Chelsea. It means addressing these concerns that create anger and resentment amongst the unfits and getting to the root of these problems before they get out of hand. We need to recognize that there may be some things we can do to rectify living standards in the Facility that will make all of us outside the Wall safer. We have an obligation to act. And then let the results speak for themselves."

Harold felt pure exhilaration as most in the room applauded, taking in the praise of the self-important plutocracy. Joe had driven home to Harold the rumblings and intrigue that came with higher-tier Party membership: the emerging factions, the mined paths to success, Leader

Wright's growing obsession with proscription and adulation and the new round of purges in DC. Joe Grant had explained it all to Harold Maguire. Tonight was a function filled with guests sympathetic to Grant's new vision for Chelsea…it just needed the right packaging.

"Thank you all for your service to Boston and our country," said Harold as he raised his glass to the applauding partygoers. "And may God bless Leader Wright and the Restoration. I can't wait to serve alongside you."

Harold accepted congratulations and moved on through the crowd, drinking in the night's success. He stopped suddenly when a smiling man with sharp facial features appeared in front of him, patting him on the shoulder and congratulating him on his remarks. He recognized this angular man from the flash drive the PRF gave him.

"We all look forward to seeing this new administration in action. Leader Wright will be watching your progress with great interest. Let me introduce myself-"

"Cantwell," Harold said, staring through the angular man.

"Have we met?"

"I'm familiar with your work."

"Very good. Then you won't mind my interest in your new position. The Leader is very thorough, but he's a fair man. He is willing to wait and see how well this new strategy works. The costs, the benefits and so on must be weighed."

"Then you'll be staying in the area for a while?"

"I will be."

"Where are you staying?"

"Hotel nearby. The new Emerson Mandrake." Cantwell poked Harold lightly with his index finger, gesturing to him. "Perhaps we could meet later for a nightcap after this is over. Celebrate your newfound success with a few associates. What do you say?"

"I think I would like that."

"Your remarks were very impressive, Mr. Maguire. You've got a real outside of the box approach. Here's hoping that it all works out. To your tenure at Chelsea!" Cantwell raised his glass to Harold and they each took a sip. Cantwell drank generously from his glass as Harold eyed him, barely noticing the woman about a decade younger than him in a sharp business suit sidle up to him for conversation.

"Harold! I had to tell you congratulations," the woman said as she boxed Cantwell out slightly, playing with the small stirrer in her glass. "Your remarks were wonderful."

"Thank you," said Harold, looking past her at Cantwell as he began chatting with other party guests. "I'm sorry, where do I know you from?"

"It's Lauren, Harold. Lauren Meyers. I swear we've met before." Lauren grabbed Harold's arm firmly. She leaned into Harold's ear, speaking at a near-whisper as the hum of conversation amongst the partygoers filled the hall. "Maybe at the dark end of the street?"

"Lauren, you said?"

"That's right, Harold. I'm a friend. Why don't you laugh a little, you look like you've seen a ghost."

Harold smiled somewhat awkwardly. "You work at Arbitrage now, Lauren?"

"I used to work for Homeland Security before I became a department liaison with Protection Services."

"So how did you end up doing this?"

"Why don't we talk about this at my place? I have a car waiting outside."

"I'm meeting Cantwell at his hotel later-"

"Skip it. I know him; he'll be far more intrigued with you if you blow him off tonight. It'll give us a chance to get to know each other."

"I don't trust you."

"Then this plays out two ways, right? Either come with me or say no, and you're already done for." Lauren leaned in close and whispered in Harold's ear. "You think you have an idea as to what's going on. Let me start filling in the details for you."

*   *   *

Lauren led Harold into her penthouse in a Back Bay skyscraper still under construction. Echoes danced through the place as Harold followed Lauren to her living room, all white and black. It was glossy and soulless, telling of great fortune. Lauren Meyers made her way to a flat screen monster of a television hanging over her fireplace which ignited at her say so. The embers glowed brightly, and Harold couldn't tell if the thing was real or a hologram. The screen clicked and glowed and Lauren started playing with a small tablet. Cantwell's face appeared on the screen and his biographical information displayed alongside his avatar.

"Why don't you have a seat, Harold? Domestic!"

A generic man's voice came over the entire household. *At your service, Lauren.*

"Cue my new playlist."

Very good, ma'am.

Eye in the Sky by the Alan Parsons Project came on, booming through the penthouse.

"I enjoy the irony," said Lauren. "This also makes for good cover. In case anyone is listening."

"Why are you helping me? You work for Arbitrage."

"You think you're the only person the Front has on the inside? I've lost myself working for these people and now I'm finally in a position to do something. Just like you, Harold. Wright is paranoid beyond description; he's starting to pick off his best people with these show trials, all the renditions and detentions. He's constantly purging people on his periphery and in the Party, save for a few trusted advisers. The higher-ups at Arbitrage want him gone. If we can eliminate Wright and his top foot soldiers, then all the dominoes fall. Maybe then we can take this country back." Lauren scrolled through Cantwell's biography. "Have you ever heard of the Genisys Program?"

"I'm becoming more familiar with it."

"I've got some secured downloads from the database. You're looking at Richard Cantwell. He's one of Leader Wright's top enforcers and-"

"Leona gave me a rundown on him. I want to know more about Eckart."

Lauren pulled up Eckart's file with a few taps of her tablet, his biography scrolling down the television screen. "Before all of this he was just some poor kid on white supremacist message boards who convinced himself to join the army. After he got his Beret, he was loaned out to the CIA for dirty work all over the world. He spent some time in Iran and Egypt scuttling insurgents, same in some Yugoslav countries. In Guatemala and Honduras, he undermined the activists opposed to corporate drilling and foresting operations. It was only a matter of time before Wright's people found him. He's been working for Cantwell's dirty tricks squad ever since. When they want something done or someone taken care of, Eckart's one of the dogs Cantwell lets off the leash."

"He got Aiden and my wife killed."

"There's more, Harold. Wright's extended terror campaign isn't just the low-boil terrorist bombings they perpetrate."

"What do you mean?"

"It's called Operation Orchestra. The last phase of the Restoration. The Leader wants to clean out the internment camps across the country to implement a Final Solution."

"Alt-right ideologues with Special Forces training – what were we supposed to expect?"

"The only thing stopping him is enough people at Arbitrage who don't think that's such a good idea."

"Why are Arbitrage and Wright at odds with each other?"

"This all started because corporate interests wanted a government they could do business with. They thought Robert Wright was going to be the usual puppet backing whatever it was they wanted to do. Then the Exchange happened, biological warfare, Black Friday... suddenly Robert Wright wasn't some amusing puppet anymore. Then we got the National Party, internment – which ProServ pushed for – it all goes on. Wall construction on the southern border, occupations worldwide. Big business got so used to footing the bill for lunatic political candidates they couldn't even see the ledge when they drove off it. They never counted on men like Cantwell orchestrating chaos on a global scale."

"So, the two of them together...they joined forces and started remaking the world into a fucked-up warzone? Just to have some master race reign supreme?"

"For them, it's not capitalism or conservativism anymore. That's old hat. I don't know what else to call them, it's neo-Nazis with an agenda." Lauren Meyers sat in a chair adjacent to the couch, leaning into Harold. "We found the intel – buried and redacted, scattered like breadcrumbs all across Genisys. Memos and briefings and reports all suggesting that a massive attack – likely with Pakistani nuclear material – would take place in New York. Surveillance teams were reassigned and shuffled around. The authors of all those documents issuing those warnings don't exist anymore. After that, President Wright had all the authority he could have ever dreamed of. He rechristened himself the Leader. And now we're here."

"Jesus," said Harold. He stood up and started pacing before stopping, grabbing his hair and pushing it straight back.

"I'm sorry Harold. I'm sorry this is what it is, but you were brought in because we think that you knowing this is better than you flaming out. We think that you'll want to help us try and do something.

Whatever it is you want to call it."

Harold stood for some time. He made his way to Lauren's minibar, and poured himself bourbon into a small glass he found there. *Aviation* by The Last Shadow Puppets came over her speaker system. He took a long swig and looked back at Lauren with a distance on his face that grew steadily into steel. "What do you have in mind?"

CHAPTER XIV

Blair's hair was pure grease, unwashed for three days. His clothes were ragged: he had two holes in his jeans as a third tear was becoming apparent on his left inner thigh. The bulky bubble coat he wore offered great warmth and it would have kept his hands from shaking had it not been for the cigarette he carried in between drags, keeping one of his hands out of his pockets at all times. He switched so that the cold was not so biting as he strode calmly down Dorchester Avenue, following a young man in his early 20s with a navy blue backpack slung over his shoulders. The voice in Blair's head started again.

"Blair, this is control. How are we looking?"

"I'm on the mark. He's still wandering up Dot Ave."

"Stay on him. Wait for our say so."

"You got it. How's our B-Team looking?" The thing had a weird hum to it and it was dancing around in his head. Just the hum and no answer. "I say again, sit rep on Bravo?" Blair paused for a moment. "This is Blair, copy? Can you hear me?"

"Blair, move in! I repeat, kill or capture. Retrieve the package."

"What? Control, come in!"

The young man with the backpack across the street was making a run for it before Blair could get a response. He flicked his half-smoked cigarette into the street and sprinted for the mark. A truck halted in front of him and Blair used his hands to bounce off from the fender. Blair was barreling down the sidewalk, dodging an overturned set of trash cans.

As the mark came up onto an intersection, an old white van screeched up, spinning sideways and screaming to a halt. The mark chucked his backpack directly at the van as two plainclothes ProServ officers dove out onto the street. Blair saw a bright flash before falling backwards several feet and the loudest boom he had ever heard in his life.

He could still feel the shockwave as he looked up and saw the van was flaming wreckage. Blair scrambled up, holding his hand to his earpiece.

"Bravo is down! I can't see the mark! He detonated the package!"

Blair stumbled before falling on his knee. The pain shot up his leg. He saw the mark through black billowing smoke. Blair was darting for him at his fastest clip. There was no pain in his knee anymore. The adrenaline was pumping. He reported back in hurried breaths.

"Control, this is Blair! Explosion on Dot and Green! ProServ officers down! I think the mark's going for the T!"

"Stay on him! Don't lose your visual."

The mark ducked around a corner and started up Columbia Road as Blair tried to keep up. Blair didn't feel his legs moving. The mark shoved an older man down as he sprinted across the highway connector and under the bridge, cars honking. Blair began to close in as the mark climbed the guard fence of JFK/UMass Station, climbing on top of the structure. Blair scrambled up the fence as the mark looked around. He drew his pistol and pointed it at the young man as soon as he was on top of the structure.

"Stop where you are! Get those hands up!"

The young man started to raise his hands and slowly turned around to face Blair. They weren't more than a few feet away from one another.

"What are you, BPD?"

"ProServ! Get on the ground!"

The young man laughed. "Then I took down some of your merc

friends, right? How many were in the van? Three? Four?"

"Shut your mouth!"

"You think you people are going to win? You can't win. How much you make a year?" The mark started moving closer to the edge of the structure, eyeing the train tracks below.

"I count to three and you're a dead man…"

"ProServ grunts get paid for their work. I don't."

"One."

"You have no idea what you're up against."

"Two." The grinding of the train intensified as it pulled into the station.

"Send my best to the suits that got your boys killed."

The mark simply fell backwards onto the tracks just before the train roared into the station. Blair ran to the edge and looked over, only to find the train slowing down and stopping on top of the spot where the young man had fallen. Screams came up from below and Blair could taste liquid rust on his lips. He looked at the front of his coat and put his hand to his face. His nose was bleeding profusely and he was covered in his own blood. The van, he thought. How many were still alive?

*   *   *

First responders doused the smoldering wreckage in the Dot Ave intersection with extinguishers and fire hoses. Windows were blown in, small flames still cackling around the initial blast as the charred remains of surveillance agents were wrapped in body bags. Blair presented his badge and was let into the blast zone as ProServ monitored city cops setting up a perimeter. He held his forearm against his nose to stop the bleeding and saw Eckart talking with officials already on the scene. Eckart pulled away when he saw Blair walking up.

"What the hell happened here?" Eckart screamed at Blair.

He was always right and you were always a fuckup, Blair thought. He changed his tune as he saw that Blair was a bleeding mess. "Jesus Christ. Medic! Over here!"

Blair waved off the paramedic. "I'll live. Just get me something I can use to clean myself up." Blair turned to Eckart. "How did you get here so fast?"

"I was in the neighborhood. What happened to you?"

"I wasn't too far away when the bomb went off. He bought it at JFK. Dove in front of a moving train before I could get to him. Transit cops are scraping body parts off the rails now."

"How long has this operation been going on for? A week?"

"A little less than that."

"So, what's the final tally on this? One dead terrorist, an explosion in a busy street, and nearly your entire backup team wiped out?"

Blair pounded his fist on the nearest metal mailbox. "We weren't expecting this! He was supposed to be dropping a bomb making kit, it wasn't supposed to be live."

"Your informer fed you a line, then?"

"Everything we collected up to this point suggested a dead drop of raw materials. Only one thing in my mind stands out."

"What is that?"

"Control went dead just before the mark noticed me." The medic came back up with a damp hand towel and Blair started wiping his face down. "What do you make of that?"

"Counterintelligence operation; we know the PRF are technically proficient. He might have had a jack into our frequency. Looks like as soon as the mark figured out he was being tailed, he waited for an opportunity to make us hurt worse than him. He'd rather kill himself than be taken alive. This isn't farm league anymore, Blair. We're dealing with a whole new breed and you're not used to this yet."

Blair wiped the rest of the blood off of his face before he started on his jacket. "Yeah, well I'm a fast learner. I chased him down on foot, didn't I?"

"After the damage was already done."

"Better here with minimal casualties than on a train full of passengers that would have derailed! We lost men today, I can't whitewash that. But we kept this from reaching the intended target and that's a victory in and of itself."

"And now we have four less officers because of your carelessness."

"My carelessness? Take a look at my face, goddamnit! Where were you? Off shining a seat with your ass? I lost men today! My fucking team, not yours! Go fuck yourself."

"Upset is a good start. Let's go find your informant." Eckart grabbed Blair by the back of his shirt and forced him to walk along with him. Eckart released his grip after a few steps and turned back to Blair. "Are you sure you're all right? You could be hemorrhaging right now and not even know it."

"Well if I drop dead then we'll know I should have gone to the hospital."

Blair climbed into Eckart's unmarked sedan parked close to the yellow tape being strung up around the blast area. "Give him a call. Tell him to meet us at one of your usual places." Eckart rolled Blair's side window down halfway as the car sped off. The air was frigid and biting. "You really went all out with that disguise. I could smell you coming from down the street."

"No need to question my resolve, then." Blair patted his coat for his phone and pulled it out from one of the pockets, scrolling furiously until he reached his informant's number. "Hey, it's you know who. We need to meet right now. I don't care what you're up to, you get yourself in gear and meet me at the car park – yeah, that one – half hour. Half hour, goddammit, or consider yourself burned!" The phone beeped off.

"Where are we going?"

"Garage on Necco Street in Southie. It's not far."

Blair slipped the phone back into his pocket. He pulled a smoke from the pack and fished for his cheap plastic lighter.

"You don't mind, do you?"

"Where's your Zippo?"

"Oh, I ran out of lighter fluid."

Eckart eyed him. "By all means."

"I know you don't like it in the car, but I did just get blown up. I feel like I've earned one." Blair knew he sounded callous. Four of his fellow officers were just killed and it was barely registering. Until now. Don't crack up, Blair thought. Use it and twist this contact into a pretzel. If there was ever a time to turn up the heat on an informant, it was now. Blair took a long drag, his nerves starting to mellow. "All four, huh?"

"I got to the scene not long before you came back from JFK. I don't think there was any suffering and no one else seemed to be hurt badly. For something that seemed like your standard public bombing it was very surgical."

"Maybe I am in over my head. I only cooked this up because of this slippery prick. He tipped us off about some kind of dead drop he heard about second hand. He gave me a name and an apartment address in Dorchester, so I let our undercovers in on it. I wasn't qualified for this."

"We're not all rock stars from birth. You have high expectations for yourself."

The smoke from Blair's cigarette billowed out of the window as the cold air stabbed at Blair's face and hands. "That could be," he said as he exhaled.

* * *

Eckart wound his way up the ramps of the Necco Street Garage, each turn echoing awful shrieks like a high-speed chase. "So, what's your contact's story?"

"Everett PD picked his little brother up on some drug charges," said Blair. "Started singing about as soon as he could. We used the kid as leverage to get at the older brother. Then we flipped him and put him back on the street. This is the first time anything he's fed us went straight to hell."

The car emerged on the top of the garage. Skyscrapers and cranes were not far off in the distance, stretching the length of the Back Bay, into the Innovation District and Cambridge beyond that. Eckart and Blair could make out a lone figure standing at the far side of the garage roof.

Eckart stopped a few yards shy of the young man. He was pacing back and forth, holding the back of his head with both hands with a look of pain on his face. "What's this kid's name?"

"Lucas, but he goes by his last name. Fenster."

Blair slammed the car door behind him, balling his fist. Fenster took a step back and put his hands up. He didn't speak. Blair socked him hard in the gut before Eckart had even shut the car door. Fenster keeled over, falling to his knees. Blair grabbed him by the hair.

"Did you lie to me, you sack of shit? Did you?"

Fenster wheezed through his bared teeth. "Wh- what?"

"You said somebody was making a dead drop. I nearly got fried on Dot Ave today!"

"What?"

"Say what again and I'm gonna skull fuck you!"

Eckart grabbed Blair by the shoulder. "Come on, Blair. Come on. Let me talk to him." Eckart took a knee next to Fenster. "Stand back up." Eckart grabbed the young man by his arm and helped him to his feet. "Stand up straight. Start breathing deep, you'll be fine."

Fenster took a few pained breathes and then looked at Eckart's face. The fear gripped him as he looked him in the eyes. He already knew the answer to the only thing he could muster. "Who are you?"

"Consider me the good cop. The person you gave up to Blair had the drop on us. It was a set up. Four Servicemen are dead because of the information you provided. You've got some explaining to do."

"Oh my God."

"God's not going to save you. Maybe we can. Tell me what you know."

Blair paced, staring Fenster down.

"It was a drop-off bag. That's all I heard. It was materials for a big hit they were planning. I swear to you that's all I heard, and I told you all as soon as I heard."

Eckart took two steps up to Fenster's face, staring into his eyes. He didn't blink as Fenster fidgeted nervously. Eckart took three sniffs around Fenster's neck. They were inches away from each other for what felt like far too long. Eckart turned to Blair. "He's not lying."

"How the hell do you know that?"

"I'm telling you." He turned back to Fenster and put his hand on his shoulder. "The Front just used you, Fenster. They think you're an informant, so they gave you garbage to feed to us and you were too weak to realize it."

"No."

"Right now, Corporal Blair and I are your best friends in this world. The PRF will probably kill you the next time they see you. But you shouldn't worry about that at the moment because what you've done is more than enough for me to declare you an unfit."

"But I didn't do anything! I told you the truth, you said so!"

"The truth isn't enough. Men died today because of how weak you are." Eckart grabbed Fenster by his neck and kicked him to his knees. He started screaming as he shoved him onto his face. "You're going to Chelsea, young man."

"Wait! Wait! I can give you someone…someone important!"

"Who can you give me?"

"Harold...Harold Maguire!"

Eckart stopped and pulled Fenster back up so that he was on his knees. Blair moved closer to the pair. Eckart stared at Fenster as the young man fought back sobbing. There was dirt on Fenster's clothing and some blood was trickling out of his mouth. Eckart put his hand on the back of Fenster's head and brought him in close. He took his hand off of the back of his head and used his thumb to wipe a tear from the boy's cheek. "Tell me about him."

CHAPTER XV

"Do you believe that shit?" Blair was sitting back in the passenger seat of Eckart's sedan. They watched Lucas Fenster wander off, a jittering wreck.

"He made very serious accusations, but I think there may be something there. We don't get to take a man like Harold Maguire in for questioning. We don't get to lean on him, and we don't even make a hint of what it is he's doing – even if we're being targeted."

"You actually believe that kid? After today?"

"How else would he know about the Vice Chancellor?"

"If Maguire were a potential lead, why did he wait until now to tell us? I think he's feeding us a line and he's got exactly jack shit. He's fishing…"

"We need to check him out. The kid might have been trying to insulate him up to this point. I want to pull Harold Maguire's Genisys file and get everything we can on him. It just needs to be quiet. Leave it to me." Eckart rolled the passenger side window down. "I'm bringing you back to the barracks. You smell like an unfit."

*   *   *

Harold Maguire was sitting in a military Humvee as it rolled through the streets of Chelsea, one vehicle in a convoy of many ProServ officers in full tactical gear. A staffer sat next to him, the agony apparent on his face. Harold adjusted his tie. He had never worn a dress shirt in his life that had fit him properly – and the bulletproof vest wasn't helping. Outside his window, he saw a slew of ragged human beings, all fighting over something he couldn't figure out. There had to have been a dozen, all beating on each other.

"How much longer until we get to the Chelsea Council?" said Harold.

"We're almost there," said his aide, a short, wiry man.

"Thanks, Brian."

"Of course, Vice Chancellor."

"Are you alright, Brian?" Harold tilted his head slightly as he furrowed his brow at the aide.

"Yeah…yes, sir. I'm OK. We who are about to die salute you, right?"

"That's the Romans, isn't it?"

"Yeah, they would stage fake naval battles for the pleasure of an audience."

"Is that what you think this is?"

"Faking it? No. I think this is for real. That's why I'm terrified."

"We've got an army with us, kiddo. They've tripled flyovers for the last week, they've been up and down and all around where we're going. I'm sure we'll be fine."

Brian still looked pained.

"You're a real history buff, huh?"

"It's valuable to know, so we don't repeat the same mistakes and all."

Harold chuckled. "Right…tell me what's on the docket."

"We'll be meeting with Councilor Sonedis Cuaron. He goes by Sonny – he's been pretty effective at distributing foodstuffs and teaching subsistence farming. Rootless, since the soil is polluted." Brian looked out the window for the hundredth time as the Humvee convoy tore up near-dirt roads and passed burned-out buildings, street fires, and garbage-lined sidewalks packed with people all generally wandering or standing about.

"Is there anything else you can think of?

"I gave you my report, sir?"

"Yes, I read it. It was well done. You're a sharp kid, Mr. Henry. I'm glad you're on the team."

"Thank you, sir."

"Can you please call me Harold?"

"Harold. Thank you." Brian Henry leaned out of his seat and tapped the shoulder of the ProServ sentry sitting in the passenger seat of the Humvee. The two exchanged some talk before Brian settled himself back in the rear seat of the Humvee next to Harold and put his seatbelt back on.

"We're very close."

"Thank you, Brian."

"So – our first meeting is with Councilor Cuaron, after that, we visit some of his constituents who are into urban agriculture, and then after that we're off to some of the trouble-spot housing…"

"I think we're going to have to end up bolstering the food programs for sure, and if there's anything we can do with the utilities we should do it. The distribution is completely screwed up – we're underselling calorie counts per head and I don't think we have accurate totals for how many people are even in here. My first impressions, at least."

One of the ProServ sentries sitting in the front seat turned to look at Harold. As he did, the driver screeched to a halt. Harold pushed his door open and stepped out of the military vehicle before the ProServ sentries could scramble to open the door for him. A dark-skinned man with jet black hair and a thick overcoat patched with grime approached the Humvee to greet Harold, extending his hand. He was flanked by his own entourage.

"Vice Chancellor – I am very happy to see you here!" The

Councilor yelled the words.

A helicopter hovered low above their heads, and Harold reached out to the man and shook his hand as commandos surrounded the two.

"Thank you very much – I assume you're Councilor Cuaron?"

"Call me Sonny! Everyone here does." The Councilor moved him into the busy streets of Chelsea. A slew of ProServ commandos began shoving people and overturning shopping carts and moving makeshift stands, creating a six or seven foot gap between all the people huddling on the street and Harold Maguire and Councilor Cuaron.

People were at a distance but stood shoulder-to-shoulder. Harold began looking them in the eye – most wouldn't return his gaze. The pain was etched in every gaunt shadow and furrowed brow and watery eye. Some were skeletal. Sonny led the party across the packed street and waited patiently for everyone to catch up. There was an overwhelming smell of rot and death hanging in the air. Harold half-tripped over the sidewalk crossing, and in his clumsiness he noticed several bodies that lay in a gutter at the other end of the streetscape. He stared at it, and after a few moments Councilor Cuaron approached him. He yelled over the packed crowd in the streets.

"To be blunt, we're running out of places to put the dead. It's causing disease to spread since the typhoid outbreak a month ago. We don't have the protective gear necessary to handle the bodies…"

"Listen, Sonny – can we take this to a place where we can talk quietly? I want you to be candid with me."

"I'm not entirely sure you do, Vice Chancellor." Cuaron gave Harold a hard look.

Harold grabbed Cuaron by his arm. "Try me."

Suddenly the ProServ sentries were converging on someone in the crowd and shots were being fired. Panic gripped Harold, who was immediately being flanked by other sentries and rushed out of the place. Sonny fell down as Harold lost his grip on the man's arm. He pushed a

ProServ sentry off of him and shoved Sonny into the Humvee with Brian. The helicopter flew lower, firing shots in the air above the heads of unfits. Harold slammed the door shut behind himself.

"Drive!"

The Humvee peeled out in reverse as the helicopter tailed the vehicle. Sonny began muttering to himself in Spanish. Harold took his pocket square out and balled it up, pressing it hard on the gunshot wound in Sonny's stomach. The Humvee slammed on the brakes and started barreling in another direction altogether. The driver said something about getting to an extraction zone. Harold looked out of the back window. The crowd of unfits who had come to see what this outsider could do for them had retreated into the distance.

* * *

"We have a serious concern to address," said Eckart as he gripped the railing of the Mass Ave Bridge. "You know a Harold Maguire?"

Cantwell stood with his hands in his pockets, dignified as always. "I know of him. Just became a Party member, he's managing operations with Joe Grant. They're lifelong friends, which is how he got that job. I plan on meeting with him soon. From what I've heard he's had a harrowing day…"

"His daughter was killed at the Dissenter's March. We got information so I checked it out – daughter Aiden has a cover story and a redacted Genisys file. His wife Janet Maguire worked for Grant when he was in Congress. She was at Orient Heights when the bomb went off."

"That is a lot of bad luck for one nobody."

"He's not a nobody anymore. He's a high-level executive and a Party member now. We have to do something about him."

"You propose what, exactly?"

"He needs to be put down, and we need to follow the trail to everyone else involved. If there is even a one percent chance that what I've heard of him is true, then we need to act now."

Cantwell started laughing. "Absolutely not."

"Why?"

"After your ridiculous stunts? Your success rate has become somewhat troubling."

"I can handle Blair…I just need another chance."

"I'm not just talking about Blair. I just got off the phone on the way here with my contacts in the Truth – they say they're sitting on a story about the attempted assassination of Harold Maguire in Chelsea until we figure out exactly what to do with it. You insult my intelligence acting like what happened today wasn't you're doing."

"I don't know what you're talking about…"

"You keep distracting yourself with these people and you start putting our plans in jeopardy."

Eckart was all gritted teeth and menace. "Harold Maguire puts our plans in jeopardy! Along with David Blair digging into what's actually going on."

"I won't have you fuck this up any more than you already have!" Cantwell sneered at Eckart, staring him down. "The Orchestra will be initiated when the Leader wants it. When all the conditions are met. It is out of your hands. Or have you changed your mind as to how these things should work?"

"No. I haven't."

"Good."

"We're talking about a matter of months anyway, maybe a year. What's the difference whether they die now or during the Orchestra?"

"This is the end of this conversation. I will meet with Harold and determine whether or not he's a threat – I don't need you engaging in extracurricular activities. You've probably increased his clout after a fucking shooting attempt inside the Facility. As for Stephen's little brother?

Give him a wide birth and steer clear." Cantwell turned to face out over the Charles. He started walking and Eckart followed him. "You forget how much we've already accomplished. We've come too far to ruin everything now. They'll be powerless anyway when all the stars align."

"What does the Leader think of all this?"

"He thinks it's quite amusing. Watching all these characters scurry around without a shred of an idea as to what is going to come."

"I just want to ensure that it does come. That's all."

"When the strikes are authorized – when the ghettos are cleared – all of this will cease to be an issue. The Leader will be secure and there will be no more fighting him." Cantwell stopped and inched closer to Eckart's face, staring him down. "So until that time, you cross no names off on that hit list of yours without my express permission. Keep in mind you aren't the only person who acts unofficially on my behalf. Am I clear?"

"Yes."

"Outstanding. Don't contact me directly again unless it is absolutely necessary. I have a phone call to make." Eckart watched with impotence as Cantwell made to leave. He turned his back slightly. "Just be patient, Frederick. It won't be much longer now." He raised his right hand, covered in a skintight black leather glove. "I promise."

*   *   *

Harold Maguire sat hunched over in his leather desk chair, his hands covering his face. All around him were administrators for the Chelsea Internment Facility, including Ed McGonagall. Harold looked around and straightened himself in his chair. He stood up and scanned the room, putting his hands on his waist.

"Tyler," said Harold, "do we have an idea as to when we'll know how Sonny is doing?"

"Sure, I'll try my contact again at the hospital." He pulled out his phone and began texting furiously.

"Vice Chancellor," said another, "we should really start thinking about getting some Truth cameras in here."

"I'm not doing that right now," said Harold. "We're not capitalizing on this. This is a God damn disaster. I don't know if we'll get the opportunity to ever try to go back inside again."

"Sir," said Tyler, "Sonedis is in surgery now. It seemed like they stopped the bleeding. You might have saved his life."

"Well, at least we can all be thankful for that. Thank you, Tyler. Stay in contact with the folks at MGH, will you?"

"Sure thing, sir."

"Really?" said Ed McGonagall. "We can all be thankful for that? I hate to bring you all back to reality, but I have to remind you that you pulled an unfit out of the Facility in order to take them to one of the best hospitals in the country after he tried to have you killed. That's not something to be thankful for, it makes you look weak."

"That man took a bullet for me," said Harold. "I wasn't leaving him inside to die after that."

"He should have considered that before being declared an unfit!"

"Fuck you, Ed!" Stunned silence filled the room. "He saved my life."

"You should have never been in there in the first place," said Ed. "This was ridiculous from the get-go. You want to get nominated for sainthood or what?"

"You can leave now."

"I was asked to sit in by Joe Grant."

"Well you can tell him I told you to get the fuck out."

"I'm not going anywhere."

"Listen to me you entitled shit – you don't walk out of here right now I remove you. Is that something you want?"

"I'd love to see it."

The office door creaked open, and Joe Grant stuck his head in before barreling forward. He nudged Ed out of the way and put both his hands on Harold's shoulders. "Christ, Harold," he said. "I thought you might have been done for."

"I was lucky," said Harold. "Sonny took a bullet for me. We don't know who's responsible. Patrols are on a sweep and the whole area has been put on high alert."

Joe released Harold from his grip. "I heard Sonny is at MGH now."

Harold swallowed hard. "I made a judgement call and I brought him with us to the extraction zone. Last thing I remember was him pushing me out of the way and him taking a bullet." Harold glanced at Ed. "ProServ has his room guarded, they'll be bringing him back in after he recuperates."

"We might get some grief for it, but I don't think anyone is going to fault you. I'll work with our folks at the Truth and we'll come up with a good narrative. You're a hero, man. Even if the public will never get to know that."

Ed's face dropped. "Chancellor?"

"Yes, Ed?"

"I think it might be better if we suppress this. I don't know if the Leader would appreciate this, considering very few other administrative staff for internment facilities have been doing this kind of...outreach."

"That will be our decision to make," Joe said. "If I want your input on it, I'll let you know."

Ed licked his lips. "Very good, Chancellor."

"Harold, why don't you head home? You can take the rest of the week, just relax a bit. Maybe we've been pushing this too hard..."

"I may take the rest of the day or two, but I'd like to stay on. If they're not going to stop, we shouldn't either."

Joe put his hands on his hips. "I understand." He turned to the rest of the crowd. "Why don't we wrap this, guys? It's been a long day, I'm sure, for all of you. Thanks all."

The room cleared out. McGonagall eyed Harold as he left his office.

"Bye Edward," said Harold.

Joe nodded at Harold as he was the last to leave. "Call me when you get back to the house, huh?"

"Will do."

"Thanks, Harold. We'll get in front of this. By the way, how's the new place on Marlborough Street?"

"It's big." Harold fidgeted. "It's good."

"That real estate agent is something else, isn't she?" Joe said with a smile.

"She sure is."

"Glad you're settling in, my friend. I'll talk to you soon."

The door shut and Harold was left by himself in the expanse of his large office, stately and dignified. Like a lord or land baron of old, Harold thought. A land baron of sorts still. Harold moved for his desk and pulled from the bottom drawer a small flask-sized bottle of Irish whiskey. He took a long swig, letting out a deep breath. He jumped at the sound of his desk phone ringing. A shiver left his body before he picked up. His assistant told him Richard Cantwell was on the line. He put the bottle down and cracked his knuckles, inhaling deeply before the call went through.

"Harold Maguire speaking."

"Harold, it's Richard. How are you doing?"

"Mr. Cantwell. Good, fine. I'm just fine."

"I heard about what happened; are you sure you're alright?"

"It was scary, for sure, but I'm OK. I promise you, Mr. Cantwell."

"Well that is certainly a relief, Harold. We're all happy to know it."

"Thank you, sir."

"You know, I feel a bit behind having not appropriately

spoken with you before your visit to the Facility. Why didn't we see you the other night?"

"Well, I, uh, had an impromptu meeting."

"I saw, Harold…I saw. Lauren was always quite the number, a real crackerjack. Top notch girl. Did you enjoy her company?" Cantwell had a laugh.

"Yes, I did. I mean, she's a nice person."

"My apologies. I don't mean to pry. Anyway, I wanted to know if you're free for dinner this week. After today, I think you've earned a good meal."

"Dinner? I don't know…"

"I really must insist. I feel that we have a lot to discuss. You know, usually people are banging down the door to try to get me one on one. You retreat. Why is that so?"

"I don't think it's a matter of retreating, it's just a crazy time for me now. But I suppose we should make time."

"Excellent. Joe should have cleared your schedule. I'll have our people arrange something before the end of the week."

"Ok. Sounds good, Richard."

"I look forward to it."

Harold's mind went in a thousand different directions as soon as he hung up the phone. He picked up the whiskey again.

*   *   *

Blair picked up the mail laying on the entryway floor of his apartment building. Before climbing the stairs, he thumbed through the junk until he came across a letter inscribed with the ProServ insignia labeled RELATIONS OF S. BLAIR. He let the rest of the mail fall from his hands as he tore the envelope open. He unfurled the letter and began reading at a clipped pace. The words were all a jumble in his mind, but it was a letter he feared getting since his brother left for his stint in Iran. Stephen was dead.

The letter went on to offer the deepest of condolences. Blair put the letter down on a small, flimsy hutch that sat next to his front door in his small entryway. He held the hutch for some time before lifting it up and throwing it into his staircase. The wood fragmented across the stairs and his entryway, and he went for some of the pieces and started slamming them into the stairs. Blair kicked the banister until it came loose and tore it off of the stairs eventually. He started prying individual posts from the banister and used them to smash the walls until several holes grew large and exposed the lath and insulation behind the aged plaster. He yelled at the top of his lungs until he finally put his fist through the wall a few times.

Blair pulled his fist out slowly, his hand covered in splintered wood and dust. His fist and forearm were slightly bloodied, so he picked up some of the mail and used it to cover the cuts and wipe off his hand. He dropped the bloody mail, kept the ProServ letter, and left his apartment about as soon as he had arrived.

*　*　*

Harold and Lauren walked down a meandering path in Boston Common. The park was mostly empty due to the cold snap. Each had their hands buried in their heavy coat pockets. Harold popped up his overcoat lapel to deflect a sudden gust of wind and, looking up, noticed heavy clouds blocking out the stars of the night sky. Harold made his face inscrutable as he waited for the surveillance drone to make a pass before he spoke.

"Thanks for meeting me on such short notice."

"Of course, Harold. How are you feeling?"

"Like God is a child and he's fond of magnifying glasses."

"You know from what I'm hearing, Sonny Cuaron is going to live. That has huge ramifications. Regardless of what we decide to report, it's going to get around in there that you saved his life. There's no doubt in my mind that Cantwell knows."

"Good. At least I can annoy them before they have me dragged off to be shot."

Lauren took a long step over a small pile of snow. "I want you to take my hand in just a few seconds."

"Alright."

Harold held out his hand for Lauren, who reached over and pressed a small object firmly into his palm. She gripped and interlocked fingers with Harold.

"You are going to bring this to your dinner with Cantwell and put some of it in his drink. He'll have massive respiratory failure in six to eight hours. We tried to get something that could hopefully not register in an autopsy."

Harold stood up straighter. "Jesus."

"This is everything you wanted, Harold."

"How do I apply it? How can I guarantee anyone won't see me?"

"However you like, and there's no guarantee."

"You want me to go on a suicide mission."

"You wanted to go on one, and now you're backing out. I can let them know you're not going to do it. I'm sure that'll go well for you." Lauren gripped Harold's hand harder and stopped walking. She inched closer to Harold. "I shouldn't have said that to you." Lauren was whispering the words, close to Harold's face. "I know how hard this has to be for you."

Harold let go of Lauren's hand and put the small vial in his coat pocket. "I don't even know if this matters anymore. I mean, what happens after he dies? Someone takes his place and it all keeps going?"

"It's part of a strike at the Leader's top cadre – Leader included.

It's going to completely destabilize the regime. When they're all gone, we will be in a position to regain the controls. You're going to have to do this alone – but know that there are people just like you all over the country doing the same thing, and they'll feel just as alone. You just have to know that you won't be when you do it. We'll take this country back, Harold."

"Let me show you something." Harold broke his eye contact with Lauren and looked ahead. They continued towards the Public Garden. "You know, I was with Aiden more than my wife was. My daughter, Aiden I mean. Janet was always working, and I could never really find anything that made me happy. Don't get me wrong, I'm not complaining. Owning a couple buildings is a pretty easy gig. It gave me a lot of free time and before my daughter was born, I was political. After she was born, I was happy to just be with her and put all the rest aside. When I was younger, though, I loved it. Activism. When I was my daughter's age it started taking a turn. All of a sudden, the next big attack became the only thing that people cared about. Then the real scary people in power started treating fear like currency. Dealing in it. Strange…when she was young, I thought it was starting to shift back and all of a sudden, I had hope again. I thought maybe we could turn the page or at least start to make the pendulum swing back in a better direction. But that ended badly and then Janet was at Orient Heights."

Harold rubbed his wet eyes. The pair came upon a young tree, a few steps from the Boston Garden Suspension Bridge, and stood in observation. Harold's voice shook slightly as he read the plaque near the tree out loud.

"*Dedicated to Janet Olmstead Maguire. An unbroken spirit, and always in our hearts.*"

"From everything I've heard about her, she was an incredible person."

"Joe Grant organized this. My wife told me a long time ago that she wished she could be buried in one of those pods that feeds a tree. We would have done it if we could."

"That's original."

"I remember this day. Me and my daughter, the irrepressible teen. We were sitting right next to Congressman Joseph Grant. He invited Aiden and I up to speak with some preapproved remarks. He knew my daughter was a wreck and she'd start crying, and then I broke just watching my daughter's world come apart. Then Joe came up from behind us and hugged us both. We were on the cover of the Globe and the Herald. He got up to that podium and started his usual oil-slick bullshit, and then I knew. Joe Grant didn't do this because I was his friend or because he cared about Janet. Joe did this because it was good for Joe. Even the person I thought of as a dear friend wasn't above riding my wife's corpse to a bigger and better national profile."

Lauren looked at the plaque and then the tree. "I'm so sorry, Harold. I really am." She patted Harold's back slightly, on his shoulder. "A lot of these pols, they're just users. And liars. Even the better ones."

"All along there was something in me that I couldn't explain. I knew – deep down I knew – something was going to go wrong. There was always something ominous that I could never place; always something that just didn't feel right...and I couldn't rectify it. My whole life feels like one big hex. Like I didn't deserve good things, and then even when I had them I could barely compute how to appreciate it all. Maybe there were a few years when it was good, but then things just kept spiraling out of control and the less I spoke out it seemed like the more Aiden did. She was picking up the slack." Harold laughed as he spoke the words.

Lauren smiled out of the corner of her mouth. "She sounds brave."

"She was." Harold looked down as their steps took them back towards the Commons. "I'm afraid all the time. I feel like my door will be busted in at any moment. Like they'll find me and there's nothing I can do to stop it. Then I realize I'm totally forgetting what I'm doing here."

"Harold, that's not something to be ashamed of. We're all afraid."

"Then I really start to think, and I'm more afraid that I didn't love them enough."

"What do you mean?"

"My wife. My daughter. I should want to crawl into a hole with them."

"There's nothing wrong with wanting to keep going. Even if you feel like you've lost everything. You're going to live to see the ones who did this pay, and you'll have a part in it."

"I'm afraid I didn't love them enough. Not so much my daughter, but Janet. We had problems. She was always invested in work more than in us. At least I thought."

"You can't knock her for wanting to get ahead."

"I'm concerned there was something going on between her and Joe."

"Well, that's a little different, I suppose…"

"And because of that I was able to justify moving on. Sort of. And it never hurt me as much as it hurt our daughter."

Lauren stopped, and Harold turned around and met her glare. "Do you still feel like you can go through with all this?"

"The rest of my life could be good. I'd have it easy from now on if I just followed the program. I've still got time. But then it wouldn't mean anything. I'd have had an opportunity just like I had dreamed of my whole life, and when it mattered the most, I would have done nothing. My daughter really was the genuine article. She figured something out it took me this long to get to."

Lauren gave Harold a dry smile. "And what's that?"

"I'd rather be obliterated doing the right thing."

CHAPTER XVI

Frederick Eckart sat in a crowded bar in East Boston. It was a Servicemen's haunt, brimming with young recruits all drinking and smoking. The men all alternately avoided his stare or gawked at him in awe. He raised the vodka to his lips and took a long swig, finishing it in one gulp.

"Go get me another one." Eckart slid the glass to Jansen, sitting across from him.

"Sure thing, Sarge. Fuck those hajjis, anyway. Did you hear they let out that looker Blair screwed a few months back? She's here tonight."

Eckart didn't blink but seemed to take issue holding his head steady. "Yeah. I did. Go get another round."

"Yes, sir." Jansen disappeared into the crowd.

Eckart stood up and walked towards the back of the place. He went through a doorway and moved up a flight of stairs. A door opened and he saw Asiyah, sitting at a small vanity as she put on a pair of shoes.

"How's tricks, sweetheart?" Eckart crossed his arms and leaned in the doorway.

Asiyah stood up. "I was wondering if you would ever come up here to see me."

"I heard you were some kind of doctor where you were from."

"Yes. I was."

"What kind?"

"I was a trauma surgeon."

"You were doing a lot over there before Raikenov pulled you out." He cracked his knuckles and moved closer to Asiyah. "In Chelsea, I mean."

"People needed help. I did what I could."

"That's going around. We're all just trying to help, aren't we?" Eckart slurred his words slightly.

"Maybe we can do this another time." Asiyah backed up slightly placing her hand behind her back.

"A good friend of mine died. In Tehran." Eckart moved closer to her and stared her down. "What kind of name is Asiyah? Huh? Is that Arab? Maybe from Iran?"

Asiyah swung her hand out from behind her back, brandishing a knife. She took a stab at Eckart's gut. He managed to catch her wrist, twisted it, and made her wince in pain. The knife dropped to the floor.

"Look at the bright side," said Eckart. He moved in close to Asiyah's ear. "At least I'm not going to kill you." He gripped her head and smashed it into the bedroom's vanity mirror.

*   *   *

Blair was slumped over drunk, sitting with Clark in some hole in the wall. Clark was coming back to the table with a round of whiskey. He passed a glass of bourbon to Blair as he raised his drink.

"To Stephen!"

"To my brother."

Clark took a small sip as Blair downed his glass.

"I was over there for a year and a half before I got assigned to my new division," said Clark. "I can't believe the rebels got their hands on rockets."

"Yeah."

"Stephen was an ace. I mean it, man. He was skilled - he could have spent his whole life in special ops if he wanted to. He would have made a fine career man."

"What's done is done. I'm wondering where that girl is, you know the one. The darker girl from Joy Division. Asiyah. I need to talk to her."

"She's at that place a few blocks away. Coyle's in Maverick Square. Working there is part of her release program."

"Fuck. What are we still doing here?"

"You wanna check it out? Go for it. Eckart and Jansen are already there. I'm heading back for the night."

"Come on, don't be a pussy."

"I'm telling you, I'm out. Early day tomorrow."

"Whatever. I'm leaving. Thanks for meeting up with me man."

Clark rose to his feet as Blair got up clumsily. He grabbed him and hugged him. "Absolutely. You still got brothers in this world, alright? I mean that."

Blair felt the lump in his throat, so he just nodded and hugged the man back. "Take it easy, I'll see you around."

Blair stumbled as he reached the exit. He swung the door open and unlocked his car. It beeped once and Blair sat down in his sedan before slamming the door shut. He placed his hands on the steering wheel and began to bawl. He shoved his hand into the steering wheel and beeped the car horn without laying off, drawing looks from passersby. Blair eyeballed them and rolled down the driver's side window.

"The fuck are you looking at? Keep walking!"

He got the keys into the ignition on the second try and started the car, peeling out from his parking space on the side of the road as he turned a corner. The barracks were in East Boston, which meant ProServ's hardest partiers were in Eastie as well. Not quite as hard as the ones who dipped in and out of the choice haunts of the Chelsea Ghetto, but enough to be known as a presence. He fumbled for a cigarette as he swerved on the road. He had managed to cut back in the past few days until his brother's death.

Coyle's had an inviting nature to it if you considered yourself a true Serviceman, Blair thought as he pulled up across the street from the place. The green and red and blue neon signs advertising the beer and the liquor, the dingy front windows, the stream of fools flowing in and out of the place looking for cheap drinks and cheaper living. Exactly what those grunts deserved. Most of them had BORN TO LOSE tattooed on their foreheads.

Blair pushed the doors open hard with the cigarette half ash hanging from his mouth and a bad look on his face. He could smell the wickedness in the air, thick with smoke and the aroma of spilled liquor and vomit and then he saw Jansen, groping some poor girl who had a look of put on seduction on her face. He shoved his way through the crowd and stood in front of Jansen as he laughed at something. His face changed when he saw Blair.

"Hey David. What's up man?"

"I'm looking for Asiyah. Where is she?"

"Eckart's with her…you should have got here earlier, bro. She's turned out." Jansen laughed.

"What?" Blair stumbled a bit as he grabbed Jansen by his shirt and pushed him into the bar. The girl moved away from the two. Blair put his cigarette out on Jansen's face.

His shriek filled the room. Blair shoved Jansen sideways as he kicked his legs out from under him. When Jansen hit the floor, Blair grabbed him by the throat and started squeezing. Jansen fumbled stupidly and swung at Blair, hitting him in the face. Blair kept choking him until someone pulled him off. Blair swung around wildly and nearly fell off his feet. Eckart was standing eye to eye with him, stone-faced and intense.

"Come with me," he said. Eckart took out his SubCrimes ID and flashed it at the bartender staring angrily at them. "Let's take a walk, Blair." The two made their way through a crowd into a stairway.

Eckart closed the door behind them and turned back to Blair. "What was that about?"

"Jansen's a fucking idiot!"

"He listens. He does as he's told."

"If I see him again...I'm breaking his head open." Blair slowly backed up to the wall, hunching into it.

"You want to hit somebody? Hit me." Eckart put his own face inches away from Blair and stared him down. "You want to kill somebody..."

"My brother's dead, Eckart." Blair took a long deep breathe. "How the fuck am I supposed to feel?"

"Now you see what they're capable of taking from you."

"Who is they, Eckart? What the fuck are we doing? We chase them around and they chase us and we're all dying."

"We're making the world safe for Americans...for all of Western Civilization. There's a price to be paid. We pay it so others can be free."

"Who's free? People like Asiyah? I heard she was with you."

"She was. She's upstairs. But you know nothing good will come of that." Eckart pointed at Blair, and Blair noticed his knuckles. They were cracked red with blood and had swelled. "You're getting a taste now – just now – of how heinous these people are. They come here and they leech and multiply and the moment you turn your back on them, they'll have gotten the best of you. They've been trying to destroy us for centuries. They ended your brother's life. So, if I were you, I'd let that anger power you forward until we win."

Blair swallowed hard. There were fine fingernail scratches on Eckart's neck.

"Just know I did what I did for your brother. And for you. Because this needs to come to an end. If you get out of line one more time, I'll see you driven out of ProServ. Do you get me?"

Without another word, Eckart turned out of the stairwell and went to the bar. Blair rushed himself up the stairs and started checking rooms. He frantically turned knobs and threw open doors and flicked on lights. When he got to the door at the end of the dimly lit hall, he saw Asiyah. Blair ran to her and dropped to his knees as he propped her up to hold her. The blood soaked his overcoat and his hands. He picked her head up from the floor and she choked and lay bleeding in his arms, her throat looking caved in and her arm lifted limp and mangled. Bones all over were broken and her face was half shattered. Her eyes were swelled shut and the sight of her made Blair shake violently. She could barely mouth for help.

*   *   *

Lucas Fenster paced underneath the raised highway next to a mountain of broken concrete as his eyes got used to the night and the distant faded points of yellowish light. The rush of the cars passing overhead whirred in his ears, suddenly overcome by a gust of hard wind that shook the chain link fences around the underpass. Fenster raised the collar of his winter jacket. He eyed the concrete slabs holding it all up, all rusted and chipping and exposed like it might crumble at any moment. Off in the distance there was nothing but empty street. Then Fenster heard footsteps.

"Hello?"

"Fenster…"

"Eckart?"

"Care to let me know what was so important you had to tell me right now?" Eckart stood a few feet from Fenster with his hands in his coat pockets.

"I tried calling Blair. He wouldn't answer."

"He's tied up tonight. Get to the point."

"They're going to kill Richard Cantwell tonight. They've got a lock on him through Harold Maguire and they're going to try and kill him."

"How did you hear about this?"

"It's supposed to be part of some coordinated strike against the Party. I don't know how many people are going to be targeted, but it's happening now. You promised me that you could protect me if I brought you something. I'll give you everyone I know. I need out. I can't do it anymore!"

"Calm down, Fenster. How many people have you talked to about this outside of your immediate network in the Front?"

"Nobody. I was lucky I found out in time. I think they tried to keep it away from me because they know, they fucking know…"

"They don't know. They don't know anything."

"They fucking do!" Fenster pushed his hair back, starting to pace. "I called Blair and he didn't answer. I knew this was important, so I called right away. I swear. You have to get me out – they know that I'm talking to you. I can feel it, I-I know it!"

Eckart put his hands up and walked slowly toward Fenster. "You did the right thing. You will be protected, I promise you. Believe it or not, you're not the only person inside that cell who's on our side."

"Really?"

Eckart unbuttoned his jacket and put his hands on his hips. "Really. I promise you, I'll get you out." He placed his left hand on Fenster's shoulder. "Right now."

Fenster felt the sharp pain deep in his gut, radiating instantly to the top of his ears and into his toes. It was everywhere all at once, and the pain made him stiffen. He looked into Eckart's eyes and knew. Fenster moved his hand to his stomach and felt the blood flowing freely. Eckart turned the knife clockwise and pulled it out just as quickly as he put it in. Fenster fell to the ground without much fight. The wind picked up again and rattled the chain link fences. His vision went blurry, and the last thing he ever saw was Frederick Eckart standing over him cleaning his combat knife.

CHAPTER XVII

The general hum of the restaurant was a dull roar and it was a good sized space with fairly high ceilings that had art all over. Renaissance Florence looking stuff that made you seem like a fool or an appraiser if you were caught staring at it all too long, Harold thought. The idle rich enjoyed their night out, dining on small portions for stupid prices. Harold was guided through the posh Beacon Hill restaurant to Cantwell's table, where he was already seated and swirling a glass of red wine. Cantwell stood up.

"Harold! It is good to finally see you away from the working world. Have a seat."

Harold shook Cantwell's hand and took a seat across from the man. He draped the table napkin over his lap.

"It's good to see you, Mr. Cantwell."

Cantwell lifted the bottle to Harold's empty glass. "I've already put in an order for myself. This particular wine is an excellent pairing with the duck: I recommend it."

"Thank you. I'll take a look at the menu."

The waiter held his hands interlocked. "I'll be back in a few moments after you have acquainted yourself with the offerings this evening." He made his way through the restaurant to another table.

"So, Harold, we're all very impressed with your fortitude. How are you feeling?"

"A bit wound up, to be blunt. We spent a lot of time working on the strategy and how we planned on reducing violence inside Chelsea – in all the ancillary facilities, for that matter. In one instant, it blew up. We're keen to carry on, though. All of our plans. We have to be prepared to take a few on the chin to really make a difference for the better." He rubbed his pant legs with both hands and cracked his knuckles discreetly, under the table. Harold's fingers were a cascade tapping on his knee.

Cantwell looked at Harold without expression. "Have a drink of that wine. It's a cabernet. I know the family that owns the vineyard."

"Where is that, France? Wine country there?"

Cantwell laughed. "I think not! The French have turned it around, but it will be some time before I opt for their product over Napa. Besides, their climate is not what it once was."

"I suppose so. I forgot about that. Well, Mr. Cantwell, I understand that you've wanted to sit down with me for some time, one on one. I'm sorry we couldn't do this sooner."

"I understand that you have had a friendship with the Chancellor for some time?"

"Yes, yes, I have. My wife Janet worked in his office when he was in Congress." Harold pored over every entrée item on the menu and couldn't remember one of them after he finished.

"Our friend Joe has been very good for this city and this country."

"It was funny. I always got the impression that he half-liked and half-hated being a congressman. His passions made him a good candidate, but I remember his early days and he told me that as soon as he got there he wanted to be doing something else."

"Is that so?"

"Well, I mean when he began it was a different climate. Politically. After things turned…I think it really refocused him. Now I think he has great potential to reinvent himself as a real policy innovator for homeland security. And he'll be doing it from the private sector, which is important."

"I do agree with you, Harold. Joe's a treasured friend and colleague.

But I must admit that I'm curious about your arrival. To my understanding you have had no traditional experience? You have an alternative set of experiences. Largely work with at-risk populations and groups, some of whom have been deemed unfit and are currently interned."

"That's true."

"You could understand how a less educated and aware individual may take that as something to be wary of, yes?"

"I could."

The waiter returned and placed a plate between Harold and Cantwell. "For the table: Ukrainian-style blini served with crème fraiche and sturgeon caviar."

Cantwell grinned. "Have you had caviar before, Harold?"

"Nope."

"You're in for a treat."

The waiter took out a notepad. "Have you decided?"

"Yeah," said Harold hastily. "Um, I think the duck will be fine."

The waiter collected the menus. "Very good, sir. We'll have your meals out to you shortly."

"You were saying, Harold?" Cantwell took a bite of the blini.

"Right. Well, when Joe asked me to come on, he said that he wanted me because of my experience with these groups."

"Harold, I don't want you to feel as though that sort of thing is going to disqualify you. It was a different world. We have all had to do some adjusting to the new reality."

"Good." Harold took a bite of the appetizer. "What is this, like a pancake?"

"Something like that. They're much larger in Russia and the Ukraine. They also traditionally pair better with a dry white wine. But this cab…"

"Not bad." Harold wiped his mouth and put the napkin back on the table. "Will you excuse me?"

"Of course."

Harold walked to the back of the restaurant to the bathroom and locked the door behind himself. Alone, he pulled the vial from his coat and exhaled deeply. He looked at himself in the bathroom mirror, one hand on the sink and another gripping his poison. Harold ran the tap and splashed cold water on his face before he reached for some paper towels to dry himself. His phone pinged and he checked it. The notification was a text message from a private number. CANCEL TONIGHT. MADE ALTERNATE PLANS. ENJOY DINNER! Panic crashed over Harold. He stood stupefied looking into the bathroom vanity mirror. The vial came back out, and Harold dug to the bottom of a waste barrel to put the poison before refilling the basket with damp paper towels. After cleaning up he left the bathroom and rejoined Cantwell. Their duck confit were just arriving.

"This looks good," said Harold.

"I was worried that you might miss the entrée while it was still fresh." Cantwell carefully cut into the meat, dicing it into small slivers which he wouldn't touch until the entire portion was cut up.

Harold took a gulp of wine and started coughing.

"Take care," Cantwell said with a laugh. "Are you alright?"

"I'm fine." Harold cleared his throat. "Wrong pipe."

"Harold, I have found that Leader Wright was quite uneasy for some time with the Arbitrage decision to appoint Joseph Grant as chancellor here. As you know from his days as a representative, he had been more of an activist than the Leader was comfortable with."

"Maybe in the past, but Joe's been a Party member for years now. He's the reason Boston's been so accommodating to business and all the relocating from New York."

"You see, I understand completely. I'm afraid it is the Leader's will." Cantwell took a bite of his sliced thin duck. "And if we are to consider ourselves patriots and good stewards of the Restoration, we follow the Leader's will."

"What are you saying exactly?"

"I am saying that you are in a precarious position. I understand that your family is no longer with you, is that correct?"

"Yes, it is."

"That your wife Janet Maguire was killed in the Orient Heights Bombing?"

"That's true."

"Bad luck, eh Harold? And your daughter as well, and so recently. I understand she was killed in a car accident?"

"Yeah."

"You have my sincerest condolences. What was the date of her death, again?"

"The day after Christmas." Harold's ears darted back as he stared into Cantwell's face.

"It is to my understanding that there are a handful of well-respected, highly valued members of the Party who have lost members of their families on that day. Quite separate from the Dissenter's March."

"What do you want me to tell you, Cantwell?"

"Nothing – nothing at all. You just sit there and listen to me as if my word is gospel because in your case it is. I'm telling you that I know your daughter was there. And before you say anything else, I want you to get it into your head that you belong to me. You will not move amongst the unfits and act as though you are the patron saint of the poor and the starving and the huddled masses and attempt to reform the status quo. From this moment on you do exactly as I tell you to do or your newfound good luck ends and ends badly. If you don't – and I do remind you that in these matters speaking to me is speaking to Leader Wright himself – that bit about your daughter and her dissent crimes will become public knowledge. You will be fired, stripped of your Party membership, and your belongings. You will be deemed unfit for trial and relegated to residence in Chelsea permanently. Or you'll wish you had escaped with such a fate. I do promise you that much. Do I make myself absolutely clear?"

Harold felt into the inside of his coat pocket. He wished he still had his gun. "Yes."

Cantwell smiled. "Excellent. Then let's eat, shall we?"

"That's it?"

Cantwell went back to the caviar. "That's it."

"What do you mean that's it? I'm a radical agitator. I'm a closet socialist. I should be made an unfit."

"No…you may be all those things, Harold. But you won't be an unfit." Cantwell took another bite of the duck and spoke with his mouth full. "There's no need for it. You're not a killer or a revolutionary."

"How do you know?"

"I read your Genisys file."

"My file? What is that?"

"Think of it as your entire existence in the digital world. Your music, your programming choices, your movements, purchasing habits. All of it. Any of it. I even know what you jerk off to. It took me a while to make eye contact with you again." Cantwell laughed loudly and kept drinking. "I'm joking. Kind of."

"What does that have to do with anything?"

"We started coupling these files with some powerful algorithms… quantum computing or something. I don't know all the details. Anyway, we've begun to map every file and ultimately predict and weed out real unfits from the ultimately harmless. It's remarkable. We've done significant heavy lifting up to this point. I mean logistically, do you have any idea what it is to intern what – 35 million people? Round them up? Contain them? We've moved to a near-command economy, it all effectively revolves around doing just that. That's less than 10% of the total population. We've barely scratched the surface. This is the next phase, Harold."

"You're going to unleash some AI to hunt down anyone who doesn't think right? That's what makes you think I won't kill you? That I'm harmless?"

Cantwell put his silverware down. "Do not get me wrong. You've got some measure of bravery, you've got lots of compassion, I get it. But you won't take a life. Even if they've wronged you. Same reason you never cheated on Janet – even when she was cuckolding you with our dear friend Joe."

"You don't know that."

"That's the thing though, Harold. I really do. You stayed in a loveless marriage all for your daughter. Ultimately, something in you has resentment for both of them. I think you've been through enough, and this new life isn't lost on you. You know the alternative and you're not going back. You're still young enough to enjoy life."

"I haven't been getting much joy out of it as of late. You killed them both."

"I'm sorry it came to that, Harold. I really am." Cantwell held his hands over his heart, a vague grin on his face. "None of this is easy. But look around you. You've arrived." He reached for his wine and took a small sip. "If we really wanted to destroy you, we would have done it already."

"You're probably right."

Cantwell smiled more broadly. "That's the genius of all this. My greatest point of pride. We beat you into submission a long time ago and we never laid a hand on you."

"So, you've got nuclear bombings, biological warfare, terrorist attacks, and God knows what else sprinkled in between, and now we're here. I don't need it spelled out for me. I know what's next."

Cantwell crossed his arms. "You do, yes?"

"You're going to be proud architect of the worst genocide in human history."

"Deep down, you know this is what we have to do to keep this country from coming completely undone. It's like cutting out rot from an otherwise good piece of wood. Just tear it out. Then we scrape the harder bits. It's us or them. It's always been us or them. Any good wood gets snagged, it's simply part of the process. We've been doing it for centuries now, Harold. Indians, blacks, immigrants, the Japanese. It's as American as apple pie."

"What's so American? Your fucked-up White American Death Cult? Because that's all I'm really hearing from you. That's all I get out of this." Harold leaned closer to Cantwell. "This country never really belonged to you. However much you want to pretend you're restoring it. It was never yours to take. It's supposed to belong to all of us."

"Not on your life." Cantwell scowled. "This country nearly gave itself over to it, that multiracial communist bullshit you think is so righteous. We've been living with you your entire life. We exercised the discipline to be ignored or laughed at before we took the reins back. We served in the military and we worked in the Pentagon. We became lawyers and doctors and writers and politicians. We became teachers and police officers. And we realized suddenly that there were enough of us to have leverage. At that point, the Leader followed us to power. Do not be fooled, though. It hasn't been easy. Far from it. We have much work to be done yet. And we'll get it done."

"So that's it? White supremacy now and forever, even if it means all you get to inherit are the ashes? The fucking radioactive dust in the wind?"

"The life of this country has to move forward. When we're done, everything you stood for in the times before will be legend. All of this will be forgotten when the new world is built." Cantwell stared down Harold and finished his wine. "I can give you something to put you more at ease, though."

Harold drank much of his wine in one long gulp. "What?"

"I'll make sure the person who killed your daughter Aiden is disposed of. He's become nonessential to the process of building our better world."

"And who would that be?"

"Eckart. Frederick Eckart. He's grown into a significant problem. Erratic. So, if it makes you feel better, I'm willing to give you your pound of flesh as a measure of goodwill. I mean it."

"I don't believe you."

"You don't have to."

The waiter sidled up to the two men and displayed another bottle of the same wine. Cantwell waved him on to pour it. He raised his glass to Harold as the waiter placed the bottle on the table and made a hasty exit.

"Drink with me, Harold. This is cause for celebration. This is a triumph for the regime that can finally benefit us both."

"What do you want to drink to? White power?" Harold's glass stayed on the table.

Cantwell laughed and smiled wide. "Sure." He took another sip. "Why not?"

*   *   *

Harold stood with Cantwell outside the entrance of the restaurant. Cantwell's chauffeur opened the door for him.

"I'll be in touch, Harold."

Harold's town car pulled up behind Cantwell's stretch limousine. Before Cantwell's chauffeur closed the door, Cantwell leaned out.

"By the way, we've got to do something about your title. Outreach?" Cantwell laughed. "Christ!"

Harold's own driver emerged to open the door for him as Cantwell's vehicle drove off.

"Where to?" said the driver as he sat down behind the wheel and started the car.

Harold balled up his fist and put it to his mouth. He looked out the window without enthusiasm. "Home."

"Yes sir."

The car weaved in and out of the tight cobblestone streets, passing the red brick town houses. The traffic was light and Harold stared out onto the passing sidewalks, wordless.

"Bad night, sir?"

Harold scoffed. "Bad life."

"It can't be that bad, Mr. Maguire. You've got me to drive you around. You've got your health. You have to be making a fortune over there, Vice Chancellor."

"I don't know why people feel like whoever dies with the most toys and the fattest bank accounts won at life. You hoard old magazines and newspapers and you're deranged; do it with cash and they put you on the front page."

"The more things change the more they stay the same. We all do what we can. We hope you didn't go through with dosing Cantwell. You received your message?"

"What?"

"I'm a friend at the dark end of the street."

Harold was wordless.

"Did you, Harold?"

"No, I didn't."

"Ok – hold on." The driver touched his console and then his ear slightly. "Hello? I have him. That's right – execute. I hear you, will move accordingly."

"Who are you talking to?" Harold noticed that the car had meandered onto Storrow Drive and that Cantwell's limo wasn't far ahead, only a security detail between them.

"When I give you the word you lay flat on the backseat floor. You understand?"

An unmarked white van shot ahead of Harold's car and reached Cantwell's limousine. The side door slid open.

"Get down, Harold!"

Harold could see muzzle flash and heard the sound of machine guns opening fire on Cantwell's limo and the security detail. He hit the sedan floor hard as the driver hit the gas and kept up close to the limousine ahead. With his face buried into the leather interior, Harold closed his eyes and could hear the sound of more machine gun fire. There was a bump after swerving and then a crash. Harold's driver swerved to avoid hitting the limo and the car came to a stop with Harold heaving forward, nearly hitting the middle console. More machine gun fire erupted and the only thing Harold could make out was muffled screaming.

"Harold, stay in the car."

Harold heard the front door open and his driver step out. He opened his eyes and lifted his head to see out the side window. The security detail vehicle was overturned and blocking half of Storrow Drive and the limousine was riddled with bullet holes and had hit a tree head-on after it swerved onto the Esplanade. Smoke was beginning to billow out of the crumpled front end. Several masked men with machine guns emerged from the van and surrounded the car. One opened the back limousine door by smashing the window. The masked gunman climbed into the interior of the limo and appeared with Cantwell. He was shoved violently into Harold's view, screaming. Harold crawled for the side door and opened it. He fell from the backseat of the vehicle and stood up to yell.

"Stop!"

Harold walked purposefully to the wreckage as one of the gunmen trained his weapon on him. He instinctively raised his hands towards the masked shooters and looked around at all of them. The ski masks they wore all looked familiar. Each set of eyes had stared him down at Trocoa Mill months ago. Cantwell was sitting with his hands raised in surrender, looking around frantic at the gunmen standing around the wreckage of the vehicle. Harold felt a machine gun jab him in the back as he was just a few feet from the man now begging for his life.

"New plan," said Leona. "You're coming with us."

"And Cantwell dies here?"

"That's right." Leona pulled a pistol from the back of her pants waistband. "Now you can put this to better use." She handed Harold's pistol back to him.

Harold took the gun and turned towards Cantwell. As Harold approached him, the gunmen raised Cantwell to his feet. The fire from the overturned wreckage on the Esplanade had kicked up, and a plume of smoke shot up into the sky. The cackling grew to a high roar.

"You said earlier that you were all just waiting for the right time to make your move," said Harold. "That your people were everywhere, all around us. Just waiting for the right moment to strike."

Cantwell's face was contorted in rage. "Fuck you." He looked around at his captors. "Fuck all of you! You're all dead by sunrise!"

Harold took the safety off of his pistol and raised it, gesturing to the people around him. "I guess we were doing the same!"

"Fuck you, you goddamn cuck!"

Harold saw his child on the slab and squeezed the trigger. Cantwell fell backwards hard onto the side of the limo, reaching to his chest to feel the bullet hole in his rib. He looked up stunned.

"Still think I don't have it in me?" yelled Harold.

Cantwell raised his hand and looked down, bracing himself. Harold backed away as the group raised their machine guns and opened fire. The man looked like he was exploding as he was riddled with bullets. When the firing stopped, Cantwell fell down covered in blood and sagging with the awful, contorted posture of a corpse.

"Now we have to take you," said Leona.

"Where?" said Harold.

"We can't tell you now, but we'll cut you loose in a few days. We're staging your kidnapping."

"Wait."

Harold walked over to Cantwell, slumped up against the side of the car. The limo had begun to spurt flames from the front end. He searched his own coat pocket and pulled out a small blue rose and shoved it in Cantwell's lapel buttonhole. His eyes were still wide open. He had a look of absolute horror, his last moments of fear etched on his face forever. The glow of the flames silhouetted Harold and Cantwell's crumpled corpse. Harold turned to face the Front's hit squad.

"Now I'm ready."

CHAPTER XVIII

The room was beige with ceramic subway tile, some having cracked and others missing, and a few still permanently stained an off-red color. Blair watched Lucas Fenster through the two-way mirror. Fenster's face was buried in his arms on the metal table. Blair turned to Clark.

"Thanks for letting me run with this one. You got any suggestions?"

"Apparently, the cops here found his brother with a kilo of heroin and nearly as much fentanyl." Clark crossed his arms. "His brother could not sing fast enough."

"Nothing more important in life than family."

"That's right."

"Does he know that's the reason why he's here?"

"He's got no idea whatsoever. Baby brother hasn't spoken to this one since he fell into the wonderful world of smack."

"Are you thinking about what I am?"

"I don't know..."

"Tell Everett PD that the Fensters are ProServ assets. Including the druggie. They never picked him up. If anyone asks, we just sniffed this one out all our own. We tell this one that if he doesn't collaborate, the junkie eats a bullet."

"Can you handle this?"

"We're gonna find out." Blair entered the off-white room. Lucas Fenster sat up straight.

Blair stared down at Lucas Fenster and the puddle of blood underneath him. Blair was behind the yellow CAUTION tape with a local detective who had escorted him onto the scene. Kneeling down, he stared at the large, precise hole in his gut.

"I've never seen a stab wound look like this in my life," the detective said.

"Do you have any surveillance in the area?" said Blair.

"Traffic cameras, but they're city-owned so they're probably dead."

"Well I'd check anyway. Run into trouble, drop my name, and tell them this is tied to an ongoing ProServ operation. Anything you come up with here goes directly to me. You're investigating this on my behalf, and we have jurisdiction. Go to anyone but me directly I'll see you busted down, detective. You understand?"

"What the hell is going on here?"

Blair stared for some time at Fenster's lifeless face. He looked squarely at the detective and thought back to Eckart stabbing the interrogation room table so the knife stood upright as a taunt to Abd al-Haqq.

"The knife is custom. The wound is something they teach you in Special Forces." The buzzing in Blair's coat pocket made him reach for his phone. "One minute."

Blair took steps away from the scene and answered.

"Clark...what's going on? How's...how's the girl?"

"It's still touch-and-go. But that's not why I'm calling..."

"Remember Lucas Fenster?"

"The informant?"

"He's dead. And I think it's our mutual friend."

"You're in for a long night, kid. It's all hands on deck as of right now."

"What do you mean?"

Clark exhaled loudly through the phone. *"We're under attack."*

* * *

Sergeant Eckart stood staring at Cantwell's dead body. The

sirens could be heard up and down Storrow and the blue and red lights flashed like a distant storm. The police were cordoning off the area as emergency responders put out flames in the car wreckage. The scabs on Eckart's knuckles strained as he made tight fists.

"How could this have happened?" said Crenna.

Eckart turned around to face the Colonel. "The murder, or the fact that the local cops beat us to the scene? By the time I got here the State Police and BPD were directing traffic."

Crenna's aide handed him a tablet after pulling up a video and showed it to Eckart. Cantwell's limo came into sharp focus as it made its way around the Esplanade. Then the video slowly turned to static before the transmission ended.

"Whoever murdered Cantwell had the know-how to disable the surveillance drone we assigned to him," said the Colonel. "The tech boys thought it was limited interference, but it turns out it was a jamming signal."

"You've had him under surveillance?"

"For his protection, of course." Crenna turned to his aide and dismissed him. "Why don't we talk, just the two of us?"

"How long have you been watching Cantwell?"

"Since he left the airport. So, I have to ask...why did you meet with him the day of the Dissenter's March? Then again after Vice Chancellor Maguire's tour of Chelsea? He was having dinner with Maguire tonight and so far, he's unaccounted for."

Eckart swallowed hard and kept his composure. "We've known each other for some time. He wanted a rundown on what had happened at the Facility and he trusts my judgment. There's no relevance to what's happened here."

"Do you think this has anything to do with the Restoration? The Leader's purges?"

"This man was an architect of the Restoration. He orchestrated purges. This is unmitigated disaster."

"We're getting reports of some of the highest-ranking Party members in the country being targeted," said Colonel Crenna. "Bombings, shootings, attacks just like this. It wreaks of the PRF or some other dissenters. My thoughts are Harold Maguire has been abducted and he'll be held for some kind of leverage."

"I think we need to run plates on all these vehicles and cross-reference who was on duty transporting everyone, then-"

"I appreciate the spirit but I'm afraid you won't have point on this, Sergeant. I'll be overseeing this matter personally and we have plenty of Servicemen in the SubCrimes Division who are up to this investigation."

"Colonel, I think that's a mistake."

"You're too close to it. Don't think for a moment I don't know the relationship between the two of you. He was the only reason you weren't crucified by the higher ups at your disciplinary hearing. I recommend you scale back...with everything. Is that understood?"

"Who are you handing this off to?"

"Don't you worry, Sergeant. I'm sure at some point the Leader will have his personal agents on the scene. Although from the sound of things, those numbers are starting to dwindle."

Eckart gritted his teeth. "And what if one of them turns out to be me, Colonel? What would you do then?" The wind whistled and whipped around the two of them.

Crenna stuck his hands in his coat pockets. "Go home, Sergeant."

"You didn't answer my question."

"I'd pray, I think." He patted Eckart on the shoulder. The Colonel walked brusquely through the crime scene and his aide went along with him.

Eckart turned back to face the fallen Party leader and saw the strange ornament on Cantwell's corpse. He knelt down on one knee and leaned in closely to look at it. Glancing around himself, he snatched the blue flower up and tucked it into his pocket. He dusted off his knee as he stood back up and turned to face Ed McGonagall standing behind him.

"Sergeant." McGonagall propped his collar up as the wind whipped off of the Charles River. "We need to talk."

* * *

"How long do you plan on keeping me here?" said Harold. The room was dimly lit, all flimsy folding chairs made of wood and cracked plaster walls with exposed gaff. A lamplight and a radio sat on an old, scratched dresser. It all smelled of dust and mold.

"We need to let the heat die down," Leona said. "After that, we'll have you 'escape.' Right now, you're safer with us than you are at the Facility. They're going to round up the administration and contain them at the fortified command center there."

"That's what they told us if something serious were breaking out. It would have to be something like a containment breach in Chelsea, or…"

"I've heard."

"You're going to break the Wall?"

"We're going to try. The strike nationwide against the Leader's inner circle hasn't been as effective as we hoped. Our operation isn't as secure as we would have liked. Why don't you listen for yourself? The Truth is starting to pick up the attacks." Leona moved to turn the radio knob to the right station.

* * *

"*The following is a special report from the Truth — an Arbitrage Media Partner. Terror on the Esplanade in Boston tonight. Richard Cantwell, co-chair of the National Party Central Committee and top adviser to Leader Wright, was brutally murdered hours ago in an apparent assassination. Five security officials were also shot, four fatally, in this act of insurrection. Cantwell has been the highest-profile victim in a flurry of attacks on Party officials in business and government posts throughout the country. Leader Wright has been summoned to a secure location and is assessing the situation personally. The death toll is as of yet unaccounted for, but some reports have attacks occurring in Washington DC, Philadelphia, Chicago, Los Angeles, and Seattle with casualties exceeding-"*

Eckart turned the car radio off and saw McGonagall on the banks of the Charles River across Soldier's Field. He stepped out of the car and hurried himself across the grass median. Morning light was just starting to break over the skyscrapers and the steel girders rising high above the city. Arbitrage Tower had a glow of blue and orange and it calmed Eckart. He walked towards McGonagall with his hands shoved into his coat pockets.

"I just got word," said McGonagall. "The Orchestra has been initiated. Nationwide – effective immediately."

"The Leader's hand has been forced," said Eckart. "He's got no other options with Cantwell dead. Now there's no turning back. The timetable is out of our hands. We have to move now, or we risk losing everything we've worked for."

"Finally these security gaps have served their purpose? I don't have to keep greasing the wheels for you?"

"We needed the gaps to justify the entire operation."

"I get it. I just want it over with."

"This will be wrapped up before you know it. But there are a few loose ends that need tying." Eckart pulled the blue flower from his pocket. "I need the Colonel off my back for an operation involving Harold Maguire. I know where he's been taken. I can finish him once and for all."

"Consider it done. What about David Blair? You killed his informant. He's got to be suspicious."

"Leave him to me. Raikenov and his people have been activated. They're on it."

"You know, I was beginning to wonder if the Leader had all the resolve we thought. Maybe it doesn't matter. Not as long as he has followers like you."

"Keep it to yourself. By day's end you'll be sitting in Joe Grant's chair."

"Just one thing, Fred."

"What?"

"I grew up in Chelsea – before all of this, obviously. Born and raised." McGonagall moved closer to Eckart and placed his hands on the railing. He gripped it and looked out at the Charles River, churning and glimmering as the sun started to rise. The emerging skyscrapers all half-constructed started reflecting the early morning sun. "You gambled when you let the PRF take out Cantwell, and you happened to win. You and your nationwide cadre of true believers made the Leader panic and now everything you've worked for is here. But do not let your little covert ops get away from you. Do not let a few loose ends destroy everything we stand to gain today. Because I'm not going back to Chelsea." Ed McGonagall stared Eckart in the eyes as he let go of the railing to face him. "Not ever."

CHAPTER XIX

There were intense streaks of light, like lasers. Harold was gripping the side of something, hunched over and terrified. The light was loud and blistering. It rattled him, and suddenly Harold was sprinting as fast as he could, but he was a snail. Then he saw the thousand-yard stare of a dead man, and he was on top of the corpse. The dead man turned to him and locked eyes, and the smile on his face grew wide and deranged. Harold gripped his head and started tearing at the flesh, and he recognized Cantwell's laugh. He tore through the skin and there was only blood and muscle and bone left on the man as he laughed at Harold – he actually laughed at him. He laughed and laughed harder the more Harold stripped him down and destroyed him – and Harold knew that somewhere his daughter Aiden was crying.

Harold sprung up straight on the small mattress. He rubbed his eyes and ran his fingers through his hair. It was greasy, and he moved to finally remove his loosened tie. The item went into his side jacket pocket. He swallowed hard and started looking around after he smelled the mold and the dead air again. Some kind of muck blocked out the windows and the only light in the room was a lamp. Cracks ran through the old, plastered walls and only now Harold was making out the lime green color they had once been. There was an intense funk living in the place that only a complete gutting could get out. A door opened, and a young man with a tattered brown leather jacket and heavy scarf walked through and sat himself on the edge of the dresser. He was holding a machine pistol.

"Sleep well, Harold?" He lowered the scarf and showed his unshaven face.

Harold's head tilted slightly. "Nigel?"

The scarf came off. "You must be hungry."

"Yeah. You have anything to eat?"

Nigel Whitmore pulled a nutrition bar from his coat and tossed it at Harold. He placed his free hand on the gun after he did. Harold caught the bar, tore the wrapper open, and ate half of it in one bite.

"What's going on out there?" said Harold.

"We're preparing for a serious offensive at Chelsea. That's all I can tell you. Frankly, I don't think they'd like it if I shared much more with you."

"Oh," said Harold with a mouth half-full. "Have I not committed enough to the movement yet?"

"It's not that Harold. It's just need-to-know...and you don't right now."

Harold swallowed. "Well then tell me when the hell I'm allowed to get out of here. Give me that much at least."

"I volunteered to do this."

"Why is that?"

Nigel put the machine pistol down on the dresser. "You're gonna be here for a while, Harold."

* * *

Blair was winding through the streets of Cambridge in his unmarked sedan, smoking his umpteenth cigarette when he got the call from Clark.

"Blair?"

"Yeah, I'm here."

"Listen up: it's not being put over the wire yet but I wanted you to know.

Head to Everett. There's an auto body shop on Nichols Street near the old Chelsea city limits. Same make and model van involved in the Cantwell assassination was seen pulling into a repair bay there not twenty minutes ago. Do you know where that is?"

Blair began pulling up his phone's GPS with a half lit cigarette in his mouth. "I will in about ten seconds. I owe you one."

"You don't owe me anything. I'll meet you there. There's a tactical team en route as well. Follow their lead."

"Thanks, brother. I'll see you."

*   *   *

Clark hung up his cell phone and placed it in one of his pockets. He was dressed in full tactical gear, his balaclava pulled just below his face. Eckart stared at Clark, a grin growing on his face as he placed his machine gun in his chest holster.

"One down," said Eckart. "Now we take the other."

Clark couldn't bring himself to return the smile.

*   *   *

Joe Grant was standing outside of the Command Center for the Chelsea Internment Facility. He stared out at the flurry of ProServ Humvees and tanks preparing to move into Chelsea for added security. Servicemen in tactical gear hustled around the Chancellor. Ed McGonagall walked through the maze of vehicles, flanked by ProServ sentries who peeled off and stood near the entrance.

"This is quite the cluster we've got for ourselves, isn't it, Chancellor?"

"Harold's been kidnapped."

"I heard. We should really get you into the secure station, don't you think?"

"I don't care. We need to get him, right now!"

The personnel nearby slowed and stared at the Chancellor as he screamed. The McArdle Bridge lumbered open, and ProServ vehicles flanked by tactical units began their steady march inside. The streets cleared, save for some concrete barriers scattered in the road and a handful of Servicemen.

"Joe – I understand. I get it. But we can't have something happen to you, especially with Harold gone. The chain of command would collapse. We need to get to safety so we can help manage everything. I've got word myself that they've got a lead on a location in Everett and they're organizing a response."

"Fine. Fine. Let's go, then."

Ed McGonagall checked his watch and saw an incoming truck in the distance. "OK."

As McGonagall reached the glass doors, he let himself in and closed the doors in Joe Grant's face.

"What are you doing, Ed? Open up!"

McGonagall locked the door and stared out past Grant, watching as the large, unmarked truck bore down on the building. He turned and ran inside the lobby and started screaming just before the explosion shattered the glass, sprinting up steps and away from the detonation.

*　*　*

Blair was driving in Everett as the sun broke over the slum buildings and trash-lined streets. He was bearing down on the location of the tactical team at the Chelsea border wall.

"Dispatch, this is Blair – 2R91. What's the status on the body shop off Nichols in Everett?"

"*2R91, this is Dispatch. Reports of a vehicle fitting the description of the van last seen at the Esplanade Attack. Hold on, I'm picking up that State Police have just arrived on site. You're up 2R91. Coordinate on site."*

"Dispatch – what are you talking about? Where's the tactical team?"

"2R91 – no tac as of yet. You're first on site for ProServ."

When was the last time the Staties beat ProServ to the scene? Blair turned down the road, tight with rusted-out cars parked on either side of the one-way street. State Police cruiser lights flashed, bathing the slouched buildings in waves of blue and red. Blair pulled to a stop when he noticed flames breaking the windows of the auto body shop. State troopers stood and stared as the black smoke billowed out of the building.

"David – David!"

Blair raised his hand to his ear. "Carlos?"

"Get out! It's a trap!"

Bullets tore through a squad car ahead of him and more zigzagged up to the hood of Blair's car. He threw his vehicle in reverse, peeling out on the street. Looking back at the scene, he saw several cops shooting up at a third story window of a nearby house before they started sprinting. One was incinerated by a missile that hit a nearby squad car. Blair swerved and hit two parked cars, then dove out of his car and sprinted away from it and onto the porch of a house. He felt intense heat as an explosion rocked his sedan. He saw another trooper down the street jump from the wreckage of a squad car completely in flames, taking a few steps before falling to the ground. Bullets ripped through the street as Blair dashed to the next house, closing in on the shooter's nest. He peeked from around the front porch and estimated the auto shop only six more houses away.

"Carlos – what the fuck is happening?"

"Eckart sold you out. I'll explain everything, first get to cover. I've got something that can help. Keep your eyes peeled."

Blair looked in the distance and saw one small surveillance drone, and then another. Soon, three started converging on the shooter's nest. One fell from the sky as gunfire hit it.

"Blair, move through the backyards. They're distracted. Go now, get out of there!"

He saw the holes form in the street less than a second before he heard the machine gun fire. Blair barged into the backyard of a house and started climbing the low metal fence to the neighboring house. There was more gunfire but further away, towards the shop. Keeping low through backyards, Blair moved closer to the shooters' triple-decker. He crouched behind the tall wooden fence of the neighboring house and scanned through the small spaces between bits of wood. There was a hole in one of the posts so Blair made over to it and watched the backyard. There was no one until a man hustled through the back door and moved to the far end of the house where the cellar entrance doors were hanging open. The wood on the fence was rotted and warped.

"Blair, what are you doing – get out of there!"

"I can't let them die out there."

"Christ, sit tight. I think the backyard is clear. Can you hop the fence in time?"

Blair put his shoulder into it hard and was on the other side, landing on his stomach. Another man rushed out of the back door with an AK-47 and Blair raised his pistol and fired three rounds into his chest before the man went sideways off the steps. He got up fast and scrambled to the dead man, holstering his pistol, and picking up his machine gun.

"I guess that works, too."

Blair slammed the cellar doors shut and locked them in place. Bullet holes dented the doors from the other side. Blair fell backwards when he saw the first few materialize. He scrambled up and rushed into the house and the back flight of stairs. Gunfire lit up the stairway and Blair burst through the back door of the second story unit, finding the kitchen empty. Screaming came down the stairwell in a language Blair couldn't make out.

"What is that? Slavic?"

"It's Russian."

"How the hell do you know?"

"Find some cover, now!"

Blair flipped a round kitchen table over and hid behind it, checking his clip and seeing it half gone already. He shoved the magazine back in and pulled back the charging handle, sweat dripping from his forehead in the bitter cold of the abandoned building. Another gunman charged down the stairwell, and Blair fired wildly into the wall of the kitchen, emptying his machine gun. He dropped it and pulled his pistol from his holster as the gunman yelped, slumped over the railing and having dropped his weapon down the stairs. Blair stormed up to the third floor, skipping steps. He kicked the door in to the third unit and ducked back immediately as a hail of machine gun fire hit the door.

"Blair, wait for my word to rush him."

"How the hell are you doing this?" Blair heard a loud buzzing come into the house, followed by gunfire.

"Go!"

Blair turned the corner with his gun drawn, and saw the man bashing a drone with the butt of his gun. By the time he turned to face Blair, he had emptied his clip. Blair fired at the man, who turned a corner and vanished from sight. The drone moved into another room of the house. *"Blair, he's dropped the gun and he has a knife. Keep your distance and you can take him."* Clutching his pistol handle with both hands, Blair moved around the corner only to feel the gun being ripped from him. Blair struggled and managed to throw his gun into another room. The man grabbed his knife and pointed it at Blair, growling.

"Hang on, State Police are moving into the house!"

The man moved to stab Blair in the gut, but Blair pulled his arm along and moved to the side, bending the man's wrist in the wrong direction until the knife slipped from his hands. Blair kicked him hard in his balls before punching him square in his eye. The man fell backwards, and Blair went for his pistol, but felt his leg caught in his hands. The man tore him down to the floor and forced Blair to turn back and kick him in the face with the heel of his boot. Blair reached for his pistol and steadied it between his thighs after flipping onto his back, and saw the man run for the back staircase. It was then he heard the State Police screaming.

"Don't move! Get on the ground now!"

The drone moved through the house and flew away through the open front porch door with deft speed.

"Damn, dude. I was like half-sure that would work."

Blair exhaled. "You should start playing roulette."

"I took the usual idiot-bots off their routes and put them to better use. Got manual control over one. Hang tight at the scene, I'm coming myself with a friend. I'll be there as soon as I can."

"I'm going to deal with the Staties."

Blair got back on his feet. Two cops stood in front of him in the kitchen with their guns drawn.

"ProServ! Don't shoot!" Blair put his hands up as he yelled the words.

"Hold fire! Let me see ID!"

Blair saw the man who had given him such trouble being handcuffed on his knees in the kitchen. Blair showed his ProServ ID to the troopers.

Blair put his ID away and spoke through panting, trying to catch his breath. "Keep him here – I want words with him. We still need to sweep this place. All units and the cellar. At least one of those fuckers is locked in there." Blair saw some machine guns scattered throughout the living room and an economical Russian-made rocket launcher lying against the side of an old, ripped-open sofa. The stairs thudded and creaked as yet more cops flowed into the property. One started speaking to him.

"Don't worry, guy. We just went through floor one and the basement, it's clean."

"That's impossible," said Blair. "There's a guy who went into that basement."

"Nobody's down there. Our guys are in there now. Maybe you're confused, you came in here like a demon. We just followed you in."

Blair readied his pistol and made his way towards the door leading to the front porch of the third story unit. He heard the trooper on his radio talking. *We may have hostiles still in the house, hold fire unless fired upon.* The door slammed open and Blair checked the deck, checking around the small, crowded porch and seeing nothing. He made a motion to an officer on the street below. *Third story clear.* Blair drew a cigarette from his pack and lit it, taking a drag and sliding down the siding on the porch. Sirens wailed outside as ProServ vehicles pulled up to the place, officers scrambling out and securing the site. His hands were trembling now and he was having a hard time holding on to his cigarette. He stood and looked out in the general direction of Boston and the Internment Facility. Massive plumes of smoke were rising out of Chelsea. He went back inside and saw two troopers, sizing up the weaponry.

"What's your name, Officer?"

"Carelli. You David Blair?"

"What the hell is going on out there?"

"Terrorists are bombing Chelsea and they're arming the unfits. They blew up parts of the Wall and a few dinghies landed on the shore with weapons and enemy fighters. It looks like a rebellion. We thought you'd know more…"

Carelli's radio clicked and he reached his hand up to his shoulder. *"We've cleared the cellar. Nobody's down here."*

"Copy that."

"No, we need to get down there now. I locked somebody in the cellar – they were shooting at me."

"That's not possible. We've been through the basement twice now."

"Then show me."

Blair took one last drag of his cigarette and flicked it into the dirt of the backyard, drawing his pistol and heading into the cellar with Carelli and some other State Police through the bulkhead door entrance. It was all rust and jagged rock and Blair splashed into a puddle as he scanned the bare basement. He saw a tall locker that took up a good portion of a wall and motioned to the other officers. Blair flung the door open. Looking in, they saw a flight of wooden stairs that went deep underground.

CHAPTER XX

Ed McGonagall stood in the secure wing of the Chelsea Command Center, his arms crossed and flanked by Arbitrage executives and Facility administrators trying to make sense of events. A large screen at the center of a far wall illuminated. The face of Julian Mura lorded over them.

"Hello everyone," said Mura. "Who is accounted for here?"

One of the administrators looked up. "Sir, we think Chancellor Grant was killed earlier in the attack. We're down to a skeletal staff. Key personnel didn't make it into the Facility Command Center before the fighting started. We've been attempting to direct ProServ operations inside and around the Facility."

Another administrator chimed in, "We don't know what we're dealing with and we're doing this on the fly." A chorus began to erupt.

"Our Vice Chancellor is being held by these people!"

"It has to be the PRF!"

"That's enough," said Mura. "Protection Services tactical command structure is being directed competently and will keep you updated. We may be forced to subcontract to Security Solutions personnel if the fighting continues beyond today. Let's hope we don't end up running to traditional law enforcement for assistance containing this. Mr. McGonagall – you have more information on Vice Chancellor Maguire?"

"That's correct," said McGonagall. "We think he'll be used as a bargaining chip as part of some negotiated pullout from Chelsea on our end."

"Well then, these terrorists are sorely mistaken."

"I agree, sir. But we need a clear command structure if we want to move forward and repel these attacks. We run the risk of losing complete control otherwise."

"Based on the readouts and reports I'm seeing the Containment Wall has been breached in several areas. Unfits attempting to burst out in every direction. Why?"

"Internment center closures and consolidations," said McGonagall. "We've got over half a million people inside Chelsea and even more being sent to Birch Tree. I know it was our hope to begin the process of moving some of the most problematic unfits out to Amherst by the summer, but I'm afraid we waited too long. The element inside has become too dangerous, obviously. This is part of a national attack and we need to strike now."

"In the event of Chancellor Grant's incapacitation, Harold Maguire was meant to take his place as per his succession orders."

"That's not possible anymore," said McGonagall.

"I'm fully aware of this, Mr. McGonagall." Mura took a long pause. "I just spoke on a secure line with the Leader." A stillness filled the room. "His top concern now is the implementation of a contingency plan to neutralize all overtaken internment facilities nationwide. The coordinated nature of these attacks means we need a swift and unforgiving counterweight to these terrorists. He has asked me to personally designate Edward McGonagall as acting Chancellor and to authorize him to launch air strikes inside all internment zones under his jurisdiction with priority for Chelsea. You will all be notified when the strike capability is readied and available for launch – if you deem it necessary."

McGonagall uncrossed his arms. "I am honored and humbled to have the Leader's faith and confidence. I will do all that is necessary to end the fighting."

"Not yet," said Mura. "We should give our forces enough time to try and end the fighting without tactical missile strikes first. The casualties alone on our side would be a nightmare and leave us untenably diminished. But the discretion is yours when missiles become operational and our forces can make a tactical retreat. I'm moving to a secure site – all administrators shall report directly to Edward McGonagall and address him as Chancellor."

The screen buzzed off and administrators began turning to McGonagall. He smiled through his words. "Any questions?"

*   *   *

The door of Harold Maguire's small room opened and a satchel bag was thrown at him, which he didn't catch.

"Open it," said Nigel.

"What is it?"

"Change of clothes. You're not gonna do well around here with what you're wearing right now."

Harold pulled an old, dusty topcoat from the contents of the bag, along with a pair of jeans and a sweater. At the bottom of the bag was a pair of running sneakers.

"How do you know my shoe size?"

"We know everything we need to know about you. Put it on and let us know when you're finished. We need to move you soon."

"What's going on?"

"The fighting is getting closer."

Harold started taking off his suit jacket and his dress pants. "Where are we?"

"A safehouse."

"No shit. Where?" The sweater went on over his head.

"We're inside Chelsea now."

"You've got to be shitting me."

"It's safer for you in here than anywhere else. We're organizing you to get to the Forbidden City. The Auxiliary Forces will claim they found you and ProServ will organize a rescue. After that, you're not our problem anymore."

"How did you get me inside?"

"You're not exactly running a top-flight security operation here, Harold. We told you before…we've got our ways. I guess you don't remember the chloroform."

Harold stood up and put his long topcoat jacket on. "Let's just get the hell out of here."

Nigel held his gun up in front of him with both hands, low at hip-level. "Not yet. I need to wait for a signal before I can bring you anywhere. Then we move. Do you understood?"

"Don't fuck with me, kid."

Nigel cocked the machine pistol. "I'll make you regret coldcocking me at the funeral."

"Alright." Harold put his hands up slightly. "Alright."

"It shouldn't be long." Nigel looked at his watch. He didn't put the machine gun down.

Harold sat at the edge of his bed. He pinched the bridge of his nose and squinted hard, hunched over. "You know, a couple of months ago you were at my house having dinner. I honestly can't believe how far we got from there. I'm sorry, Nigel. I'm so sorry about how all this played out."

"I was at the Esplanade when you shot him." Nigel lowered his gun slightly. "Cantwell."

"You were?"

"I couldn't bring myself to say anything to you after. It was too much. I closed my eyes when I shot at him with everyone."

"That's not a bad thing, Nigel. Not wanting to be a killer."

"He needed to die. He killed Aiden. Who knows how many people he's killed."

"I thought I knew what loss was, honestly. I really did. But you lose something of yourself when you kill someone. I felt it when my family died. But I can feel the part inside of me that I lost when I shot him. I feel the emptiness. The part that I lost of myself, not just someone I loved." Harold looked down and played with his wedding ring, sliding it on to each hand repeatedly. He looked up at Nigel. "You think someone like Cantwell had to have felt empty like that when he started doing what he did. Then you realize he must have done it a hundred times. Or a thousand. There must have been nothing there where you expect to find a soul. Now I'm left with more questions than answers."

"That's their greatest power, Harold. They've made us all feel like we have none. Like we're just rocketing towards something and we don't get to choose what the world becomes. We don't get to protect people we care about, we just get to watch. War, genocide, misery at the industrial scale. All of it. Take your pick."

"I like to think that's why I did it. That I was going to make the world different than it is now. It doesn't feel like it panned out very well. Most people don't talk about it, but a lot of this country looked like it was falling apart before Robert Wright. They just systemized it after that. This is everything that was going to happen put in an accelerator."

"Do you regret it?"

"What?"

"Shooting him?" Nigel checked his watch. "Getting involved with this?"

"It didn't give me what I wanted. What I want, there's no getting back."

"I regret it." Nigel's eyes welled up. "I wish I never came here. I never wanted it to turn in to this."

"What are you talking about?"

"You'd do anything to get Aiden back, wouldn't you? You'd tear someone's heart out if you could get her back again? Wouldn't you? That's revenge, we think they're waiting on the other side for us. But she's still alive, Harold. She's alive and I can still get her back."

Harold stood up and took a step towards Nigel, balling up his fists. "What did you do?"

"I'm sorry, Harold. They took her. They took her and they said that this was the only way I'd ever see her again. She's my sister, Harold! I had to do it!" Shooting erupted outside of the room.

"You son of a bitch!" Harold ran towards Nigel and knocked the gun out of his hands. "You sold us out!" He started punching Nigel, grabbing at his shirt and beating him until he hit the ground. He kept hitting him.

The cheap wooden door exploded and a ProServ tactical squad flowed into the room. Their guns were drawn and they all converged on Harold, screaming at him to put his hands up. One commando ripped Harold off of Nigel and after some resistance another commando joined him. After the butt of a commando's gun hit him several times, Harold stopped. His hands went up and one of the ProServ commandos patted him down. The panic started washing over him and pulling him away. Harold had given himself over to it entirely.

"We have him, sir," said a commando. "Location is secure."

Harold looked over to Nigel, who was bleeding from his lip. "You had the balls to call me a fucking coward."

"Quiet!" The command came with a kick to the back of Harold's knees. The pain radiated up his thighs and through his legs as he landed on the ground. The machine gun was cocked and he could feel it near his head, pointed at him. All he could do now was look away and listen as footsteps echoed through the hallways, into the apartment closing in on him.

Harold glanced up and saw a pair of boots before one of them moved fast and struck him in the face. He fell over onto his side and saw blood from his mouth dripping onto the floor before he felt the stun of the kick. Panting coughs came out of his throat as he collapsed. A hand gripped his hair hard, pulling him up.

"Now I've got you," Eckart said. "Now you're mine."

CHAPTER XXI

Blair stood with his hands in his coat pockets in the den of the third story unit, flanked by State Police troopers. He stared intensely at the man who tried to stab him earlier, handcuffed to an old radiator and sitting on the floor. Blood was dripping down part of his face and he had a surly look on. Then it clicked: the man had stared at him with the same surly look at the Joy Division the first time he was there. The only difference was then he was flanked by cronies, now they were all dead and littered the triple-decker. At least the ones that didn't disappear through the basement. Blair heard the rumbling from the back of the kitchen make its way into the den, where State Police began to leave the apartment and more ProServ officers started flowing in. Colonel Crenna appeared next to Blair. Carlos Contreras followed him.

"Colonel," said Blair. "I wasn't expecting you."

"I told you I was bringing a friend," said Carlos. He put a cigarette in his mouth and lit it.

Colonel Crenna straightened his overcoat sleeves. "By my count, this is the second time Frederick Eckart has tried to have you killed."

"Clark sent me here," said Blair. "He knew it was a death trap. He wanted me to show up."

"Why don't we move to another room?" The Colonel motioned to one of his mainstay aides. "Secure the area. Watch him." He pointed to the handcuffed man.

The three of them moved into one of the bedrooms of the

apartment, and Carlos shut the door behind him.

"Remember our conversation," said Carlos. "About Raikenov and Eckart?"

"I do," said Blair.

"Well I looked into it, and I kept hitting brick walls. I bypassed those and kept hitting more. It went slow because I needed to cover my tracks, but I finally figured it out. When Eckart was still Special Forces doing work for the CIA he had a stopover in Eastern Europe. He met someone who could help him arm some of the right-wing forces in Central America without US fingerprints on the guns. The guy was a former spook himself: he was Russian military before he moved to FSB. He went freelance and started dealing arms with the unofficial blessing of the Kremlin." Carlos blew smoke from the side of his mouth.

"Grigori Raikenov," Blair realized.

"Raikenov worked for a Russian politician who wins the presidential election in a squeaker. He's not very popular and he already looks like a lame duck. Then bombs start going off all over St. Petersburg and Moscow. Before you know it, unpopular politician becomes the indispensable leader Russia needs for the next 20 or so years. You get my drift?"

"Raikenov was a protected ProServ asset," said Colonel Crenna. "I didn't even know about his status in the company until now. Apparently, Cantwell and Eckart built the model with Raikenov in Chelsea. Cantwell's inner circle ensured to place assets just like Raikenov across internment centers all over the country. I had a surveillance drone placed on Cantwell every time he came to Boston. He would almost always meet with Eckart in a very public place, and one of them always jammed the drone's audio recording capacity. We never heard the contents of their conversations."

"Raikenov gave Eckart and his band of lunatics a playbook to turn this country upside down," said Carlos. "Waves of low-intensity terrorist attacks to justify internment, the guns in Chelsea, the unfits slipping out of the Facility, and now the upheaval inside the Walls…it's been Eckart pulling the strings on the ground. He even infiltrated a PRF cell to orchestrate Cantwell's death and accelerate the Leader's timetable."

"Timetable for what?" said Blair.

"The Leader and his top movers call it Operation Orchestra," said the Colonel. "It's a protocol where every internment facility in the United States is obliterated in coordinated air strikes. The Leader's plan all along was to murder tens of millions of Americans and call America greater for it. The final phase of the Restoration."

"I found out almost too late to warn you," said Carlos. "This whole place was a ruse to justify Orchestra and lure you into a trap. But we've got a plan. It's an op. Totally off the record. No official support – part of a coup to depose Robert Wright. We report to the Colonel through back channels, we move fast, and we neutralize these two once and for all."

"Do we get any backup?" said Blair.

Carlos looked to the Colonel. "Right now, we don't know exactly who we can trust." He looked back to Blair. "We make a wrong move and we potentially lose Eckart and Raikenov in the wind. This is something we have to do ourselves."

"What about the air strikes?" said Blair. "How do we stop them?"

"You leave that to me," said the Colonel. "I'm coordinating with some of the higher ups at Arbitrage to scrub the strikes. We're working with law enforcement and the military. The Leader is going to be neutralized, his top lieutenants nationwide are the targets. You two would be part of the operation that cuts off all the heads of the hydra at once. That's the only thing that's going to stop Orchestra at this point."

"There's a passageway in the basement," said Blair. "I wouldn't be surprised if there was a direct shot between this house underground and the Forbidden City. We're that close to the Wall here."

"There are guys surveying it right now," Carlos said. "That's probably the case. But they'll expect us to come up that way if we were to go through."

"Not if they think this was a success," said Blair. "What if we get the mouthbreather chained up outside to give them word that I'm dead and the ambush worked? Then we get a better idea of what happens next. Maybe they welcome us back with open arms, right into the heart of where they're operating from inside. That's Raikenov – where's Eckart now?"

"Officially, he's operating as part of a tac unit in Chelsea quelling the rebellion," said Colonel Crenna. "Unofficially, we think he's taken Vice Chancellor Harold Maguire, along with any others who joined in the resistance against the Leader. Eckart's taking the opportunity to clean house and tie up loose ends during the chaos. We're almost certain Clark has joined them. He's probably retreated to a hardened, reinforced location within the Chelsea Facility protected from any planned air strikes. He's likely close to Raikenov in the Forbidden City."

"Do we try and save the people he's holding?" said Blair.

"Only if you can," said the Colonel. "Harold may already be dead; in which case we don't have time to waste. We do have someone who could potentially help – they served under me years ago and have been part of the small group we've cultivated working against the Leader. They grabbed her before Cantwell was killed last night and moved her into Chelsea. She's got a subdermal transponder that responds to a specific frequency we're using, the standard scans wouldn't pick it up. According to the signal, she's in the Forbidden City."

"Is she still alive?" said Blair.

"The signal picks up her vitals," said Carlos. "So far, she's under duress but she's alive. She's someone you can trust."

"We've been able to take an educated guess that they're all likely in the same location in Chelsea," said the Colonel. "You can use it to find her. Now let's move you out and get you prepped."

The three exited the room and went back into the den, where the handcuffed man stared up at them. Blair eased himself into a crouch, balancing himself on his toes and resting his elbows on his knees. He leaned in closer to the man, stern and staring intensely into his eyes without blinking.

"We'd like to have a word with you."

*   *   *

The walls were taupe cinderblock and cracking badly, making veins that let in a draft. The windows were worse: some blacked out, others broken. Dirt film covered each of them, but you could still see outside. The ceiling was dropped-in with half of the pieces missing. Harold Maguire was staring up at one of the mucked-out windows when the fist hit his face. Cartoons got it right a long time ago, Harold thought. A pop of light, sharp squiggles all around. Instant and disorienting. He noticed the burn mark on the face of the man pummeling him, a small circle that looked nearly infected. The door of the room opened, and Lauren Meyers was shoved in with her hands tied in front of her. Her mascara had run down her face and her hair was a tangled mess. She had on her mainstay gray suit and white blouse, but the sleeve on one arm was ripped and one of her heels was broken.

"Jansen, tie this one up next to Maguire."

"Sure thing, Clark." The man with the burn on his face looked at Harold and grinned before he cracked his knuckles, moving for Lauren. He grabbed her hard by her hair and jerked her toward the closest chair.

"Let me go!" Lauren's words came off more as a plea than a demand.

Jansen took his free hand and smacked her in the face, his hand open moving fast upwards and into her nose. Lauren let out a terrible noise as her nose began to bleed. She half-fell into the chair as Jansen landed a punch into her gut, and she doubled over and end up on the floor. Harold squirmed around, but he had been tied to a chair of his own. He watched as Lauren writhed, holding her face as she bellowed and tried to catch her breath.

"How much longer does this go on?" said Harold.

"As long as we want," said Jansen. "Want to try and stop me?"

Jansen wound up and kicked Lauren in the gut as she still lay on her side. Her breathing became erratic and gasping. No matter how much she tried there was no oxygen to be had, nothing to feed her.

"You two must have really pissed off the Sergeant. He never lets me have at people like this. You two don't want to know how bad it's gonna get. This is just the beginning."

"You're going to kill her," said Harold. "Why don't you bring it back to me now, huh?"

"Shut the fuck up," said Jansen. He turned back to Harold and smacked him in the face. "I speak, you listen."

"Then kill me now! You got me. It's over." Harold licked some of the blood from the corner of his mouth. "You win."

"It can't be that easy. Not for you. Not after all you've done."

Harold looked up and saw the man who said the words. He walked in holding his bulletproof vest by the collar around his shoulders, dressed in the all-black tactical gear of Servicemen sent out to do riot duty or go on special operations. PROSERV was stamped on the front of the vest, and his combat boots clunked on the hollow wood floor with each step he took. His tongue pushed out the side of part of his mouth and slowly became a grin.

"Frederick Eckart," said Harold.

"Harold Maguire," said Eckart. There was a calm in his face as he said Harold's name. "Did you really think you would be able to kill me? Hell, did you think you'd be able to kill Cantwell if I didn't want you to? You understand that don't you? He nearly derailed all of this."

"That's it, then?" said Harold. "You knew all along?"

"I was on to you from the beginning," said Eckart. "I reviewed each casualty after the Dissenter's March. I'd have to have been a fool not to. Your daughter obviously stood out. Those cover stories don't protect you from everyone." Eckart leaned somewhat closer to Harold's face. "This would have been a lot neater had you just blown your fucking head off that night, alone in your shitty two-bedroom. You got so much more adventurous after that. You just had to know who did it. You had to get to the bottom of things and save these poor souls like the hero you wish you could be, you white savior, you!" He let out a laugh.

"You're out of your mind," said Harold. "It was you that day in Chelsea, wasn't it? You tried to have me killed."

"The world has made us surprisingly resilient, hasn't it? I can't take full credit, though. I have a tremendous support system inside this place. You'll meet them later. We'll have a bird land for us here, just in time to pull us out before the bombs start falling. You'll get to see it all – but not before I break you."

"You think there's more to break?" Harold tried to struggle out of the ropes around him. "Look at me for Christ's sake! It's over!"

"No!" yelled Eckart as he punched Harold hard in the stomach. Eckart placed both his hands on the sides of Harold's head, raising it so they locked eyes. "You killed my mentor. Do you understand what that means? You took the life of a good man."

Harold spit, trying to send it at Eckart. He moved back effortlessly.

"How many times do I have to say it?" said Harold. "You got me. You won. Just kill me already!"

"That's right, Harold. I do have you. That means I set the agenda. After all the bullshit you've put me through – demotion, Cantwell, trying to stop this – it can't just end now. You have to suffer. You need to see this city in ash and rubble. Then and only then do I get to do something I've always wanted to do."

Harold caught his breath, but his pain was constant and his eyes watered. "What?"

Eckart smiled. "I get to give two communists a free helicopter ride."

Jansen laughed. He was still trying to tie up Lauren to the chair close to Harold, who hung his head.

"This faggot," said Jansen.

The door unbolted and swung open. Eckart turned to face Clark, who lumbered in with two large metal buckets he all but dragged across the floor. He set them at the corner of the room and retrieved from inside one of the two large buckets a smaller one. It was filled with water, some of which he poured back in to one of the larger buckets. He set it down at his feet and took off his jacket, rolling up his sleeves. Clark stared at Harold, and then at Lauren. They were both fastened to loose wooden chairs, rope chafing at their skin. Eckart took several steps back from the two of them.

"In order to get your Beret, you have to be abducted by your own people. They take you and they hold you for a few days." Eckart removed a cloth from his pocket. "They used to subject you to what they used to call 'enhanced interrogation techniques' – it used to be so sanitized. I never understood why they didn't just call it what it is. It's torture. Very simple."

Harold squirmed in his chair. Eckart approached him and wrapped a cloth around his face, tying it tightly in a large knot at the back of his head. Harold began to writhe and thrash with little to show for it. Eckart put his foot on the chair, in between Harold's legs. He leaned in and smiled at his captive. Lauren looked on in shock.

"I've done this to more people than I can count. Do you know how much actionable information I've been able to gather from doing it? How many lives I've saved?"

"I don't know," said Harold, stammering.

"None. I've never saved a single life or stopped one bomb

from going off because I did this. People say torture doesn't work – but it depends entirely on *why* we torture. Do you understand? If you're attempting to get good information out of someone, then it doesn't. We've known that forever. But if your goal is to cause pain or break someone completely, then it's more than worthwhile. That's why we kept doing it, Harold – because it felt good to do this to our enemies." Eckart shoved the chair and Harold fell backwards with a yelp. He went for the small bucket and stood over Harold's head as he poured some of the water onto the cloth wrapped tightly around Harold's face. "Because it feels right! That's the whole point!"

Harold began coughing and inhaling fast, desperate not to drown. He felt the water getting into his throat and it was like he was being washed away, rushing down a river he couldn't climb out from. He was flailing deep in the water and he couldn't catch his breath. The only thing to do was scream through it, and he began bellowing with water in his mouth. Harold heard Lauren yell for him. The chair he was tied to flipped, and Harold was suddenly on his side. The cloth was raised at the mouth and he coughed furiously.

"Breathe," said Eckart. "Breathe deep, Harold. We've got some time to kill."

CHAPTER XXII

Ed McGonagall watched a wall-sized map of the Chelsea Internment Facility light up.

"Each red area represents some major disturbance," said Brian. "As you can see, virtually every sector of Chelsea has some form of fighting going on, besides a small quarter near Route 1 where the former municipal housing authority was established."

"Then it's time for us to initiate air strikes. I want to give an order for as many of our men to pull back now as is possible before we scramble air support."

"Sir," said Tyler. "If we pull our men back now then we guarantee that they aren't able to overcome the fighting going on."

"Or we risk their lives for little to no reason," said McGonagall. "I'm not willing to shed the blood of our fighters as long as we can bring about a resolution that will finish this once and for all." McGonagall, flanked by his fellow administrators, looked in the direction of Brian Henry. Henry was standing nearby, scrawling furiously on a tablet. "Mr. Henry?"

"Yes?"

"Check the status. If the jets aren't ready for maneuvers, we need to get word out and see if we can scramble something for the strikes."

Henry grimaced. "I'll do that now, sir."

"Good. We want to be sure that we're able to move when we need to."

"How can you justify this?" said Tyler. "Our forces are making headway and most of the people inside Chelsea aren't fighting directly with us!"

"Take a look at the map," said McGonagall. "There isn't a section of the Facility that isn't in disarray! We need to quell this before it puts the entire region at risk. We're seeing the same thing nationwide – shall we log your insubordination for the Leader's personal records? Would you prefer to make official your disagreement with his direct orders?"

Tyler sunk into his chair. "No, Chancellor."

"Good thinking, Mr. Tyler. Get in touch with air command now. We'll take them before the sun goes down."

*   *   *

Blair made his way through a dark dirt tunnel, with large sections held up by wooden scaffolding. The man who had been handcuffed to the radiator not long ago walked just ahead of him, and Blair occasionally jabbed Yevgeny with the barrel of his automatic rifle. He held the gun with both hands and moved nimbly on his feet, keeping a close eye on the man in front of him. Yevgeny kept his hands held to the back of his head. Behind Blair, Carelli stood with his police-issued shotgun drawn, aiming at Yevgeny. Blair had changed into a ratty coat, dirty jeans, and soiled shirt before entering the tunnel. The look was complete with an Auxiliary Force armband.

Blair turned the light off on his rifle as a light bulb hanging from the ceiling of the tunnel came into view and lit up the area. He took a deep breath in, feeling nauseous. Carelli and Blair had marched Yevgeny more than a mile through subterranean passages and into the sewers before coming back into a dug-out corridor.

"It's not far now," said Yevgeny.

"Remember – if you comply, we let you live. If you do anything out of order, I put a bullet in you myself."

"I understand."

Blair reached for his earpiece. "This is Blair. We're at the doorstep. Holding until you're in position."

"*I got you,*" said Carlos. The words sounded choppy and distorted. "*Wait for my word, then move. Based on your position you should be popping into the basement of a house right next to the old housing authority buildings. You'll be inside the Forbidden City perimeter. Send Yevgeny in with the package, and if he tries anything yo-*"

"Copy that," said Blair. "I'll wait for your word."

Blair lowered his rifle slightly and eyed the backpack slung over Yevgeny's shoulders. The bag was worn and a faded blue. One of the straps was half-ripped off and the logo of the company that made it had faded off it completely. Yevgeny turned to face Blair and Carelli behind himself with his hands slightly raised and in sight.

"You promise me you don't kill me for no reason?" said Yevgeny.

Blair raised his gun. "You almost killed me for no reason. Or I suppose it was just a bad reason, right?"

"You don't know what happens to me if I don't work for Raikenov."

"It's the same thing we would do to you if you don't follow through now." Blair lowered his gun slightly. "I promise you we will not kill you. Not if you do everything you need to do. You go in, drop that bag off, and make yourself scarce fast. Understand? When we go in, it's going to get serious. You run out and keep running, and you get to disappear forever."

"I understand." Yevgeny turned back around and braced himself to get through the door, into the house where he knew others were waiting for something on the other side. Cold sweat dripped from his forehead as he started trembling. "I understand."

"Good," said Blair. He turned away from Yevgeny and faced Carelli, speaking to him in hushed tones. "Thank you for going this far…

but this has to be the end of the line for you."

"What do you mean?" said Carelli.

"I mean take this," said Blair. He took a small backpack off his back and pulled out a block of tan clay, handing it to Carelli. "This is C4. I want you to take twenty steps back and insert it at the base of one of the scaffolds in here as you're leaving, and just run like hell. Get back to where State Police have the house cordoned. You understand? That's all I need you to do."

"I want to come with you," said Carelli. "I can help!"

"You are helping," said Blair. He leaned in closer still. "Understand me when I say this. They're not sending me in because I'm some hotshot. This is a suicide mission. Unfits are going to overrun the place at any moment. You don't want to be on the wrong side of that. You can make sure the people who are responsible for all this don't get away with it if you set the charge and evacuate. You understand? I'll set it off when you're long gone."

"I understand."

"Get going – it's not gonna be long now."

* * *

Harold's coughs were violent, and he had started to drool on himself again. The water had washed his wounds a little cleaner, but they were still throbbing. His lip was fat and split open. The rest of his face was bruised and puffy. He saw someone standing in the corner of the room – his vision was blurry, but he knew what he was looking at. She leaned down next to her father and caressed his face. He felt the touch, and he knew he was home. After months of feeling adrift, his feet were touching the ground. *"You're going to be a great martyr, Dad."*

Eckart gripped Harold's hair and propped him up. He removed the cloth from his face, and Harold could finally breathe again. Eckart moved to Lauren and held clenched in his fist the same cloth that had been wrapped around Harold's face. She began pleading.

"Eckart, please stop. Just stop. Stop!" The cloth wrapped tight around her face and her screaming became muffled. "Stop! Stop!"

This time Eckart placed the chair on the floor. Clark handed him a full bucket, but he didn't pour it immediately. He stared at Harold, and Harold returned the gaze. Eckart started slowly with drips of water, but he couldn't take his eyes off the man tied to the chair who had given him so much grief.

"Are you done with me?" said Harold. "She doesn't know anything, it's me you want."

"What?" said Eckart. His eyes were wide, and he scowled. Clark looked on suspiciously.

"I think you broke him," said Clark with a laugh. "His brain isn't wired right anymore."

Eckart stopped pouring the water and looked at Clark. "Now this is something I haven't seen in a long time. I've seen people break. I've seen people admit to all kinds of things. But I rarely see someone dig down and ask for more…all that heart, and all for nothing."

"Not for nothing," said Harold. "If you kill me, I'll be with them again. If you don't, I walk away from you. And I know what I have to do for the rest of my days."

Eckart ripped the rag off Lauren's face, who gasped for air. "Harold don't do this! Just be quiet!"

"There's nothing he can do to me anymore," said Harold. He started laughing. "You did all of it!"

"I'm gonna show you how much more I can do to you!" said Eckart.

An explosion rattled the building, shaking the grounds. Clark went to one knee and steadied himself before he fell over. Eckart dropped his bucket, the water crisscrossing the floor. Lauren shut her eyes tightly and gritted her teeth. Harold felt as if he had been ripped back off his feet, left to float. He struggled with the rope keeping him bound to the chair.

"What the hell was that?" said Eckart.

"I don't know," said Clark. "Insurgents get through the perimeter?"

Eckart held his hand to his ear. "What's going on, Jansen? Do you have contact with Auxiliaries? Jansen?"

Harold strained to hear a whirring noise, somewhere off in the distance. The sound was low, and he felt it in his chest. He turned his head somewhat to look out the window and saw a helicopter barreling close to the building. Harold threw himself sideways, tipping the chair over and falling onto his side. The chair cracked noticeably, and Harold had more room to wiggle the rope. Bullets began ripping through the room, and then other parts of the building. Harold tried to keep his head down, but he looked up and saw red bullet streaks he saw not long ago on the Esplanade. The tracer ammunition was furious over his head, and out of the corner of his eye he saw Eckart and Clark scuttle out of the room. Harold shoved his shoulder forward and made the ropes move, and then shimmied himself out of the chair completely. He crawled on the floor towards Lauren, undoing the knots that kept her attached to the chair. The shooting was deafening.

*   *   *

Raikenov's office began to shake fiercely as the helicopter gunship tore the building apart. Dust and debris filled the air as his trusted lieutenants scrambled. Grigori Raikenov himself seemed calm, staring down the chamber of his pistol as he slid the barrel back into place. He put the gun in a side holster under a heavy winter topcoat. Dhananjay opened the door and yelled to Raikenov's crew.

"We need to get out of here!" he yelled.

"Not before we take down the gunship!" said Raikenov. He

pointed to one of his men. "Dmitri – RPG." The goon made his way to a rocket-propelled grenade launcher, picked it up, and placed it on his shoulder before hustling out of the building. Raikenov motioned to the rest of his men. "We're done here. Let's go."

The crew began running through the halls and out one of the side exits. Tall weeds grew high and gave them all some cover as they moved through the Forbidden City. Raikenov watched as Dmitri raised the rocket launcher to the moving helicopter. Dmitri fired, and the rocket left a smoke trail in its wake. The helicopter had already started in some kind of maneuver, gaining altitude and moving over Route One and beyond Chelsea after dodging the rocket. Raikenov smiled.

"That's all we needed." He motioned to his men to make their way to an old basketball court where a slew of Humvees were parked.

"These will take us to the evac point," said Dhananjay, pointing at the vehicles. "There's going to be a ProServ chopper waiting for us, Eckart set it up!"

"Good," said Raikenov. "Lead the way."

Raikenov's Auxiliary Force cadre made off towards the Humvees. Some of the cadre reached the vehicles before others and started climbing into them. The engines began to rumble. Raikenov looked off to the side to look for Dmitri but noticed that he had disappeared. He looked back to his men as they piled into the fleet. Raikenov froze in place. Two of the several vehicles erupted in flames, a large explosion setting off fireballs reaching high. Raikenov heard a rocket fire and hit another vehicle, causing another fireball to rip up the old courts and the vehicles stationed on it. One of the Auxiliary Force members ran several steps in flames before falling to his knees and letting the fire take him completely. Raikenov felt the heat tear at him and fell to his knees before going face first into the dirt. As he got his senses back, Raikenov looked up and saw a fierce ProServ grunt with a rifle pointing at him, dressed as one of the AF members.

"Corporal Blair," said Raikenov.

"I still don't think I've killed as many people as you," said Blair. "To answer your question from before."

"They'll be consequences for you."

Blair motioned to his surroundings. "These aren't consequences? Look at what you've done to us."

"No. We didn't do this to you. A few nudges was all it took, here and there. All we ever did was hold a mirror up to you people. We showed you what you really were…that's all."

Blair eyed the gun just a few inches from Raikenov's hand and shot him in the arm, and then in one of his legs. He yelled out in pain as the blood flowed freely. As he steadied his rifle, Blair placed his boot on Raikenov's forearm and applied pressure, scanning the surroundings. Raikenov cried out. It was then he saw them, off in the distance. The smoke was billowing around them, maybe a mile away where gunshots were ringing out and the occasional shout and explosion became clearer. All the defenses of the Forbidden City were fading fast. The unfits were starting to break through.

"I hope they're not hungry," said Blair. "I've heard stories about what the hungry ones do for food."

Raikenov grimaced as Blair smashed his face in by the butt of his rifle. They deserve to get their hands on you, he thought. The dirt around him began exploding up as shots rang out, and Blair moved in a zig zag motion for cover.

"Carlos, you copy? Carlos!"

"I'm here – I've got a positive ID on Eckart in the main building, not sure if I got him before the rockets. Did you take care of them?"

"I don't know – I can't guarantee that. The unfits broke through, they're in the Forbidden City."

"Christ. Get to a rooftop nearby, we've got to scrub this. I'm picking you up. We have to get you out!"

"I'm going in." Blair made for the shooter's nest, racing into the building as fast as he could. "Look for me on the roof once I confirm Eckart as dead."

CHAPTER XXIII

Julian Mura took up the large screen before the administrators at the Chelsea Internment Facility. McGonagall looked up from his planning, meeting Mura's digitized gaze. Giant and all-consuming, he stared up at Mura with a sneer.

"Your attention immediately," said Mura.

"Hello, sir," said McGonagall. "I'm afraid that our forces are coming under more resistance than they've ever experienced. We are prepared to launch strikes in the next half hour."

"I regret to inform all of you," said Mura, pausing to clear his throat. "I regret to inform you that Leader Wright has been lost. The continuity government is initiating lockdown procedures as we speak. Consider your current location sealed. State and municipal law enforcement are being dispatched along with the National Guard to fortify all serious positions and infrastructure. It's out of our hands."

McGonagall shrank into his own body, all bravado draining rapidly. "The Leader's dead?"

"I'm afraid so. We will be dispatching personnel to your location immediately in order to fortify your positions, but you are to make no executive decisions. The Orchestra is cancelled – I repeat, the Orchestra has been cancelled."

"Are you sure about that?" said McGonagall. "I want to be sure that's the case."

"Hear me now," said Mura. "Orchestra is finished! We're

planning a tactical retreat from all besieged internment centers in the Northeastern United States, and others across the country are soon to follow. These riots need containment – all private and military forces are to fall back behind border walls and keep all unfits inside the walls. That is all we can authorize at this time until we know exactly the nature of the threat."

"Our Leader has been assassinated and you want to retreat?" said McGonagall.

"Our personnel are approaching your position and will be there as soon as possible. You will hear more instructions at a later date."

Mura's face – once taking up the entire screen – fizzed out and popped into a small white dot and then a completely black screen before rioting areas of Chelsea and, in smaller screens, Lawrence and other internment centers became prominent again. McGonagall looked on, somewhat dumbfounded. One of his aides looked to him.

"Sir," he said. He choked back tears. "Is this happening?"

McGonagall turned to him. "Straighten up. The Leader's enemies are moving against him and they're hiding behind continuity protocols to do it. Get word to the fleet – the air strikes move now!"

"Sir," said Tyler. "They've grounded all air traffic. We can't get access to any of the fighter jets on call for strikes."

"What do we have that we control directly?" said McGonagall.

"We have a handful of Carnivore drones under our direct jurisdiction – they've got a couple thousand pounds of payload between them."

"Activate them – priority target is Chelsea, then other ancillary facilities. Target areas for maximum casualties right now!"

* * *

Blair rushed up the stairs of the main Housing Authority

apartment building, the butt of the machine gun dug into his shoulder. He gripped the railing and looked out the window to where he had left Raikenov, and already saw unfits picking him up and dragging him as they began to beat him. Blair grinned at the sight and continued running up to the next floor clearing when shots erupted at the other end of the hallway. He ducked behind a wall and poked the gun out from around a corner to return fire. He knew the voice without seeing who shot at him.

"I didn't think you'd make it this far!"

Blair fired more rounds as he moved into the hallway, hiding behind the doorway for cover. "Give it up, Eckart!" He leaned his assault rifle out and fired a few more times and pulled it away as more gunfire came his way.

Dust flew around him as bullets lodged into and broke the cheap cinderblock and plaster walls. Blair reached into his coat for a smoke grenade. He pulled the pin and tossed it down the hallway, hearing it detonate as he moved across the hall to another room. He heard Eckart yell.

"I think Stephen taught you a little too well. All this time I thought you were just a scared little boy!" Eckart's machine gun fire ripped through the hallways.

Blair crouched down and slid the assault rifle over his shoulder. He pulled the pistol out of his pocket, sliding off the safety. Carlos buzzed in his ear.

"*David – listen up. They just grounded most air forces, but whoever's running the Command Center just authorized a few drones to leave their hangars and unload on Chelsea. I can get you out before that happens, just get to the roof now!*"

Blair held his ear. "I can't ask you to do that. I'm staying."

"*Come on, man! Just move it now!*"

"Someone has to make sure he's dead!" Blair fired down the hallway as some of the smoke began to clear. Through the clearing he saw Jansen holding a shotgun.

Blair scrambled further into the room as part of the entry doorway to the cheap apartment exploded into a far corner of the entryway. Jansen entered the apartment, shooting in part of a dividing wall. Jansen pumped his shotgun, discharging one of the spent shells. He walked idly through the living room.

"Hey Blair! I'm gonna start by shooting you in the kneecap. You're gonna be even shorter when I'm done with you." Jansen felt uneasy in the silence as he continued looking around, sneaking into another hallway. "You hear me, you fucking traitor! You're gonna pay for what you did to my goddamn face!"

Blair grabbed the barrel of Jansen's shotgun, then used it to bash Jansen in the head. Blair kicked him in the stomach, knocking Jansen backwards as he flipped the shotgun around. As he looked up, Blair pumped the shotgun and squeezed the trigger. Jansen's head dematerialized across the living room. Blair exhaled deeply, staring at Jansen's remains.

"How's that for your goddamn face?"

* * *

Lauren Meyers shouldered Harold Maguire through a long corridor, beige and besieged as gunfire erupted in the building. Large chunks of wall and windows had been shot out. She reached for the handle of a steel door, which opened to the stairwell. Grabbing at Harold's back and under his arm, she muscled him more upwards as he continued to droop. She looked down the flight of stairs, then back up again.

"Come on," said Lauren. "Come on, Harold. We have to go up. They're going to come get us out of here, but we have to go now."

A gunshot echoed in the hallway and Lauren moved for cover, shoving Harold into a separate corner. Harold turned and saw Eckart closing in on them from down a hallway with his pistol drawn, shooting again at Lauren.

"What's the rush?" yelled Eckart.

Harold turned back to Lauren as she braced herself in the stairwell. "Run!"

"No."

Eckart made his way to the entryway of the stairwell and Harold rushed him, grabbing the gun. "Run!"

Lauren sprinted down the stairwell as the gun went off, narrowly missing her. She leaped over the bannister and bounded halfway down the opposing flight in one move, disappearing into the building. Eckart wrestled control of his gun back and grabbed Harold by his hair, jerking him around and rushing him up the flight of stairs. They reached a door at the top, Eckart quickly knocking it open to reveal the rooftop of the old public housing building. The roof was old and patchwork and some large holes were made larger by the helicopter attack. Harold straightened upwards as he felt Eckart grip his hair, pulling it tight into a fist.

"Come with me and watch what happens next." Eckart inched Harold closer to the edge of the building. They overlooked the entirety of the Chelsea Facility in the distance. "You think killing the Leader is good enough? He was a mascot. He worked for us. You can't stop what's coming. You're going to watch every second. All those filthy fuckers are about to be deep fried. You haven't stopped anything!"

"Eckart!" yelled Clark. He had appeared in the rooftop doorway. "Eckart, kill him now and let's get the hell out of here!"

"Before the fireworks?" said Eckart. The smile on his face was deranged. "You're crazy!"

Clark eyed the skies nervously and disappeared from the doorway. Harold watched helplessly as the aircraft's roar grew louder. Looking up, he could make out the drones as they spread throughout the air.

*   *   *

McGonagall lorded over his subordinates' shoulder, watching eagerly on the large screen as a scaled radar map of the drones started fanning out over Chelsea. He clenched his fist and bit the side of his cheek. A loud beeping pierced his ears. McGonagall turned to look towards the control monitor, and saw one of the designated Carnivore blips had started flashing red. Then another. A third started drifting far outside the boundaries of the Facility.

"What the hell is going on!" yelled McGonagall.

"They're malfunctioning," said Tyler. "They're losing altitude." One of the red flashing blips disappeared, and then another disappeared without lighting up first. "They're falling out of the sky…"

"Damnit!" yelled McGonagall. "Get control back now!"

"One Carnivore just delivered payload," said a nearby administrator. "Jesus Christ."

"What?" said McGonagall.

"It just hit the Containment Wall. We need a status report there right now."

"What the fuck is going on?" said McGonagall. He held his hands behind his head. "Override them manually, do something!"

Screaming erupted as everyone around him scrambled.

"Sir?" said someone.

"What?" yelled McGonagall.

"One of the Carnivores just entered East Boston airspace."

McGonagall's face dropped. He felt his bowels fall out from under him and let out a guttural scream before the Chelsea Command Center was obliterated.

CHAPTER XXIV

Blair moved down the hallways, coming up on a stairwell. His transponder locator was buzzing, and he removed it to see a radar blip he was on top of. Blair moved for the woman who appeared in the stairwell before him. She was calm and raised her hands to show him.

"Don't shoot."

"You're Lauren Meyers?"

"I am."

"I was sent by the Colonel. Where's Eckart?"

"He just took Harold Maguire, I think they went to the roof."

"Jesus – they're launching the strikes now, they're hitting Chelsea."

"Is it the Carnivore fleet?"

"Last I heard they grounded fighter jets. It's ProServ drones, why?"

Lauren smiled. "Then there's nothing to worry about."

"What do you mean?"

"Just trust me. And give me that shotgun. I've got a plan."

"The Colonel trusts you. I don't."

"Do you trust Contreras?"

Blair handed over the shotgun, and Lauren checked the chamber before pumping. She watched him as he reached around his back and grabbed the strap of his assault rifle. Blair took it off his shoulder and gripped it by the barrel. "You better not get us killed."

"Us…no. Maybe only you."

* * *

Eckart watched as the fleet of Carnivore drones flying high alternately overshot their targets and fell out of the sky. Harold felt the grip Eckart had on him loosen as one of the drones launched a missile at the Chelsea Command Center. It was enough for him to turn his body and elbow Eckart in the eye socket. Harold scrambled away from the man, sprinting and then sliding behind some rooftop equipment. He crawled on his hands and knees, taking turns throughout the maze of machinery and crouching down behind a large metal box containing a fan that had stopped spinning a long time ago.

The door to the rooftop exploded and Blair came out, shooting in Eckart's direction with an iron grip on the barrel of his rifle. Eckart fired back, and both men moved for cover behind the metal equipment littering the roof of the building. Blair fired a few more shots over the metal box he hid behind and looked back towards the door to see Lauren scuttle for cover. She steadied her shotgun and eyed Blair, nodding slightly.

"Eckart! It's finished! The Orchestra's over! If you give up now, I might be able to keep you alive!" Blair removed the clip from his assault rifle, counting the bullets. It was nearly empty.

"You think this is over," yelled Eckart. He fired three times in Blair's direction. The bullets pinged off of the metal. "This is just the beginning!"

Lauren looked out over the ledge of the roof and saw the Auxiliary Forces in the distance fight losing pitched battles with the collective strength of unfits armed with automatic weapons. They had started reaching the Housing Authority buildings. Soon they would be rushing in. She looked back towards Blair and mouthed to him. "Let's go." Blair scrambled, keeping low, towards Eckart's position.

"What, are you here for a rescue mission?" yelled Eckart. "Well tell you what, he's real close by. Introduce yourself, Harold!"

"Stay wherever you are and don't move, Vice Chancellor!" Blair steadied his rifle ahead of him, moving deliberately and hoping for a clean shot.

"You hear that, Harold? Listen close to that man. That's the voice of the man who killed your daughter!"

Blair moved in and tucked himself behind a corner of the extended equipment. "What the hell are you talking about?"

Harold sat upright, clutching at some loose gravel and preparing to sprint. Lauren moved towards Eckart's position, keeping her shotgun ready.

"You didn't know, Blair? I checked the ballistics report on her… remember the bullets I handed you? Damnedest thing. Exact match for the ones they found in her!" Eckart crept towards the edge of the tall metal box. He grew nervous as he heard the whirring of a helicopter coming for them. "Tell you what, Harold. You live through this you go ahead and see for yourself!"

Harold screamed as he turned the corner and tackled Eckart into the open of the rooftop. He wrestled Eckart for the pistol and it went off. Harold slumped and Eckart shoved him off, scrambling back up. He made eye contact with Blair, aiming the rifle directly at him. As he raised his pistol, Blair started shooting. The first bullet hit Eckart center mass and he moved backwards as more bullets hit him. Eckart fell to one knee as Blair's assault rifle clicked empty. As Blair ditched the rifle and went for his handgun, Eckart shot in Blair's direction. Blair twisted and went down. Eckart checked his body armor, feeling something hot in his gut before spitting up blood. He looked off towards Harold, who slumped onto his side with a small, dark red pool collecting underneath him. Feeling drained, he started walking towards Harold. Each step was part-shuffle. Harold looked up to him.

"At least I had something worth taking." Harold's voice was weak. It was barely audible as the helicopter came in close to the rooftop.

"You're gonna die with nothing."

Eckart turned and shot three times at the helicopter before it turned slightly, its machine gun firing off into the distance as it moved again yards away from the building. He moved towards Harold, aiming his pistol at the man's head. "I'm done listening to your bullshit."

"You're done alright." Eckart spun around to see Lauren Meyers pointing a combat shotgun directly at him. A piece of Eckart's torso flew off him as he fell backward from the blast, tumbling nearly off his feet as he watched Lauren pump the shotgun and fire a few more times. Lauren saw the final look of fear on Eckart's face as he fell backwards off the roof, landing some stories below. She rushed towards the ledge and looked over. Rebels began converging on the building, some running inside. More still began to crowd around the corpse. Lauren looked back towards Harold as the mob amassed to tear the corpse of Frederick Eckart apart.

It was then that Lauren heard a voice. She looked back down below to see Leona Davis with an AK-47, leading a band of unfits and terrorists into the building.

Blair propped himself up and checked his shoulder. He shifted his head to see the bullet hole above his clavicle and shoved his hand on it tightly, letting out a yelp as he did.

"Carlos, Blair here." He winced through his words. "I think we're ready to go now."

"Copy that, just cover me."

He looked up and saw Carlos' helicopter, a rope ladder descending from the side. "I don't know if I can climb that high. I have Meyers and Maguire here, but they're in bad shape. I need you to land!"

"You got it, bud."

Lauren stared into Harold's eyes and saw a man drifting away. "Harold – we need to go. They're coming up and we're not exactly who they want to see, ok?"

Harold glanced up and saw David Blair standing before him, a puzzled look on his face as he clutched at his shoulder. Blair stared back at Harold and saw the flash of a young girl and suddenly Blair knew it in his gut. The whirring of the helicopter's propeller intensified, and Blair screamed his words.

"Vice Chancellor – I'm sorry! I never meant to-"

"Leave me here!" yelled Harold. "I'm where I belong."

Blair choked back a lump in his throat as he watched Lauren squeeze Harold's hand for a final time. She helped Blair climb into the helicopter nearby and pulled herself into it. Once seated, Carlos lifted off the roof. The helicopter gained altitude and Blair looked out onto the roof. People had surrounded Harold and were picking him up. Around the building, hundreds of fighters could be seen taking control of the once off-limits area. The large crowd that had just taken the Forbidden City became ants as the three cleared the Wall and Route One, disappearing into the sky.

CHAPTER XXV

"This is the Truth – an Arbitrage Media Partner. One week on from the death of Leader Wright, and internment centers nationwide are still seeing violence the likes of which have been previously unknown to contracting security forces. Despite broad success in quelling insurrection and preventing large-scale rebellion, organizations like Protection Services and Praetorian Global continue to face stiff resistance on the Homefront. Traditional law enforcement has been called in to aid in the fighting, now authorized fully to operate within the private internment centers. Just yesterday alone, more than 70,000 casualties were reported in skirmishes still ongoing in facilities based near major urban areas – 2,500 or more during the Siege of Compton, with lesser casualties across the Midwest in Flint, Youngstown, and Chicago's own South Side Internment Center. Fighting in Brooklyn's Quarantine Area took a turn for the worse as defense forces lacked enough protective radiation equipment to contain Manhattan Island. Meanwhile, the National Party has worked tirelessly to fill the ranks of government and key private sector positions after coordinated terrorist attacks targeting the nation's leadership. Interim Homeland Security Secretary Joe Grant – a survivor of an attempt on his own life in Boston not long ago – had this to say-"

Asiyah lowered the volume on the television set, hanging in the far corner of her hospital room from the ceiling. Her eyes wandered outside, where from her window she could still see streaks of black smoke billowing out of Chelsea beyond the buildings that littered the bright blue sky. She shifted in her bed, propping herself up and turning the rest of her body towards the window. Much of the pain had stopped and her face had healed significantly, save for a few gashes and a scar that had formed running from her forehead down onto her cheek. The slice had missed her eye, which she could still see from. The knock at her door made her turn over to face the entranceway. She smiled slightly at the flowers that took up much of her vision.

"I hear they let you out today."

"They do. I'm going to be walking out of here in about an hour."

"What are you going to do first?"

"I'm going north. Vermont. I have some friends who can get me to Canada. I'm done with all this."

"I don't blame you." David Blair moved and sat at the foot of her bed. "Do you mind?"

"No. Thank you for those."

Blair handed them to Asiyah and forced a smile. "Sure."

"I like the blue ones. The roses."

"I hear they're new. They're springing up all over the place."

"Not as unique as they used to be, I guess."

"I guess not."

"You come here to try and talk me out of leaving?"

"I came here to apologize. I shouldn't have involved you."

"Please don't, David. I knew what I was doing. I knew the risks."

"I shouldn't have tried to get you to do my dirty work. I was too afraid to face him myself. I realize that now."

"I understand. He was horrible. But he's gone now. He's exactly where he should be."

"Thank you, Asiyah. I got you this, too." Blair reached into his coat pocket and handed a passport and several documents to Asiyah. "This should be everything you need to get out of country with no trouble. You get into anything, you call me. I'll have you out in no time."

"This was the least you could do." Asiyah shifted in her bed. "When I get there, I'm going to be a surgeon again. They're fast-tracking all the American refugees for licenses and certificates. High-skilled professionals."

"You never told me you were a surgeon." Blair looked somewhat shocked.

Asiyah looked out the window, and then back at Blair. "You never asked."

*   *   *

Carlos and Blair were in their spot, drinking pints and sitting at a booth in the dingy dive bar in Cambridge. *I Don't Belong* by Fontaines D.C. came over the place's speaker system. The table still had a stickiness to it and several glasses were left empty around them. Blair was deep in thought, looking off across the bar at nothing in particular. Carlos studied him for a moment.

"How's your clipped wing feel?"

Blair motioned his arm, tucked neatly into a dark envelope sling. He clutched his drink with his free right hand and downed the beer. "Better. It was in and out."

"You need to give it time, it's still fresh."

"No shit, I got shot like ten days ago."

"That's not what I'm talking about. I mean everything. I wasn't even on the ground and I didn't think we were going to make it through. It rattles you, man. Nothing wrong with saying it."

"I verified the ballistics on Aiden Maguire. They matched the bullets Eckart gave me the day of the Dissenter's March. If I never killed her, I don't know if all of this would be shaking out the way it did."

"That's what this is about? It's done. It's terrible and it weighs on you, but it's over. You can't blame yourself for that."

"Sure I can. I can kill a little girl, but I couldn't kill that fucking monster!"

Some heads turned in Blair's direction.

"Jesus, man keep it down." Carlos drank some of his beer. "He's dead, that's what's important. You know Lauren Meyers was in combat before she was a security analyst? She's got a chest full of medals from her time in the service. There's no shame in the fact that she closed him out."

Blair finished the rest of his drink. "Did she have something to do with the Carnivores? The way they went haywire like that?"

"Part of some hacking drive the Pentagon put together years ago, all kinds of nasty stuff that got baked into the grid. Called Jupiter Overdrive – get into the networked infrastructure anywhere and start flipping switches. It's half the reason why the rebels stand a chance now."

"So in other words, we're fucked if they lose and we're fucked if they win?"

"Maybe they'll be some kind of national reconciliation and a negotiated peace."

"Maybe there'll be some kind of guillotine they put our heads in."

Carlos leaned in close. "At the end of the day, I think the new continuity government is interested in reforms. I think they'll fight the rebels because they have to, grind them down, and eventually shut down the camps. I think Arbitrage wants out of the internment-for-profit racket if this is what it's getting them."

"Does it matter? The more I think about it, the more I think Robert Wright won even in death. Orchestra killed millions of people. We still don't even know exactly how many."

"And the resistance saved millions more. I know it's bad, but it can always be worse. Always."

"What's your next move after this?"

"Me? I don't know yet. The Colonel's been looking to bring me back into the fold, but I don't know. I half-hope the rebels win."

"Why?"

"Because I'm tired of being half-American. I want to live in a country where I can be me."

"I don't know what to think anymore."

"Yes you do. When the chips were down and you needed my help you didn't ask for Carl Carver. I'm not ever gonna forget that."

"You know, I don't feel bad about the op. I can live with knowing that I've killed bad people – terrible people. I just. You know." He took a long swig. His eyes shifted down. "I went to Harold Maguire's apartment and his storage unit. It was like looking at two different people."

"What do you mean?"

"This apartment was everything you'd expect out of a Party member. A little too perfect. Then I checked out the storage unit he had. They didn't clean it out yet. That was him, who he actually was. The stuff he wanted to hide."

"You got to stop. It's not gonna help you to dwell on this."

"The guy had a record collection worth a small fortune. I thumbed through some of them and found this album by *The Clash* I listened to when I was a kid. Same one the al-Haqq brothers were playing when we raided Malone Park. I must not have paid close enough attention to the lyrics or something."

"Blair…"

"You know they never found Harold Maguire's body in Chelsea."

"You're still here. You can do whatever you want from now on."

"Yeah…I can. That's why I'm out of here."

"Seriously?"

"Yeah. I don't know where yet, but I asked the Colonel to get me reassigned. I'm getting as far away from here as I can."

"There's still a lot to do around here – I mean, the PRF is still picking people off left and right."

"If I don't do this now, I don't know if I'm going to have a life left to save. I mean it. Maybe a change of scene will help. Are we paid up?"

"Yeah. We are." Carlos and Blair stood up from the table, and he brought Blair in for a hug. "Take care of yourself. And stay in touch. You never know, maybe you'll land somewhere decent and I'll follow you out."

"I'll keep that in mind."

The two walked out of the bar and parted ways. The air was mild and green buds began taking shape on the trees. Blair worked to get his free hand inside his light jacket, removing a cigarette from the pack with his mouth. He fished around again in his jacket to put away the pack and get his lighter, which wouldn't catch as the wind picked up. The lighter went back into his side pocket and he traded it for his car keys. Blair climbed into his old beater of a sedan carefully, reaching across himself to shut the door tight. He glanced at the dashboard before he put the keys in the ignition and picked something up.

The blue rose was fresh and cut small so that the stem was no longer than a few inches. The petals pushed out and one slipped off gracefully, fluttering down into Blair's lap. He looked off into the distance and saw the silhouette of a man at the end of the street, standing on a corner shrouded in darkness. Blair felt jittery, an unease that took over in his gut as he squinted to make out the figure in the distance. Then he knew exactly who was staring at him and what was happening. His jaw shook and his eyes welled up. He sat for some time, shaking slightly. David Blair closed his eyes tight and inhaled deeply as he turned the keys in the ignition, bracing himself.

THE END

JAMES TARR

is a government services consultant and writer. Born and raised in Lynn, Massachusetts, he earned two degrees in Criminal Justice and Political Science from the University of Massachusetts Lowell and a Master of Science in Urban and Regional Policy from Northeastern University. He lives with his wife Christina in the Boston Area. *These Troubled Days* is his first novel.

For more info, follow his works here:
Facebook: facebook.com/james.a.tarr
Instagram: @thesetroubleddays
Medium: jimtarr.medium.com
Twitter: @james_tarr_